THE
GLARE

ANISSA STRINGER

ISBN-13: 978-1502304384
ISBN-10: 1502304384

Thanks for purchasing this book.

StringerStories.com

The Glare Series
The Glare
The Glare Continues
The Glare Ends
Since the Glare: Susan's Journal
Before the Glare

Other Novels
Blood of an Elf: Quinn's Story
My Virtual Life
Regrets

Non-Fiction
A Year of Guided Gratitude: 365 Gratitude Prompts for
Your Favorite Journal
Scrapbooking Games and More

DEDICATION

This book is dedicated to my daughter, Jessica. She was the first person to read this story, just as she's the first to read most of my manuscripts.

ACKNOWLEDGMENTS

I'd like to acknowledge my good friend, Donna Taylor, for her editing expertise. She catches errors and inconsistencies like nobody's business—any errors that remain are mine and mine alone.

Special thanks to Carolynn, Rebecca, and Marla—three of my oldest friends and the first to tell me I should write a book (even if this isn't the one they were talking about)!

A big thanks goes out to Diane and Kim as well. They called me out on my "can't do" attitude more than once; and another thank you to Jolie for the countless hours we "talked shop" as we walked.

SEPTEMBER: THE END

I was homeless when I was thirteen.

Homeless. That word doesn't mean much anymore. Not when there are so few of us left. Not when you can walk into any home, on any street, anywhere in the country—maybe in the world even, and claim the house as your own. Once you drag the corpses out, of course. And deal with the smell. The bodies don't look much like bodies anymore. It's been too long for that. But the stench of their decay has a way of sinking deep into the furniture, the carpet, even the curtains, and it takes a while to get used to.

***

Somewhere in the distance, someone called my name. The voice floated across the water as I paddled toward my dad. Beneath me, the water was icy cold and dark, but the sun was hot and its warmth pushed away scary thoughts of big fish with sharp teeth. Besides, my dad was there, right in front of me, just a few yards away. His arms were stretched toward me and he smiled and laughed. My mom and sister, Laney, were on the shore. When the small waves pushed me higher in the water, I caught glimpses of them behind Dad. They clapped and cheered for me.

"C'mon kiddo! You can do it! Kick! Kick your feet! You

can do this!" Dad said.

I kicked hard and gulped for another breath of air. I was almost there! My dad grinned and took a tiny step back. I gasped for air as I felt my body start to sink, but he urged me on.

"You can do it! You're almost there!"

Just as I started to panic, he reached out for me. I kicked harder—hard enough to push myself right into the safety of his arms—when I heard my name again. Dad shook me and yelled my name, but the voice was wrong. It wasn't his voice anymore. And he would have never shaken me like that. It was Laney. And I wasn't a little kid anymore—I was thirteen. The image of my dad disappeared in a dark swirl like the last bit of scummy gray water that swirls down the bathtub drain.

It was only a dream. Dad was dead, but Laney's voice was real. She shook me again, harder, and she wasn't yelling my name, but whispering it, her lips pressed against my ear. A strand of her soft blonde hair tickled my cheek—or maybe it was my hair. Hers was only a little darker than mine was.

Before I could respond, she hissed, "Listen!"

I froze and finally heard the screaming and swearing that would have ordinarily woken me up.

There was a loud *thunk* as something big hit a wall. Laney and I both jumped.

Our mother screamed. "Just who do you think you are?" she yelled.

Her words slurred together the way they always did when she was drunk, and her voice screeched like a nail on glass. "This is *my* house! Do you hear me? You're in *my* house!"

There was a loud scraping noise. She must have picked up something big—a chair maybe. Then there was a crash. And it was his turn to yell.

"I hate you!" he snarled. Only the words came out long

2

and drawn out like he was yelling in slow motion: "I haaaaate yeeeeew!"

Laney and I had peeked around the corner often enough during their fights to know what would come next.

We held our breath and clung to one another. We waited for that thundering sound that meant he was running toward her, ready to tackle her. Then they'd fight. Really fight. He would punch and hit and slap. And Mom would fight back, clawing and biting and kicking. They would fight like that for a long time. Sometimes the cops would come, and that was almost scarier than the fighting. We learned to hide when they came to the door. If they didn't know we were there, they wouldn't threaten to take us away. Usually, when the fighting began, we snuck around the house and closed the windows and blinds so the neighbors couldn't see or hear what was happening inside and call the police. Instead, Mom and Rich would beat each other up until neither one of them could move anymore.

In the morning, there would be drops of blood on the carpet in the living room and the hall and on the peeling linoleum in the bathroom. Mom would always accuse us of spilling something on the carpet even though, just as often as not, she'd have blood smeared across her face or still dripping from her nose as proof of what really happened. Or he would. And the house would be littered with empty bottles and cans and gallon-sized jugs of whatever alcohol was strongest and cheapest that week.

When she woke up, Mom would tremble and shake. She'd yell for one of us to bring her a straw and we'd put it in a bottle of whatever was left over from the night before and hold it steady so she could drink. She'd swallow it down the way a runner gulps down sports drinks after a race on a long, hot day. Mom could hold the bottle for herself after her second drink if we put the straw in it for her; watching her aim it at the opening was like watching a toddler try to string beads for the first time. After the third drink, she could take a shower, and if Rich spent the night passed out on the floor or the couch, that's when he'd leave. The tires of his beat-up car would hit the curb or a garbage can when he drove off. Neither one of them would remember anything that happened. Or at least they would pretend they didn't.

This time, the sounds were different. Laney and I looked at each other, our eyes big and full of fear. We strained to hear their conversation.

Mom's voice was high pitched with terror. The fear brought her out of her alcohol-induced stupor for the moment. "Put it down, Rich. Just put the gun down…"

Laney and I slithered off my bed and dropped to the floor. We huddled in the corner, and Laney wrapped her arms around me when she realized I was shaking. I wasn't shivering from cold—we lived in Arizona and it was almost ninety degrees most days in early fall.

It was silent for a moment and we breathed again. Then Mom laughed. Not the happy laugh that used to make me think of tinkling bells. Not the laugh I dreamt about from that day on the beach when I was still little. This was her hard laugh. The mean one. Laney called it Mom's cynical laugh. She said it was all the anger and hurt and sadness coming out because Mom didn't have any happiness left inside her anymore, not even for us.

And even though she was drunk, she was really angry. Her voice was hard and mean when she screamed at Rich. "You're nothing but a big chicken. Do you hear me? A chicken!" She made squawking sounds and she laughed viciously. "You couldn't shoot a…"

He screamed back at her. His voice was garbled and slurred—it belonged to a crazed beast, not a man.

Then, BANG.

Part of my mind got lost for a moment. It was as if I'd been dreaming or watching TV. I remember thinking, *I wonder if the neighbors heard that. It wasn't nearly as loud as I*

4

thought a gun would be…

And then I snapped back to reality like a rubber band that's been shot across the room. We heard another thump.

"Oh, God! Babe! I'm sorry!" he sobbed. "Oh, no! Oh, no!" he cried. "What did I do?"

He brayed like a sick donkey. "I didn't mean it! I swear! I didn't mean it!"

I tried to wriggle out of my sister's arms. I needed to see Mom! I needed to know if any of this was real. I thought it might be part of the dream. Sometimes I'd have the good dream, the lake dream that was my favorite real-life memory, but then it would morph and change into a nightmare before I woke up. This had to be part of the nightmare. But Laney held on to me.

"It's too dangerous. *He's* dangerous," she whispered in my ear. I felt her body shaking behind me and her voice quivered.

I stopped struggling. He *was* dangerous. Rich was never nice, but when he was drunk, he was really mean. He once slapped Laney across the face when she tried to convince Mom to stay home instead of going out with him when they were both already plastered. And drunk or not, there was always danger in his face, hidden by angry-looking eyebrows and the scrapes and scratches Mom clawed into his cheeks when they fought. The danger was always building, always getting closer. We felt it. Laney woke me up not because they were fighting again, but because we were scared of what might happen if Rich found us while he was drunk. Instinctively, we knew it was safer if we were together, but it was safer still if we were together and he couldn't find us at all.

On the nights he was at the house, we hid. Sometimes we slept on the back patio, wrapped in old sleeping bags, more to keep the bugs away than for the warmth, at least during the fall and summer. Other times we hid in the back of Mom's closet where we buried ourselves in dirty clothes.

We fell asleep there, safely hidden where no one would think to look: among dirty socks and Dad's old clothes, fallen from their hangers and nearly forgotten. In the morning we woke up long before Mom or Rich did, and we would make our way back to my room or Laney's where we would cuddle up together and sleep a little longer.

In the other room, Rich stopped crying. He was talking to himself, muttering, but we couldn't make out the words. Now and then he'd try to revive Mom and then he'd start sobbing again.

We jumped again when he yelled, "Why?" It came out long and strangled—a coyote's howl coming from deep inside a man's body. He sobbed again. The gun went off once more and then there was silence.

***

"Two years, Jenna. Just two years," Laney pleaded with me. "That's all we have to get through. Then I'll be eighteen and out of school, and I can work full time and we won't have to worry about them separating us."

My hand faltered over the numbers on Mom's cell phone. Back in those days, if you had an emergency, you dialed nine-one-one on the phone and someone would come help. Firemen would put out fires, the paramedics would come if someone was hurt or sick, and of course, there were the police, too.

One time Laney threatened to tell someone about the drinking, just to get Mom some help. But Mom was already drunk, and she only laughed her mean laugh.

"No one can help me. As for you two, all they'd do is take you away and separate you. No one wants two mouthy, know-it-all teenage daughters," she snarled at Laney's hurt face. "You'd never see each other again," she finished with a slurred sneer.

That's when we knew she wasn't really our mother

anymore. She was an alien who had taken over our mother's body or something, but she wasn't our mom. Our mom, the one with the tinkling laugh and the smile that made everyone smile back at her, was gone. Laney said that something inside of her was broken and that's why she changed. Not that it mattered.

I had already dialed the nine and the first one. I hesitated for a moment and then clicked the talk button to hang up.

I looked up at Laney. Tears dripped down her face just as they did on mine. She was all I had and I was all she had, but that wasn't anything new. "What do we do?" I asked.

We stared at their bodies—at Mom and Rich—and the blood pooling beneath them. It sunk into the dirty fibers of the carpet like the cheap red wine they sometimes drank. Then Laney looked away. I saw sweat bead up on her hairline and on her upper lip. Her face got even paler than it had been.

"We have to bury them," she whispered. Her voice cracked as she spoke.

"What if someone looks for them?"

She gulped. She was trying so hard to be a good big sister. She didn't want me to worry. She swallowed again and lifted her chin.

"They won't. Everything will be the same as it is now. I already pretend I'm Mom if one of us is sick and we have to let school know we'll be absent, right? And whenever someone comes to the door and wants to talk to Mom, I always say she's in the shower or at work even though she hasn't had a job in months. I already pretend to be her if one of our friends' moms wants to talk to her about a sleepover or something. And sometimes she has me get money for her out of the ATM. And I've been depositing Dad's social security checks ever since she had to get them to start sending it instead of automatically depositing it because the old bank closed her account. Everything will be exactly the same. Mom just won't be here getting drunk, and Rich won't be here fighting with her."

"Oh."

Laney nodded firmly, trying to convince herself that everything she said was true. "It'll be exactly the same as before," she said again, more to herself than to me.

OCTOBER: HOMELESS

I guess it's not really fair to say we were homeless. We had a home, after all. When Dad died, back before Mom started drinking and stopped being our real mom, she paid off the house with his life insurance money. But the rest of the money disappeared a long time ago, and the social security checks we lived on were pretty small. Still, Laney did just as she promised. She took care of me. She and I walked to the bank together, and she deposited the checks in the ATM. She forged Mom's signature on the checks she wrote to pay the electricity and water bills. After that, there wasn't much money left over, especially when we got surprise bills in the mail like property taxes and home owner's association dues. There were also credit card bills Mom had racked up since she lost her last job and a couple of parking tickets, too. Paying the bills was the important thing, the most important thing. An unpaid bill would Arouse Suspicion. When we talked about it, we said it just like that, too, as if the words had capital letters because that was the thing we had to avoid at all costs: Arousing Suspicion.

***

We had a home, it's true, but with so little money we

didn't have much food. Rich used to bring over bags of groceries—things like frozen pizzas and soda and stuff to make sandwiches. We didn't realize how much he'd helped us until after he was dead. At school I started to tell people about the imaginary bunny in our backyard. I snuck it into conversation every time I could.

"Did I tell you my sister found a bunny in our yard? I've been bringing home my extras from lunch for it," I would hint. "We're trying to tame it."

My friends oohed and aahed at the thought of a cute little bunny, and since no one really ate their apples or carrots anyway, they always gave them to me. Laney and I were both already in the free lunch program at our schools and it kept us from starving. We filled our trays with every bit of food we were allowed, and we ate until we were stuffed. My brain always felt foggy during my afternoon classes because of it, but it was better than the way my stomach growled before lunch every day, making it hard to concentrate.

The extra food we collected from our friends went home with us, hidden in our backpacks. That became a secret code we shared. "I got two apples to feed the bunny," I said one day when I got home from school. Laney was already there. Her high school had early release days on Fridays. The rest of the week, she met me at my school and we walked home together.

"I did, too."

"At least that's breakfast for tomorrow and Sunday," I said. I tried not to sound too eager when I asked, "When can we buy more food?"

Laney kept careful track of our money and always made sure she didn't get any cash out of the ATM unless she was sure we'd have enough to pay the next bill that came in; right after Rich killed Mom, we spent too much money and had to pay Mom's credit card bill late.

I had watched as Laney opened the late notice from the

credit card company. She unfolded the paper and I tried to read it over her shoulder, but her hands shook too much. I watched her face instead. Her eyebrows had furrowed with concentration as her blue eyes—just a little darker than mine—raced back and forth. She silently mouthed the words as she read.

She took a deep steadying breath and smiled at me. "It's okay! Everything's alright! They charged us a late fee. It's twenty bucks and it raises the amount we owe each month by…"

She looked at the bill again. "…by sixty-three cents. That's not too bad, is it?"

I looked into her eyes to make sure I understood. "So no one's going to come here asking for Mom or looking for the money? They don't know that Mom's dead?"

Laney hugged me and we both laughed with relief. "No! It's just a late fee, that's all! We're going to be okay! We can do this!"

After that, Laney was very responsible with our money, but neither one of us regretted the extra money we'd spent that first month, even though it was on plants and not food.

***

The ground had been too hard to dig up the night Rich killed Mom and then himself, so we had to bury them in the flower bed instead.

"This isn't going to work, Laney!"

I had tried to dig out a hole in the rock-hard earth using a rusty little spade. It was dark and we were both still in shock. We were panicked, too—desperate to hide their bodies once we made up our minds to do it. It was the only way we'd be able to stay together. I scraped aside the dusty red gravel, but I couldn't do more than chip out tiny bits of the hard-packed ground.

"I know, I know," Laney whispered.

She managed to dig out a bit more of the ground than I did, using a shovel she found in the garage. We both cringed with each shovel-full. The shovel clanged and scraped against the rocks and dirt and we kept looking at the neighboring houses, willing their lights to stay off and for no one to hear the noise.

"What are we going to do?" I asked. The panic that hummed in my head made my hands shake.

"Shhh!" she said, hushing me even though my voice was much quieter than the clang of her shovel. "Just...just let me think! I just need to think for a minute!"

We had both looked around the yard, desperately hoping for an idea as we sat in the moonlight.

"Mom's flower bed," she whispered.

The flower bed was on the side of the house near the gate. There weren't any flowers in it. There hadn't been any flowers since Dad died. At first, Mom said it made her too sad to remember when Dad built it for her with red bricks to raise it above the ground so he could fill it with good, soft soil instead of the red Arizona grit that was in the rest of the yard. We surprised her with it on Mother's Day. Later, when she wasn't so sad, Mom stopped caring about everything except drinking. The flower bed was just one more thing that didn't mean anything to her anymore. The only things that grew in it were tough, spiky weeds that seemed a little like Laney and me. No one watered or fertilized them, or bothered to pick the bugs off, but somehow they survived anyway.

We didn't speak as we dug all the soft, black dirt out of the bed. We sliced through the weeds and they oozed with sticky white sap. In a dazed moment of confusion I wondered if we would have bled red like Mom or white like the weeds if Rich had shot us, too.

Laney and I didn't speak when we dragged the bodies out of the living room, across the rough gravel, and to the flower bed. We carried Rich out first, then Mom. Their bodies were still warm and soft. They felt like life-sized dolls instead of people. They looked a little like that too, when their arms and legs moved in strange ways as we dragged them across the yard.

I wept while I worked, and when I looked at Laney I saw that she was crying too. The moonlight reflected off the tears that covered her face, but she didn't make a sound.

"Take Mom's arms. I'll take her feet," she whispered. I almost couldn't understand her because her voice shook so badly.

We heaved Mom's body upward and tried to lift her into the empty flower bed, but the dead weight was too much for me. I held her under the arms and blood dripped down her chest, onto my leg. I cried out, and she slipped out of my hands. The top of her body dropped over the edge of the flower bed with a flat sounding *thud*. Laney still held on to her feet. For the first time, I noticed that one of Mom's flip-flops was gone and her heel was roughed up from being dragged across the gravel. Her lifeless body was draped over the bricks, half in and half out of the hole. Laney groaned. I started sobbing hysterically.

Laney dropped Mom's feet and grabbed me by the shoulders. She smelled like dirt and blood. She shook me.

"Shh! Stop it! Stop!" she hissed.

I struggled to stop crying but I couldn't do it. I just couldn't.

"Go inside!" she hissed at me again, pointing to the house. "Now! You'll wake someone up!"

I ran inside, covering my mouth with my filthy hands and tasting dirt. I threw myself on the couch and bawled, howling with grief and fear and shock.

I don't know how long I stayed there, crying. When Laney came back in, she sat on the edge of the couch and patted my back. She brushed the hair back from my face.

"I'm sorry, Jenna," she said softly. "I'm so sorry."

I sat up and crawled into her arms. She held me and

rocked me like a baby, like she was my mother instead of my sister, and we cried together.

When our tears slowed, she said, "I got them both in the flower bed but I still need to cover them with dirt. Do you think you can help?"

Laney was so strong and so brave, but her face looked old now. She had deep circles under her eyes that hadn't been there before. I promised myself I would be stronger, like her. I nodded, not trusting myself to speak.

We buried Mom and Rich in silence. The dirt pattered down onto their bodies. I caught one last glimpse of Mom's face just as Laney shoveled a scoop of dirt over it. The lines between her eyes that made her look mad all the time were smooth, and despite the blood that had smeared across her cheek and the bruises and the bloody hole in her chest, she didn't look angry and broken anymore.

When all the dirt was back in place, we smoothed it over so it was level. It had been so long since anything had been planted in the flower bed that a lot of the soil had blown away despite the weeds. Now, with the bodies buried in it, the flower bed was full all the way to the top again.

"We need to plant something since it's all dug out. It might look suspicious otherwise," she whispered. "No one weeds a flower bed unless they're going to plant it."

I reminded myself to be strong like Laney. "Mint," I whispered. The word came out weakly. I tried again. "Mint. Remember how Mom wouldn't let us buy mint the year she planted all those herbs? She said it would take over the whole flower bed..."

Laney nodded. "Okay. Tomorrow we'll find some."

She put her arm around my shoulder. I put mine around her waist and we leaned on each other as we went back into the house. We staggered as we walked, almost as if we were as drunk as Mom and Rich always used to be.

We found a few scraggly pots of peppermint and spearmint at the grocery store the next day. They sat in racks by the lawn chairs and porch swings. Someone had pushed aside the furniture to position the racks so the herbs and flowers would get a little shade and the autumn sun in Ahwatukee wouldn't fry them. We spent nearly thirty dollars buying all the mint they had. Now I know that thirty dollars would have fed us for a month or longer, but we needed the plants to fill the flower bed to hide what we had done. That was even more important than eating. That's why we didn't regret the late fee when we got the credit card bill.

***

I asked Laney again. "When can we buy more food?"

She looked like she was about to cry. "Not until next Friday."

And then she did cry. "I'm sorry," she said. "I tried to get us more food at school today but I almost got caught with the apples…"

"It's okay," I said. Normally I would be as upset as she was about our prospects for the weekend, but I had good news.

"It's okay, Laney! Amber asked if I could spend the night! I'm going over there in a couple of hours. You eat the apples for dinner tonight. I'll bring back some food, okay? I'll tell Amber that I have to be home early for chores so you don't have to wait too long to eat in the morning."

We'd been spending the night with friends every chance we got, even though it meant that one of us would be left alone in the house. I think Laney turned down some sleepovers because she knew I was afraid to be alone, but sometimes we were just too desperate for food.

Knowing Mom and Rich had died in it made the house extra spooky and scary even though we'd moved an area rug from Mom's room in order to cover most of the blood stains. We moved the furniture around to cover up some of the blood that dribbled out of Rich's head when we carried him outside, too.

Once, when Laney was at a sleepover, I lifted the corner of the rug to see what the blood stain looked like. I might have been able to imagine it was just an old wine stain except for the rusty smell of iron that came up through the carpet and almost made me throw up. Whenever I was alone in the house, I always thought about the blood on the carpet. When Laney spent the night away, I would barricade myself in my room with my dresser pushed up against the door, and I would hide under my bed with a flashlight. I'd read or do homework while I listened for sounds that my imagination turned into zombies and monsters. Sometimes I even slept under my bed until Laney came home the next morning. I felt safe in the confined space, and it was always worth it because sleepovers were such an easy way to get food. No one ever knew we raided their pantries.

***

"I've got to go to the bathroom," Amber said as we watched TV at her house.

"Thanks for telling me," I joked when she got up and walked down the hall. I was getting better at putting on a mask around other people, pretending that everything was normal when my head swirled with worries of Arousing Suspicion and feeding the bunny.

As soon as she was out of sight, I grabbed my backpack and ran to the kitchen. I peeked around the corner, but Amber's mom was out running errands, and her brothers were in their rooms with the music blaring. There wasn't much risk of getting caught. My heart raced anyway.

I slid the pantry door open and grabbed a handful of granola bars and stuffed them into my backpack. I cringed as snack-sized bags of crackers and chips crinkled in my hand. I dropped them in my backpack and searched for more snack food that could sit in my backpack overnight without going bad. Nuts! A twinge of guilt stabbed at my insides when I saw the full jar of peanuts, but the never-ending hunger was more intense than my guilt. I put the heavy glass jar in my bag with everything else.

The toilet flushed, but I was already back on the couch as if I'd been stretched out since she left. My battered backpack rested by my feet, zipped up and only slightly more full than before. I'd put my jacket on to keep my backpack from bulging too much—back then, people used to crank their air conditioners on so high that you'd freeze if you stayed inside too long. School was that way, too. I sat up when Amber came back into the room. "Hey," I said. "I'm kind of hungry. Got any good snacks?"

Amber laughed. "I swear, it's like you have a tapeworm lately. You're always hungry and you never gain an ounce! It's not fair! Everything I eat goes right to my thighs."

She grabbed some of the skin on her leg and rolled her eyes. "Go make yourself a sandwich or something," she said with a laugh.

A sandwich! I tried not to sound too eager. "Are you sure your mom won't mind?"

She laughed again. "No, it's fine!"

I stuffed a fat piece of cheese into my mouth like a squirrel stashing nuts in its cheek pouches while I made the sandwich. I chewed the cheese quickly, without tasting it, just to get more food inside my body without getting caught. I clattered the stuff in the silverware drawer so I could slide the pantry open again and steal more food. I slipped a can of tuna in each pocket. A sleeve of crackers went into the arm of my jacket. Laney and I would feast for the next few days.

NOVEMBER: SUSPICION

As the weeks passed, we developed a lot of tricks to keep from Arousing Suspicion. Most things didn't occur to us until there was a problem, like the time a neighbor came by and complained about Mom's beat-up car. He called it an eyesore, whatever that is. It hadn't moved since before Mom died. The tires were going flat and the hood and roof were covered in bird poop and dust.

"My mom is at work right now, but we'll have her move it tonight," Laney reassured the man. He lived across the street and we thought he and his wife might be Suspicious. Sometimes we'd see the blinds in their front room window tilt up and then drop back into place when we looked over at their house. That night, we waited until it was dark and their lights were out. Then Laney got the keys and climbed into the car.

"It started. That's good!" I said. There were times when Mom tried to start it and the engine wouldn't turn over. I went to the passenger door to get in, but Laney wouldn't let me.

"What are you doing? I don't know how to drive!" Her voice was high-pitched with panic. She'd had driving lessons a few times with Mom, but they hadn't ever gone well. "You need to stay back. I don't want you to get hurt!"

She didn't do too badly, though. The car lurched

forward and stalled once, but she got it into the garage. She sat in the driver's seat, shaking, while I closed the garage door. She waited until it went all the way down before she got out so it wouldn't Arouse Suspicion if the neighbors were peering through their blinds from across the street.

DECEMBER: CHRISTMAS

We had record low temperatures and frost nearly every night in December, but we didn't dare turn on the heat very often. Instead, we wore layer upon layer of clothes. We snuggled up together under a bunch of old blankets at night. We took hot baths when it was especially cold; it was the only way to really get warmed up before bed. Going to bed hungry was bad enough, but being cold *and* hungry was miserable. And we were really hungry. Christmas break meant two weeks without our free school lunches.

"It's your turn to take one first," Laney said on Christmas Eve. We splurged on the electricity and water that we had to use for the baths but we shared the bath water to compensate.

I sighed as I sank into the hot water. My toes burned after being so cold, but the agony was worth it when my skin turned pink and my body warmed up for the first time all day. I sank lower in the water to cover as much of my body as possible. It wasn't hard. There wasn't much of me to cover anymore. My legs looked longer than they really were since they were getting so bony, and the rest of me didn't look much different. I stared up at the ceiling so I didn't have to look at my knobby knees or the way my hands and feet looked too big for the rest of my body.

I kept expecting Laney to knock on the door to tell me

to get out so she could take a bath, but she didn't. I was dressed in old sweats, a tee shirt, a sweatshirt, and two pairs of socks before she finally knocked.

"I'm going to skip the bath, Jenna. I'm too tired. Leave the lights off, okay?"

"Okay," I called back.

Keeping the lights off whenever we could was one of the other ways we tried to keep the electric bill down. The lower the bills, the more food we could buy, and we were already stretching our tiny food budget to the max. Even before Rich killed Mom, our pantry hadn't been full. By the end of Christmas break, it was nearly empty.

I had dreams about cinnamon rolls that night. I could even smell them. Mom made them for us the previous Christmas even though she'd already been drinking a lot by then. I couldn't remember a Christmas morning when we didn't have them for breakfast. They weren't fancy or homemade or anything, just the tubes you buy in the refrigerated section at the grocery store. Mom always flipped a coin to decide which of us would push the tube open with the end of a spoon. If it was me, I got to spread the frosting on the rolls when they came out of the oven and lick the extra frosting off the butter knife. Then Laney got to choose the first roll from the pan.

When I'd complain because Laney took the one with the most icing, Mom would laugh her tinkling laugh and say, "Sorry, sweetie. You know the rule. If you'd put the same amount of frosting on all of them, it wouldn't matter which roll your sister chose!" Mom used to have all sorts of little tricks like that to keep things fair, back when she was still our mom.

After I woke up, I stayed in bed and fantasized about cinnamon rolls until I realized that I really could smell them! I bounced out of bed and found Laney bustling around the kitchen. She had a big smile on her face, but she looked guilty, too.

"They were on sale for $1.49," she explained.

Sheepishly, she added, "I ate two already. I couldn't help myself. I thought you'd never wake up!"

I started to explain about my dream when I noticed the tree. "You put it up?"

I stared at it. It was the same old artificial tree we'd had for as long as I could remember; a branch was missing on the back and the star always sat cock-eyed on top. If you accidentally nudged the tree, it would tumble off. The star had fallen so many times that the glitter had worn off on the edges and the tips were flattened and broken. The lights only blinked on one side of the tree, and the string of silver tinsel Laney had draped around it wasn't long enough to cover all the branches…and it was still the most beautiful tree I'd ever seen. I stared at it, noticing each of the ornaments: the expensive one Mom bought during our last trip before Dad died; the reindeer made of felt that I could just barely remember making in second grade; the dozens of cheap, shatterproof balls Mom bought every year after Christmas when they went on clearance…

I was so lost in happy memories that it took a moment before I realized that a pile of presents sat beneath the tree.

I was stunned. We didn't have enough money for food. I couldn't imagine that Laney would spend money on anything else, and we talked about the tree on the first day of Christmas break. We agreed it would be better if we didn't even pull it out of the garage since there would be no presents this year.

"It didn't seem right," she explained. "And the presents aren't a big deal," she warned. "They're from the lost and found at school."

It didn't matter. I opened each package, wrapped in newspaper taken from the neighbor's driveway, and tried to show her how excited I was about each one. There was a red fleece jacket that looked almost new and a stocking cap that almost matched the jacket. There was a paperback book, too. I turned it over and read the back. It was about a girl who found out she was half-elf and it was exactly the kind of book I liked to read to escape my real life.

"Thanks," I said as I reached for the last present. Something rolled around inside the old cereal box she'd used as a package. I opened the top. Inside was a single piece of paper, rolled like a scroll, and a pen.

"What is this?" I asked, crinkling my nose as I held the roll of paper up.

Laney laughed at the look on my face. "Do you remember when I told you about the speaker I had in one of my classes a while ago?"

I nodded. We talked about our classes sometimes, and that one was a favorite of hers.

"The speaker said that no matter how bad things are, it's better to focus on the positive, even if you have to really search for it. I thought that maybe we could start a list of the good things about all of this."

I nodded again but my expression must have given away my real feelings. It would be impossible to fill that paper with good things. There was nothing good about how we were living!

I didn't want to hurt her feelings when she always tried so hard, though. "Sure. That's a good idea."

Quickly, she said, "I'll even start it. It won't be so hard to do. You'll see!"

I handed her the paper and pen. She pulled the rubber band off of it and unrolled it. Across the top, she wrote, "Good Stuff." Under that, she wrote three things: Dad's checks, free lunches, and being in this together.

She handed it back to me and I understood. She wasn't asking me to pretend that things were great or even okay. She didn't expect me to *like* the fact that our mother was dead and that we had buried her in the backyard. She wasn't asking me to pretend that being hungry all the time was fun, or to act like I wasn't terrified of getting caught and separated. She just wanted us to remember that things could always be worse. And they could have been.

Later they were.

I looked down at my plate. A few crumbs were all that was left of the fourth cinnamon roll I'd eaten. They'd tasted so good I was almost able to ignore the way the sores around my mouth stung when I ate them. We'd started stealing oranges and grapefruits from our neighbors' trees, and all the citrus we'd been eating made our stomachs hurt and gave us raw-looking sores around our mouths. I licked one at the corner of my mouth and looked around. I was surrounded by the gifts Laney got for me, and the lights on the Christmas tree—the ones that worked—were twinkling beautifully.

I took the pen and wrote three things of my own on the list: cinnamon rolls, my new jacket, and my sister.

Laney grinned when she put the list on the fridge and helped herself to another cinnamon roll. "You can have the last one," she told me.

After that, we wrote things on the list whenever we could think of something good. It didn't fix anything, but it did help when things seemed especially bad.

I spent the rest of the day making Laney a bookmark with the tiny bits of construction paper we had in a drawer. It was lame, but it was the only gift I could think to make. She acted like Mom used to when I gave it to her.

She hugged me and said, "I love it. I can't wait to use it. Thank you."

JANUARY: DOCTOR LANEY

Christmas break ended on the second of January and we went back to school. That meant we were back to free school lunches. We also went back to one of the worst flu seasons in years, and by Friday I had it. I don't remember much about the rest of the month except for a few hazy memories of Laney leaning over me, pushing pills into my mouth, and holding a cup to my lips so I could swallow them down. It was a good thing I got sick instead of her. She always wanted to be a doctor; I wouldn't have known what to do if she'd been the one who got sick, but she was smart and she took good care of me.

FEBRUARY: YARD WORK

It was the middle of February before I felt like myself again. At the end of the month, when the day time temperatures in Ahwatukee were nearly perfect but the nights were still chilly, we found a red note taped to the front door when we got home from school. I glanced around when Laney peeled it off. The blinds in the house across the street dropped into place and we looked at each other, worried. The only other people we saw were other kids walking home from school. They ignored us just like we ignored them.

Inside, we dropped our backpacks and unfolded the note. I peered over Laney's shoulder and we read it together. It said, "You are out of compliance with the covenants issued by the Home Owner's Association. To avoid a fine, please address the following maintenance concerns within the next two weeks."

Below that, there were three boxes. Two of them were checked. The first box said, "Excessive weeds." The next one, which was not checked, said, "Home is in need of repairs." The other checked box read, "Overgrown bushes/shrubbery."

We looked at each other, then at the front room window. We stepped closer and pushed the blinds up and looked at the yard, really seeing it for the first time. Three monster-sized rosemary bushes outside the window partially blocked our view of the ground because it had been so long since they'd been pruned. Near the sidewalk, gangly weeds sprouted up through the red gravel. Wide, round mats of something low-growing made gray-green splotches everywhere in the yard. Several inches of dead leaves and faded flowers sat under the only tree in the yard, an oleander with bright yellow flowers and long leaves that stayed green all year. Back when Dad was alive, he constantly reminded us that oleanders were very poisonous whenever he pruned the tree or picked up the leaf litter beneath it. It got so that we would try to beat him to it.

"Hey, Dad!" Laney or I would say. "Be careful with that tree. It's poisonous, you know!"

"I'll show you poisonous!" he'd always say. Then he'd snap his over-sized pruning shears at us, and we'd pretend to be afraid and run away.

I looked over at Laney. Her body shook with tears.

"What's wrong?" I asked, panicked.

"I'm scared. Jenna. How much longer can we keep doing this? What if someone finds out we're alone? What if they separate us? What if…?"

I wrapped my arms around her and patted her back. For the first time, I noticed that we were nearly the same height. She was my big sister. It didn't seem right for me to be almost as tall as her. I also noticed how skinny she was. Too skinny. Far skinnier than I was, even after I'd been so sick. My mind flooded with snippets of memories of her telling me she was full, and of her giving me the last few bites of her food. But she couldn't have been full. I felt her ribs poking out beneath her skin, protruding even farther than mine did.

An image blossomed in my mind's eye: I was a loud baby bird, peeping for food, my beak aimed up at the mamma bird—a bird with Laney's face. She was probably hungrier than I was, but she still gave me some of her food because she wanted to take care of me. A cruel voice in my head that sounded like Mom's whispered that maybe it was also because I always complained about being hungry. Maybe Laney just gave me her food to shut me up. My eyes filled with tears, but I brushed them off on Laney's shirt so she wouldn't see me cry and think she needed to comfort me. Again.

I took a deep breath and squared my shoulders. I *would* be brave and strong like Laney, and I wouldn't complain anymore. Not ever.

"Well, no one's found out we're alone yet, have they? And they won't if we're smart, like you said. We'll clean up the yard—*I'll* clean it up—and we'll make sure it stays neat so no one ever has a reason to come around again."

Laney sniffed and hugged me. "I'm sorry. You shouldn't have to worry about this stuff. You should be hanging out with your friends, and having fun, and…"

My voice was hard when I answered and it scared me a little bit. "Yeah, well, so should you. But it's not like that for us, is it?"

Softer, I said, "But you know what? Even though this is horrible, it's not as bad as living with Mom the way she was, and it's a lot less horrible than having Rich around."

After that, I spent a little time outside nearly every day. I weeded the yard and used the rusted pruning shears from the garage to trim the bushes. I found that if I kept up on it, there was never much to do. In some ways, I kind of liked the work, too. My mind went sort of blank and numb when I picked weeds, but in a good way. Sometimes, when neighbors passed by, walking their dogs or pushing fat babies in strollers, I was able to pretend nothing was wrong, even if only for a few minutes at a time.

One man, who had white hair that he wore in a buzz cut, walked by at the same time every evening. He looked like he was once square and tough, but now his stomach was big and round and he kind of looked like he was pregnant. He limped a little bit as he walked a beige dog with a mop of fur, and even though he carried himself stiffly, the man was really nice.

"You're doing my yard next, right?" he'd ask. Or "Do you do windows too?"

Sometimes he told me a joke or, if he was on his phone, he would just give me a stiff salute and keep walking.

One time he stopped and said, "How on earth do your parents get you to work out here so often? My wife and I never had kids, but my brother couldn't get *his* to do a thing without bribing or threatening them."

I think he bought it when I tried to laugh naturally. I said, "Oh, bribery. Definitely bribery."

I was in seventh grade that year, and Laney was a junior in high school. If we would have known that the world would be a different place before the end of summer, maybe we would have done things differently. Instead, Laney just kept paying the bills, and we did everything we could to avoid Suspicion. When there was money left over after Laney wrote checks for everything, we'd buy groceries. When there wasn't anything left over, we searched for other ways to feed the bunny.

MARCH: SAVED BY THE BAGEL

We might have been getting the hang of things by March but it was getting harder to pretend that things were normal with my friends, and sleepovers became less frequent.

Amber had been my best friend since Kindergarten. In third grade, we even had those necklaces with the heart shaped pendant broken in half. Her side said, "Best." My side said, "Friends." The halves fit together perfectly, like a simple jigsaw puzzle, and we both wore them until fourth grade when the cheap chain on mine broke.

We still hung out together at the same lunch table in middle school, but she did stuff with other people more than with me. I couldn't really blame her. I didn't have money to go to the mall or to go ice-skating on the weekends, and I couldn't even walk to the store with her after school to buy a Popsicle or a candy bar. She made the junior varsity volleyball team earlier in the year and a lot of new friends came with being on the team. When track started up, she joined that, too. The sports fees were too much for us to afford, and they also required a physical from a doctor. And anyway, Laney didn't think it was a good idea for either of us to do anything that burned as many calories as running or playing sports.

Without as many sleepovers, we found more creative

ways to feed the bunny. Laney babysat for her friends' younger brothers and sisters sometimes. But babysitting jobs didn't come up very often. We constantly brainstormed ways to earn money, but most of our ideas required money to begin with, like bake sales or making crafts. We started planning a garage sale to get us through summer, but that was still a few months away.

One day, Laney came home more excited than I'd seen her in a long time.

"I think I might know how to get us more food!" she said.

She took Mom's cell phone into her room. I tried to follow her, but she stopped me. "I don't want to get your hopes up," she said, closing her door. I tried to eavesdrop but she opened the door and shooed me away with a big smile on her face.

The next day was Saturday. We walked to the bagel shop just a few blocks away. I knew we couldn't afford to actually buy bagels, and Laney wouldn't tell me what we were doing, but she did give me a clipboard to hold. She printed off a letter on Mom's ancient printer. The ink was almost gone and the words were gray and blotchy in places. I started to read it but she stopped me. "I want it to be a surprise," she said. "You'll understand in a couple of minutes!"

"Hi. What can I get for you?" the guy behind the counter asked. He had shaggy brown hair and a few splotchy pimples traced a line across his forehead where his hair touched his skin. He looked like he was a few years older than Laney, but it was hard to tell. She was so tiny that she looked younger than she was.

"We're here to see Mr. Black," she said.

The guy stepped toward the back room and yelled, "Dad! Someone's here to see you."

A man with a dirty white apron came out of the back room. His stomach was as round as the bagels he sold. He wiped his hands on a rag that smelled faintly of bleach before he tossed it down on the counter. He held out his hand and Laney shook it. She looked like a grown up when she talked to him even though she was my size.

"I'm Laney Peters," she said. "I talked to you on the phone yesterday."

She faltered for a moment until he smiled and nodded. "Oh, yes. Let's see…it was a weekly volunteer club, is that right?"

Laney nodded. She glanced at me. Her face turned pink, but she smiled at him. "You have a good memory," she said with a grown-up laugh. It tinkled just a little, like Mom's used to.

I stood beside her and continued to hold the clipboard. I tried to look grown up like she did. She was skinnier than I was, but she looked so graceful standing there, not scrawny and knobby-kneed like me. Everyone always said we practically looked like twins, but I felt like a bony kid next to her. I hadn't realized how pretty Laney had gotten. The guy behind the counter kept sneaking glances at her. A younger boy cleaning up a spill by the drink machine glanced at me. I thought he might go to my school but I couldn't be sure. He looked familiar, but not familiar enough that I could place him in one of my classes. He gave me a lopsided smile and went back to mopping.

"Well," Mr. Black said, "Like I told you yesterday, we're always happy to donate our leftovers. We just need a letter from your organization each time we donate to you, for tax purposes."

Laney motioned to me. I lifted the clip on the clipboard and handed her the letter. She gave it to him. "Here you are," she said.

She even sounded like a grown up. "…and we can return every Saturday to pick them up for our Sunday morning meetings, is that correct?" she asked.

He smiled at her and I saw the family resemblance to

both the boys working there. "We'll be glad to help you out, but we do need a letter each time," he said again.

"Aaron or Evan can always help you if I'm not here when you stop in. It's a family business, and one of us is always here."

The younger son, Aaron, rolled the yellow mop bucket toward the backroom. Mr. Black called after him, "Go grab those boxes from the back, would you?"

Aaron brought out two cardboard boxes of bagels. Two boxes! He sat them on the counter and carefully folded them up so they were closed tight and formed a handle at the top. I tried to dazzle him with a smile like Laney's, but he didn't seem to notice. He handed each of us a box. He didn't have his hand all the way out of the handle when I grabbed it, trapping his hand inside. He laughed it off but I was mortified. Nothing like that would have ever happened to Laney.

"Thanks so much. We'll see you again next week," Laney said. I don't think she even noticed the way Evan stared at her, or how a couple of the customers turned to watch her when we left.

Our stomachs rumbled as we walked home.

"Why are you so quiet all of the sudden," Laney asked when we were nearly home. "I thought you'd be excited about the free bagels!" She wrinkled her forehead. "You're...you're not mad at me for lying, are you?"

Laney did everything for me. She took care of me when I was sick, she held me when I cried, and she even figured out a way for us to get free food. I wasn't mad at her—I couldn't be. But I also couldn't bring myself to tell her that I was jealous of her, that I wanted to be as pretty and as smart and as strong as she was. I smiled and tried to make it look real. "I'm just hungry, I guess."

We walked the rest of the way home in silence. I mostly forgot the stupid boy in the bagel shop when we ate lunch. We shared a can of tomato soup and we each had a bagel.

We spread them with thick layers of almost-expired cream cheese that Aaron had thrown into one of the boxes at Mr. Black's suggestion. It was a feast.

Every week after that, we picked up more bagels. Sometimes, if Evan was the only one there, he'd give us each a cup for a fountain drink while he flirted with Laney. When we walked home, we were just two teenagers drinking sodas, carrying bagels, and laughing. We ate bagels for breakfast nearly every morning from then on. It was good to go to school and not starve all morning long. "Bagels" showed up on our list of good things more than once after that.

APRIL: DUMPSTER DIVING

We were hungry most of the week of spring break, even with the bagels we got. It was even worse than Christmas break had been. Spring break was only one week long instead of two and a half weeks, but we had nothing in the pantry at all, and neither of us had been invited to a sleepover for weeks. Citrus trees bear their fruit in winter so we couldn't even steal oranges from our neighbors' trees.

Laney kept saying, "I'll figure something out. Don't worry Jenna. I'll figure something out."

Near the end of spring break, when we were especially desperate, we went dumpster diving behind a fast food place down the road. Laney thought the food they threw away might not be too gross since it wasn't made to order like food in a real restaurant. It was cooked, wrapped, and set under warming lamps. She figured the extras would be thrown away all wrapped up so the food should still be clean and safe to eat.

The moon was just a sliver that night, so the only light came from passing cars and the street lamps' wide, foggy-looking pools of orange light. Music blared from a car that passed us. Faces blurred past from its open windows and a whistle faded before the car's brake lights came on. The men in the car peered backwards at us. One of them yelled something at us, but the car behind them honked so they drove on. We walked faster.

I grabbed Laney's hand. Ahead, the car's brake lights came on again and the car made a U-turn in the intersection.

"They're turning around, Laney! What do we do?"

"Keep walking," she said between gritted teeth. "And don't turn around. Maybe they just missed their turn."

We heard the car approaching us from behind as the loud thump-thump-thump of the bass sound of the stereo system crept closer. The car glided past, slow enough that we got a good look at it. It was an older model of some kind, painted over in places with the flat black color of primer. The doors and hood were deeply dented and thick black exhaust drifted from the tailpipe. It smelled like smoky, oily sludge. The two guys who leaned out the windows were probably not much older than Laney, but their faces looked dangerous, in the same rough way Rich's had. We kept walking.

"Lookin' good, ladies!" the one with long, greasy blonde hair and a face full of stubble yelled over the sound of the radio. "Wanna go to a party? We've got plenty of room for both of you!"

We walked faster. The guy with black hair, nearly shaved to his skull, and a round, brown face said, "Hey! Why you gotta be like that? You need to have some fun! Loosen up, ladies!"

Someone else inside the car said something unintelligible and all the guys started laughing. It was a rude laugh that made me sure the joke had been a gross one until I saw the greedy, leering way they looked at our legs. It *had* been gross, and it *hadn't* been a joke—whatever the guy had said—he meant it.

Laney must have been thinking the same thing. She squeezed my hand as we stepped off the curb to cross a small neighborhood street.

She whispered, "Let me handle this, okay?"

I nodded. I didn't know what to do or say anyway. If I'd

been alone, I would have started running when the car slowed down the first time.

The car pulled in front of us. It blocked us from crossing the street and black exhaust blew into our faces. I coughed. Someone inside mimicked me and pretended to have a coughing fit. All of the men inside started laughing again. Other cars passed us and sometimes a face stared out at us curiously, but no one stopped to help.

Laney still had my hand, and she pulled me toward the front of the car so we could get around it. The driver pulled up another few feet, blocking us again. The guys inside laughed more. "What do you say? You're not afraid, are you? Let's just go for a ride, that's all ladies! Just a ride."

Someone inside snickered and said, "Yeah, right. Just a ride. That's all!"

Laney pulled me back to the sidewalk and pushed me behind her. She put one hand on her hip. "I don't know," she said. Her voice sounded strong and confident...and sassy. "It looks to me like your car's pretty full already."

She pretended to peek inside but she stayed up on the sidewalk with me. The smell of alcohol and dense cigarette smoke drifted out the window now that the car was directly in front of us. A guy in the middle seat, in the back, snuck a sip of something and then belched.

"Ah geez, man. That stinks!" the guy on the far side of him said while he waved his hands in front of his face. The rest of the passengers laughed, distracted for a moment.

The one in the middle belched again and got punched in the shoulder this time. The smack turned into a scuffle between the two. The scruffy blonde on our side of the car got in a few whacks when a cigarette went flying and landed in his lap. The driver yelled at them. "Knock it off back there! You want us to get pulled over?"

"We *are* pulled over, you idiot," someone shouted back at him. "Geez, you need a drink. Here." The bottle was passed to the driver. He took a chug and then belched

37

himself.

"Hey, hey," said the blonde guy. "Don't be rude. Maybe the ladies would like a drink, too."

Laney and I had started to walk around the back of the car, hoping to slip past the guys while they were preoccupied. The driver nearly hit us when he backed the car up. We jumped back on the curb. Laney smiled without really smiling and said, "Sorry guys. Not gonna happen."

She grabbed my hand. "Look," she said. "Our dad's already pissed we're not home. He said he'd call the cops if we're not back in a few minutes."

She pointed down at the next neighborhood street as if we lived there and were practically home. She pulled me out in front of the car. The driver tried to block us with the car again. Their laughter sounded distorted and evil. The part of my imagination that always took over when I was scared whispered things to me: Those weren't men in the car. The car was really full of evil creatures that were dressed up like men; they were demons wearing man-suits.

Laney pulled me back to the curb. She stood with her arms crossed and her legs planted shoulder-width apart. She shrugged her shoulders and sighed out loud. "We can sit here all night, guys, but sooner or later our dad *will* call the police. But if you want your evening to end with a DUI, I guess that's your problem."

I nodded beside her and tried to look as confident and unfazed as she did. I probably just looked like a stupid kid who was copying her older sister.

We couldn't hear all of the conversation over the loud, thumping music but what we did hear went something like this:

"…not worth it…"

"…ah, c'mon. She's hot…both are…"

"…probably underage anyway…"

The scruffy guy argued the hardest, but Laney had said exactly the right thing.

The driver stared into his rearview mirror at each car that passed, and he yelled at the guy behind him. "Keep that bottle out of sight, for crying out loud! What if the cops drive by? That's an open container, you idiot!"

He shook his head and muttered something to himself, and then he pulled the car forward. He cranked the wheel hard to the left and turned the car around. When the car was facing the other direction, the scruffy blonde leaned over his friend and shouted though the window, "Hey, At least give me your number!"

The car rolled away and the blaring music and black fumes followed it. Laney and I watched the car disappear before we turned around and ran home. We never made it to the dumpster, and we never dared to try again.

The rest of April wasn't much better. We did a search for "wild foods" on the computers at the library one day and found out that people sometimes ate the fruit and the young pads from the prickly pear cactus, so we tried them. The pads were called *nopales* and we hated them—no matter how we cooked them, they were always sort of slimy. But food is food I guess, and there were lots of prickly pear cactuses in our neighborhood.

Even with the nopales we ate most days, I don't know how we would have survived if it hadn't been for our free bagels and the free lunch program at school that we went back to when spring break ended.

MAY: SHE FIGURED SOMETHING OUT

At the beginning of May, Laney did what she promised. She figured something out. That's when she started bringing home money. It was always cash. And there was a lot of it. She was always vague when I asked about what she was doing and where she was working.

"Don't worry about it, Jenna," she told me. "I'm taking care of everything, and you don't need to worry anymore, okay? I'll take care of you just like I promised."

She bought groceries, lots of groceries. We stopped going to the bagel shop, and she even bought us both a couple of outfits from the secondhand store, but she also stopped smiling as much. And her laugh changed a little, too. Sometimes the hair stood up on my arms when I heard her laugh. It had changed somehow and I hated it, but I didn't worry.

That's what I regret the most. That I didn't worry. Maybe if I had, she'd still be here. Maybe we would have been together when the world came crashing to an end, and I could have taken care of her and protected her the way she always took care of me.

But it was such a relief to have food in the fridge and in the pantry that it was easier than it should have been to overlook the way Laney changed, so I *didn't* worry. Not even a little. I had a normal life again, even more normal than it had been when Mom was alive. I came home from school and sat down at the table with a snack—something good like cookies and milk—and I did my homework. Sometimes I pretended everything really was normal; that Mom was alive and back to the way she used to be, and that she'd come in the kitchen any minute to check my work and ask how school was. Except that it wasn't Mom who did those things. It was Laney, but that was okay. It really was.

There were only two days left before the end of the school year when I stopped being able to pretend anything anymore. It was a Wednesday. Laney didn't meet me at school to walk home with me like she usually did. I waited around until someone from the office came out and asked if I needed to call someone to pick me up.

"No. No thanks," I said as I hurried off to avoid more questions.

Laney didn't usually carry Mom's phone with her. It was at home and besides, I convinced myself that Laney must have told me to walk home by myself and I'd just forgotten. She'd been doing that more often and when she did, she usually came home with money.

She wasn't home when I got there, and she still wasn't home at seven when I finally called one of her friends. Even with the money she brought home, we only used the phone for emergencies. I hoped Laney wouldn't be mad, but the more I thought about it, the more convinced I became that she hadn't told me to walk home alone after all. And I was sure she hadn't mentioned that she'd be late, either.

"How should I know where she is?" Sammie said. "I hardly ever see her anymore." Sammie's voice sounded wounded, and it was only the desperation in my own voice when I asked, "Do you have any idea where she might be?" that teased a response from her.

"The last time I saw her today was when she went off with that guy in the white van after school."

"What guy?" I asked, trying not to let her hear the alarm

that rang in my brain.

"I don't know his name. It's that guy who picks her up sometimes to babysit his kids. The one who looks like he's not even old enough to have kids of his own."

I knew it wasn't true. Laney wasn't babysitting. Sammie believed that's what Laney had been doing—that part was true. But Laney would have told me if she was babysitting. And even when she did babysit, she never made the kind of money she'd been bringing home for the past month. I hated myself for not seeing it sooner.

I slept under my bed that night. I hadn't done that since the last time Laney had a sleepover. I woke up three or four times, pulled myself out from under the bed and checked her bed, Mom's bed, even the couch, the back patio, and the pile of dirty clothes in Mom's closet that we'd been avoiding. But Laney wasn't there. She wasn't anywhere. The next morning I called the attendance line at her school and reported her absence. I tried my best to sound like Mom and to keep my voice from shaking. I heard Laney call our absences in often enough that I think I did a passable job of it despite the way my voice cracked.

"This is Marsha Peters. I just wanted to let you know that Laney is sick." I did my best to avoid Suspicion and protect myself and Laney for when she came back. "She might be out for a few days. I'll probably send my other daughter in to pick up Laney's stuff if she's not better by the last day of school…"

I must not have Aroused Suspicion because no one in the office ever called back or seemed particularly concerned. I was relieved. And terrified.

***

Laney didn't come home that day or the next. I left for school earlier than usual on the last day of school—Arizona schools used to get out at the end of May. I had to turn in

Laney's textbooks or we'd have to pay for them. The ladies in the front office of the high school were laughing and chatting when I walked in. They seemed just as relieved that the year was over as the students did. I held my breath while the school secretary thumbed through Laney's books, looking for marks and torn pages. She turned each book upside down and shook it. A piece of paper fell out. She laughed good-naturedly.

"I always miss something when I just flip through the pages," she explained. "Does your sister want this or should I toss it?"

I grabbed the counter to steady myself. "I'll take it." My voice came out even but my hands shook like an old man's when I took the bookmark I'd made for Laney at Christmas. It was dog eared and creased. She must have used it every time she used the book. I folded it very carefully and slid it into my pocket so it wouldn't crumple more. It was a useless scrap of paper, but it meant everything to me. It still does, even now when you can use a hundred dollar bill as a book mark if you want to.

The secretary shrugged. "Well, that's about it. Her books are in good shape, and her teachers have cleared her, so you're good to go."

She handed me a big manila envelope. "These are her last few graded assignments, her report card—that kind of thing. I hope she feels better soon. It doesn't seem fair to start summer off sick!"

"Yeah, it's not fair," I agreed. I couldn't seem to make my voice any louder than a whisper. It *wasn't* fair. Nothing was fair. I wanted to go home and crawl under my bed. Instead, I walked to school, telling myself, "Be strong. Be strong. Be strong like Laney."

I made it through my last day, but just barely. Three of my teachers asked me if I was okay. All of them let us sit and talk during class, but I didn't speak to anyone. I buried my face in a book and pretended to read. Hardly anyone spoke to me anyway. They passed around their yearbooks and read what other people had written, laughing and shrieking at their pictures and the notes from their crushes.

"What a bummer," they said when they asked where my yearbook was, and I had to tell them that I hadn't gotten one. They hurried away, uncomfortable.

Excited voices carried through the classrooms. The teachers sat at their desks, as relaxed and happy about the last day of school as the staff in the front office of the high school had been. The halls were loud and rowdy, too. Kids laughed and yelled, but the happiness and excitement skirted around me. The thick crowd parted as I walked through it.

One time in Science, we looked at amoebas through our microscopes. We watched the way their bodies enveloped their food, and that's what I felt like—an amoeba engulfing a tidbit of food. Except that I was the food and the other kids were the amoeba. I was inside the amoeba, being swallowed up by it, and there was nothing I could do about it.

My friends hung out at the wash in the neighborhood after school that day. I went with them because it would have been Suspicious if I hadn't. I was still a part of the same circle of friends that I'd always known, but I was on the fringes of things now. I didn't do any of the after-school activities they did. I didn't have the cute clothes that were so important to everyone. I couldn't afford the makeup my friends were starting to wear or those cool belt buckles all the girls had, and I couldn't even fake the right amount of interest in boys, or the latest movie, or what happened on the TV shows everyone else watched. I was tolerated only because I'd always been there with them and because, I think, a few of their parents suspected that my mom "had a problem" and they felt sorry for me.

"I've got to get home," I said when Amber tried to convince me to stay.

She didn't put much effort into it, and I didn't think I

could pretend much more, anyway—not when I wanted to crumple into a heap on the warm pavement and never move again. But that would have Aroused Suspicion.

"Mom and Laney are both sick. I've got to make dinner tonight. I might be getting sick, too," I added. My voice sounded flat and distant. Getting sick would explain why I wasn't as excited as everyone else about the start of summer. That was good.

"That sucks!" Amber said, but she'd already turned and was talking to another friend about all the fun stuff she was going to do over summer.

"I'm going away to camp again this year, and my mom signed me up for art classes and swim team and indoor volleyball, too. Oh, and we're going to my aunt's house in Denver for practically all of July!"

A few people gave me half-hearted waves when I left. As I walked away, I heard Amber finish. "I swear, I don't know *how* I'm going to survive this summer."

I asked myself the same question. *How am I going to survive this summer?*

The last day of school meant the last day of free lunches.

"Laney?" I called as I unlocked the door.

Maybe she was back. I was still telling myself that she must have gotten sick or hurt and couldn't come home, and today she'd be back. I knew she would never abandon me, so she had to be stuck somewhere. But her name disappeared into the empty house and I was still alone.

I was alone the next day, and the following one, and the one that came after that, too. I wish I had worried about the way Laney had changed. Why hadn't I worried?

JUNE: GOING BATTY

It was nearly nine and it was still light outside. The air was sweltering and heavy inside the house. Outside, it was just sweltering. A summer wind blew, but it was oven-hot. The temperature had been hovering around a hundred and ten all week and the only way to escape it was to stay inside with the air conditioner on high. I didn't have that luxury, but at least the house provided shade.

I sat at the small, dented table in the kitchen, alone, as I always was. I fanned myself with a piece of junk mail. The checkbook was out and the bills sat in front of me. The electric bill was too high because of the air conditioner, even though I barely ever turned it on. I couldn't afford to pay the electric bill and the water bill this month. Not if I had to buy groceries, pay the minimum on Mom's credit card bill, and the phone, too. I gulped and tried to swallow back the fear that wanted to eat me. I looked down. My hands were clenched and shaking. I forced them open and dropped the pen I held. My head fell to the table and I started to sob.

"Stop it!" I screamed. My voice echoed in the emptiness, and I felt even more alone and afraid. I whimpered and curled up into a ball in my chair with my feet on the seat. It wasn't hard to do. I didn't take up much space anymore; I was a skeleton with some skin and that's all. I rocked back and forth as I cried, and each sob sounded lonelier than the last. I tried to pull myself out of it, to be strong, but the silence of the house was too much. I pushed away from the table and ran to my room. I threw myself onto the floor and pulled my body under the bed in one practiced movement.

That night I had the happy dream again. At least, it started out happy. I swam into Dad's arms while Mom and Laney cheered me on from shore. But when I reached Dad, he changed and he wasn't Dad anymore. He became Rich, and he was covered in dry blood from the gunshot wound in his head. The blood flaked away when he moved. On the shore, Mom and Laney turned into skeletons. They both laughed that hard, cold laugh that meant there was no more happiness left in the world. And they both waved envelopes that looked suspiciously like bills.

***

Those first few weeks of summer were the worst. I stayed inside and waited for Laney to come back, but she never did. The longer I stayed cooped up in the house, the more afraid I got. I kept the TV turned on and the volume cranked up day and night. An image of the electric bill always floated in the back of my mind but instead of being a piece of paper, it looked like a slot machine that had dollar signs instead of lemons and cherries. Every time I turned the air conditioner on or left the TV on, the number of dollar signs went up, up, up. I kept the air conditioner off most of the time, but I couldn't turn off the television. I just couldn't. The noise and the voices and the canned applause were the only things that kept me from going batty.

I stayed under my bed and strained my ears to hear whatever show was on, afraid to come out. I felt safer in the tight space, but the loneliness and fear kept getting worse. I stayed under my bed longer each day. When I was too hungry to stand it anymore, I tiptoed through the house as if there was someone in another room I had to avoid. I crouched down in the kitchen, hidden in a corner like a mouse while I nibbled tiny bits of rationed food. I winced at the sound of my own jaws when I chewed. Then I scurried back to my bedroom and slid into the only place I felt safe. I started having sick fantasies about how my mummified and dried up body would be discovered. I was sure it was only a matter of time before I starved to death.

A reporter would interview the nosy neighbors across the street. She would start by saying, "We're here in Ahwatukee, a friendly little suburb of Phoenix, where things like this aren't supposed to happen…"

The old man would talk and his hunched-over wife would nod silently in agreement, but their beady eyes would gleam. When they went back inside, they'd call their friends and tell them to turn the news on quick.

"We thought the horrible smell was a dead roof rat or something," the man would say as he leaned into the microphone. "But eventually the smell faded so we forgot about it."

The police would have the house blocked off with yellow crime scene tape.

The reporter would tip her microphone toward a police officer and ask, "What happened here, sir?"

He would take off his hat and scratch his head. "The body seems to be that of a young female who starved to death. The whereabouts of her family are a mystery."

The reporter would end by looking directly at the camera. "And that's all the news we have on this sad and shocking story. Anyone with information about the dead girl or her missing family is urged to call the number listed at the bottom of your screen."

Every time I imagined it, the horrible fantasy became more realistic and crisp. It got so that as soon as I closed my eyes, the scene started to grow more details. One morning, I lay under my bed, sweating as I tried to stop the fantasy from starting. I watched a dust bunny drift back and forth with each breath I took as I half-listened to the television. There was a commercial on about the teen section of the Ironwood Library. The library was only a few blocks away, not far from where Laney and I had tried to go dumpster diving. The commercial was nearly over before I came out of my daze and really heard it. When the drone of the narrator's voice began to make sense, I got another chance at life.

***

No one noticed or minded if I stayed at the library all day. It was free and cool, too. Cool was important. Sometimes I just read books or thumbed through magazines. Other times I signed up for the Internet and scoured it for more wild foods I could find in my neighborhood, or for money-saving tips. At home, I became even more obsessive about the electric bill. I only turned the air conditioner on at night, and only long enough to cool the house down so I could fall asleep.

I blocked off nearly all the air vents with cardboard and duct tape from the garage. Laney and I had talked about doing that during the winter because of the expense of turning on the heat, but she decided it might be a fire hazard. The websites I went to said that it was fine to block off the air though, so I figured it must be safe.

I kept all the doors shut and I stuffed towels under the gaps at the bottom so the cool air couldn't creep into the rooms I didn't use, like Mom's room or Laney's. I unplugged everything that could be unplugged, even the washer and dryer and the stove. When I needed them, I plugged them back in. I took water bottles with me to the library and filled them from the water fountain each day before I went home. The water tasted terrible, but it was free. The bills didn't drop very much with all those changes, but it was enough that I had a few extra dollars left for food that month. If I had known that the end was as near as it was, I would have run the air conditioner on high all day and night. I would have still been hungry, but at least I wouldn't have been hot and miserable all the time, too.

Even at the library I was careful to avoid Arousing Suspicion. I alternated where I sat to keep from being noticed. On Mondays and Wednesdays I sat in an overstuffed arm chair hidden in the mystery section. On Tuesdays and Fridays I sat at the tables by the computers or used the Internet. On the weekends, I sat in the kid's section, nearly hidden by the cushions and pillows where the librarian read books to the kids during the week. The weekends were the best even though I came in later on Saturdays than I did on other days. I looked forward to dozing off in the pillows, surrounded by the sounds of mothers reading stories to their children.

One Saturday, a toddler with black curls done up in cute little pigtails stumbled up to me and handed me a book.

I took it and asked, "Did you want me to read this to you?"

The little girl nodded at me. Her mother came up behind her and smiled in apology. She told her daughter, "She doesn't want to read you a story, sweetie. Come on. Let's go look for some more books."

The little girl didn't move. She just stood there, smiling at me. Innocence shined in her round little face and her mother smiled down at her. She thought her daughter was the most beautiful thing in the world, you could tell. My mom used to look at Laney and me like that.

I took the book and said, "I don't mind."

The girl plopped down next to me, and I read the story to her. When I was done, she stuck her chubby, diapered bottom in the air to stand up. She took the book from me and then toddled off. The mom smiled at me and said, "That was really nice of you. Thank you," before she followed after her daughter. I thought about writing that on the list on the fridge, but as soon as it crossed my mind, I started to tear up. I missed Laney so much. Why hadn't I worried more?

I got to the library most mornings before the sun rose too high in the sky. I was usually there, waiting in the shade of the building for the doors to open, and I stayed until the librarian announced closing. I snuck in my lunch—whatever food I could scrounge that day or buy with the few dollars I managed to make in the Saturday morning garage sales I started having.

What did I need Mom's clothes for? Or most of the furniture in the house? If I could move it outside by myself, I sold it. I sold most of Mom's clothes, but kept Laney's. I was quickly outgrowing most of my own clothes despite my near-starvation diet, and I could fit into some of her stuff, at least sort of. Some things fit better than others. I sold the DVD player and the few DVDs we had, but I kept the TV. It used electricity and Laney had canceled cable back when we got the first bill after Mom died, but it was the closest thing I had to company. When I got really freaked out by the silence in the house, I still turned it on just to hear the voices.

***

A couple of weeds made my stomach twist with anxiety when I noticed them one evening as I came home from the library. I hadn't been keeping up with the yard work because it was so hot, but seeing the tall weeds by the side gate freaked me out. When I stepped through the yard to look at them closer, I saw that it wasn't really that bad. There were only a few. Even weeds couldn't tolerate the scorching heat of an Arizona summer very well.

While I worked, the man with the dog came around the corner. He didn't wave or tease me like he usually did. He just stood and watched me for long enough that I started to get nervous. His fuzzy little dog sniffed at the edge of the yard and raised its leg on a bush. I didn't know what else to do, so I pretended I didn't notice him until he spoke.

"You know, young lady, I have a yard full of weeds that need pulling if you're interested in making a few extra bucks this weekend."

Money! I almost forgot myself and accepted the offer immediately.

"Sure!" I said. I remembered to cover myself at the last minute and added, "I have to ask my mom if it's okay first, though. Can you wait a minute?"

He nodded and watched while I went to the front door. I stepped inside and said very loudly, "Mom, one of the neighbors asked if I can pull weeds for him this weekend. Is that okay?"

I pretended to listen for a response. I nodded my head, although I wasn't sure the man was even watching. In my mind, I imagined what my mom would have said a couple of years ago.

"As long as it doesn't interfere with your chores or homework you can pick as many weeds as you want."

Aloud I said, "Okay! Thanks, Mom!"

I turned to the man and said, "It's fine! She said I can as long as it doesn't interfere with my chores or homework— but it's on the weekend anyway and school's out for the summer…"

The man chuckled. "Spoken like a true mother. Or a wife, for that matter!"

He pointed behind me, over the roof of my house and to the side. "Our house is catty corner to yours. We're the one with the big palm tree in the back. Not behind you, but next to the guy behind you. It's taupe with dark brown trim. Think you can find it?"

I turned and looked where he was pointing. I nodded. "No problem. What time do you want me to come over?"

"Well, I'm an old military man so I'm up at oh five hundred every day. Just come by when you want to do the work. It's fine if you want to come by early, before it gets too hot."

I was more excited than I'd been in a long time. "Thanks, Mister…" I hesitated. I didn't know his name.

Gruffly, he said, "It's Branson. My name's Brian Branson."

***

I carried the bucket and stick I used to dig up the dirt around weeds when I did my own yard. I worried I might be too early, but the garage door was up and Mr. Branson was tinkering around inside. A large box fan blew air around the garage, but I didn't think it cooled things down much. A few beads of sweat dripped down his neck.

I stopped in front of the garage. I didn't want to bother him, and I was suddenly worried that maybe he hadn't really meant for me to come by. Maybe he was just asking if I'd weed for him the way he sometimes joked about whether I did windows. He smiled when he glanced up from an old burnished metal workbench. He didn't seem surprised to see me, so that was good.

"Hi there, kiddo." He did a double take at my bucket and added, "Well, you're prepared, I see. No second thoughts, then?"

"No, sir."

He stepped out of the garage and wiped his hands on an old greasy rag that smelled like motor oil.

"Well, this is it. It's not much of a yard, but it's more than I want to weed with this back of mine." He rubbed his back and winced. "You know our dog, Meatball, already. He's friendly. Just make sure you shut the gate when you go around back so he can't get out, okay?"

I nodded.

"I'll be puttering around in here for a while longer so give a shout if you need anything."

Weeding isn't a very hard job and there weren't all that many weeds in his yard anyway. I was a little disappointed. I was hoping for lots and lots of weeds so I could earn a lot of money. I figured I'd be lucky if he gave me five bucks for the work. Still, that would be enough to feed me pretty well for a couple of days if I was careful. I sighed and got to it.

It took less than an hour to pull the weeds in the front, even after checking and rechecking the yard to make sure I hadn't missed anything. I dripped with sweat when I was done, and I knew my face was as pink as the quartz gravel that was spread around the gigantic landscaping boulders in his yard. There was a breeze, but it was the same hot one we always had during summer, the kind that feels like the blast of heat from an oven. I went around back and stood in the shade of the small patio. I was wiping the sweat from my face with the hem of my shirt when the back door slid open and a petite woman stepped out and looked at me. The scent of baking cookies followed her on a wave of cool air. I wasn't sure which I was more tempted by—the icy air or the smell of the cookies that made my stomach rumble and my mouth water.

The fine lines around the woman's brown eyes crinkled when she smiled; she looked like she smiled a lot. Her brown hair had streaks of gray in it but she was trim and fit.

"I thought I heard the gate close," she said. "I'm Mary, by the way. Brian told me you were the best weeder in the neighborhood!"

Meatball stuck his head out the patio door. He stood between Mary's legs and when he realized I wasn't Brian, he bounded over to me. His claws clicked on the concrete and he put his paws up on my legs. His tongue lolled out of the side of his mouth.

"No, Meatball! Get down…"

"It's okay," I said. "I love dogs."

I crouched down and scratched him behind the ears. I always wanted a dog but Dad had been allergic, and after he died we couldn't afford one, anyway. Meatball's fur smelled like flea shampoo and cookies when I rubbed my face on the top of his head. He licked at the sweat on my face.

Mary looked at me, concerned. "Can I get you a drink? You look like you could use something. I don't want you to keel over from the heat!"

I hesitated for a moment. It was always hard for me to decide when to accept food or drinks and when to be polite and turn them down, especially since my stomach always wanted more than I had. I didn't want to risk Arousing Suspicion.

"No thanks," I started to say, thinking of the money they'd be paying me. They might decide to pay me less if they gave me a drink, but Mary had already slipped back inside. She came back out with a bottle of water and a soda.

She shook her head and smiled at me. "Brian said you were a very polite young lady, but you'll be a polite and dead young lady if you die of dehydration."

She laughed at her own joke and my stomach knotted up. She had a happy laugh that reminded me of Mom's before she started drinking.

She put the bottle and can on the patio table and added, "...and we can't have you dying of dehydration when you're pulling *our* weeds, now can we?"

I shook my head and laughed. She didn't seem to notice how shaky it sounded. Jokes about people dying or being killed made me nervous. "I guess not. Thank you."

The backyard was smaller than the front, and I was done in less than twenty minutes. I drank the water Mary left for me. It was lukewarm after just that short time outside. I put the soda at the bottom of my bucket and covered it with a few wilted weeds instead of drinking it. I threw the rest of the weeds in their trash can when I went back around to the front of the house. The sour smell of old dog poop and rotten garbage blew into my face when the lid dropped back in place. I barely noticed it—I was too busy thinking about how I would savor the soda after dinner.

Mr. Branson was still in the garage when I went around front. "Done already?" he asked.

"Yeah, you didn't have very many weeds."

I hesitated and then asked, "Do you want to check to make sure I got everything?"

I started to worry that I might have missed something after all and he wouldn't want to pay me anything. He made a show of examining the front yard and then the back.

"I see you picked the weeds in the cracks of the patio, too. I had a crew doing my yard a few months ago, and they usually missed those. Drove me crazy."

He went to the back door and poked his head inside. "Mary, bring me my wallet, would you?"

My heart thrummed like a hummingbird's wings and I tried not to lick my lips in anticipation. The smell of freshly baked cookies floated outside again, and I faked a cough to cover the rumbling of my stomach.

Mary brought him his wallet and he thumbed through it. She winked at me and handed me another bottle of water.

"Thanks," I said. I tried not to smile when she rolled her eyes at her husband.

"Here he goes," she whispered out of the side of her mouth. He ignored her and continued to make a show of considering how much to pay me.

"Hmmm. Let's see. Nearly two hours of back-breaking yard work in the hot sun, minus the cost of a bottle of water and having Meatball lick the sweat off your face. Hmmm. How does fifteen dollars sound?"

I swallowed hard. Fifteen bucks! I could buy stuff to make sandwiches for the whole week with that! And not just peanut butter and jelly. I could buy lunch meat! Or stuff to make burritos! I might even have enough left over to buy a candy bar for dessert! My stomach rumbled again.

Brian and Mary exchanged glances—they looked at each other the way people do when they're both thinking the same thing. The smile dropped from my face. I messed up. Somehow I messed up! Did I say something I shouldn't have? Or had they heard my stomach rumble? Was that it?

I swallowed hard and tried to smile again.

"That seems like a lot of money, sir." My voice sounded flat, even to me.

It took a moment before he answered. And when he did, his voice was harder than before, not playfully gruff like it had been. "You're right," he said.

He looked at Mary. "You'd better go wrap up some of those cookies you made. She'll have to take some of them home to even things out." The pretend gruffness was back.

My confusion must have shown on my face. When Mary went inside he whispered to me, "She's a terrible cook. Just terrible. Fifteen dollars is too much to pay for the yard, but I have to give you a little extra money for taking some of those awful cookies off my hands."

Mary brought out a plate filled with cookies—a dozen maybe. The chocolate chips were still shiny, the way they are when they've just come out of the oven. Plastic wrap covered the top of the plate and steam collected inside. She handed them to me and I felt the warmth of the cookies through the bottom of the thick paper plate. I could tell just by the smell that there was nothing wrong with Mary's cooking.

I tried to protest even though my mouth watered so badly I almost couldn't speak. "Are you sure…?" I looked from him to her and back again.

Brian handed me the money and Mary said, "You're probably saving Brian's life by taking the cookies. He's diabetic, you know. He begs me to make him cookies and even though he's only allowed to eat one or two with dinner, I catch him sneaking them all the time. It's enough to drive me to drink!"

She patted his cheek and smiled at him. "I wouldn't make them at all if he didn't hound me so."

"Besides," she said. "You really did a lovely job on the yard. You earned the money and the cookies. Don't worry."

I thanked them both and turned to go, my bucket in one hand, cookies in the other, and money stuffed into the only pocket of my shorts that didn't have a hole. I was the luckiest girl in the world!

"Uh, just a moment," Brian said. He and Mary exchanged that look again. She nodded at him. I would have missed it if I hadn't turned when I did.

"You know, I'm not getting any younger and besides, I really do hate yard work. Maybe you'd be willing to come by once a month to weed for us? Perhaps the first Saturday of the month?

I almost dropped the cookies in my excitement. "Yes! Sure!" My heart raced. Fifteen extra dollars every month? Wow!

"Now, the first Saturday of July is in two weeks….is that going to be a problem?"

"Oh no! It's no problem! I'll be here first thing! Thank you! Thanks!"

I didn't even feel the baking heat as I walked around the corner and back to my house. The temperature inside my house wasn't much cooler than outside and I sighed, remembering the blast of cold air from Brian and Mary's home. I left the bucket just inside the front door and dug through it for the warm soda. I stuck it in the fridge and breathed the cold air that drifted out from the open doors until the slot machine image of the electric bill was too strong to ignore.

Then I filled the bathtub with a few inches of lukewarm water. I took the cookies with me, eating while I stripped off my sweaty, dusty clothes. I sank into the water and sighed with relief as the water cooled my overheated body. I promised myself I'd save a few cookies for later, but I didn't have the willpower; I finished them all off before I even got out of the tub.

That night, for the first time since Laney disappeared, I added two things to the list on the fridge: yard work and Mary's homemade cookies.

JULY: THE END IS NEAR

Brian and Mary only paid me ten dollars when I went back at the beginning of July. I tried not to cry when Brian gave me the money. The extra five dollars would have bought five loaves of cheap bread, or two jars of peanut butter, or two dozen eggs, or a big block of cheese.

"You were just here two weeks ago," Brian said when he paid me. "But I imagine the yard will be full of weeds again by the beginning of August. The monsoons are supposed to start early this year, and the rain always makes the weeds grow like...well, like weeds."

I tried to be positive as I walked away—to see it the way Laney would have—but tears leaked from my eyes. I almost didn't hear Mary call my name.

"Wait a sec!" she called after me. I stopped and turned around, blinking the tears back. Maybe I'd forgotten something in the backyard and Brian had brought it in through the house. I glanced into my bucket, but my little spade and my pointy stick were there. I hadn't brought anything else.

"I have a favor to ask," she said, holding out a plastic grocery bag. "You know it's just Brian, Meatball, and me here, right?"

I nodded slowly.

"Well, I've been cleaning out the fridge and the pantry

and found some things that we'll never be able to use up before they expire. I thought that maybe between you and your sister and your mom, that perhaps you could eat this stuff up before the expiration dates so none of it goes bad. It seems like such a waste to throw perfectly good food away, doesn't it?

Food! I nodded. "Yeah, it would be such a waste," I said, echoing her.

"Do you think your mother would mind?"

"Oh, no. Not at all. We hate wasting food," I said. "Thank you!"

She smiled at me and then froze. "Darn it! I forgot something! One more thing. Don't go anywhere, okay?"

I didn't move. The sun blazed down on me and sweat dripped down my temples. The armpits of my shirt were soaked through, and sweat ran down my back where my shirt was too wet to absorb it, but I didn't care. I wouldn't have moved for anything.

Mary came back out with another plate of cookies. "Shh!" she said. "You know how hard it is for Brian to turn down my cookies! You'll take these so he won't ruin his diet with them, won't you?"

"Oh, yes! Your cookies are delicious! Thank you! Oh, thank you!"

I looked back once when I reached the corner. Mary hadn't moved. She stood there, just watching me as I walked away. Had I been too excited about the cookies? Had I accepted the almost-expired food too easily? I worried the rest of the way home until I put the bag on the table and pawed through it, and then I forgot everything else.

There was a package of tortillas, two cans of refried beans, a whole block of cheese, a box of pasta, a can of spaghetti sauce, three cans of tuna, a small jar of mayonnaise, and a box of crackers. I burst into tears. There was so much food! Enough for nearly the whole month if I only ate twice a day! And there were Mary's cookies, too! I couldn't forget about the cookies! Or the money I earned!

I was a little better about rationing the cookies the second time around. I ate four and saved another four for after dinner. I packed the rest for my lunch at the library. I didn't know then—no one did—that the end of everything we all knew was so near.

ZERO HOUR

I twirled a strand of hair in my fingers and stared down at the book on the scarred wooden table in front of me, but my eyelids were heavy and the book was only a prop anyway, something to give me a reason to be at the library. It wasn't even August yet, but the monsoons had already started, just like Brian said they would. The howling wind and thunder and lightning storms that struck at night made it even harder to sleep than usual. It was humid besides, but the library was comfortably cool and I felt safe there.

I half-listened to the conversations around me.

"Is it just me or is it especially bright out today?" someone whispered to a friend.

"I thought it was just me! It's weird, right? I could hardly see when I came in. My eyes have been watering all day."

Farther away, someone else talked quietly into a cell phone. "Geez, I must need new sunglasses. It's really bright out today…"

The same meaningless conversations seemed to be taking place all around me, and the talk about the weather lulled me closer to sleep.

My eyes had just fluttered to a close when the library's intercom system screeched. I lurched up with a jerk. "Library patrons, I need your attention, please."

63

I heard her talk often enough that an image of the severe-looking librarian popped into my mind as soon as I heard her voice. She sounded tinny over the intercom, but urgent. "The library will be closing in five minutes. If you need to check anything out, please do so now. The library is closing in five minutes."

A man working at a nearby computer called out, "Are you kidding? It's two o'clock in the afternoon! Is this some kind of joke?"

A few more upset voices agreed. "Yeah, I didn't see anything posted about an early closure today. You can't just close without giving us some kind of notice!"

I looked around, confused. Other people began to grumble in agreement as they looked at their watches or at the big, round clock on the wall that looked just like the ones in every classroom at school.

Wherever she was, the librarian must have heard similar complaints because her voice was a little higher when the intercom system screeched again. "The President has declared a state of emergency for the entire country. Everyone has been asked to return to their homes immediately. I repeat, the library is closing in five minutes!"

People stared at one another. A few sets of eyebrows were drawn together angrily, but most people looked as worried as I felt. The man at the table next to me pulled out his smart phone and slid his finger across the touch screen.

My water bottles! I reached down and unzipped my backpack. I knew a few more ounces of water out of the faucet at home wouldn't raise the water bill very much, but the habit was established and I wanted to fill them before I left. I watched the man at the neighboring table out of the corner of my eye as I pulled them out.

"Holy cow!" he said.

My shoulders tensed. He was going to say something about the number of bottles I'd pulled from my backpack. I glanced at him, but he was staring at his phone, not at me.

"Listen to this!" He didn't seem to care if anyone was interested or even listening when he read aloud from the small screen. "The President has asked for the citizens of the United States to return to their homes immediately and without delay. He has requested that all businesses and organizations close down immediately..."

He paused as he scrolled down the screen farther, skipping a few paragraphs and flicking his fingers apart to enlarge the words. "Hey, this says that according to the CRS report for Congress—whatever that is—that the President has the right to exercise certain powers in the event that the nation is threatened by emergency circumstances."

Without looking up, he read on. Even those sitting in front of computers or with smart phones of their own stopped what they were doing to listen to him. "It says they've verified that the brightness of the sky, which has affected not just the United States, but every country in the world, is not the result of any known phenomenon. The President has been advised to declare a national emergency until the situation stabilizes. The leaders of virtually every other nation are doing the same."

Around me, people murmured. "A global emergency for a bright sky? This is a joke, right?"

"This is ridiculous!" a woman said from behind the bookshelves. Her voice was full of disgust.

The man skimmed more of the story and glanced up with a smirk on his face. He relaxed when he summarized the article. "Ha! Aliens. Some people think it's aliens. Or the end of the world. Or some kind of biological weapon. This must be some kind of farce or an elaborate hoax like War of the Worlds or something."

A guy a couple years older than Laney sat a few seats away. He wore faded jeans and an old tee shirt. He stood up and nearly tipped over a short stack of college textbooks that were probably for summer courses.

"Whatever," he said, loud enough for everyone to hear.

"I'm not sticking around here to find out what it is. Look!" He lifted the slats of the flimsy, commercial-grade blinds from the window beside him. He shielded his eyes with his other hand.

"Look outside! That's not natural!" His eyes were wide with panic when he dropped the blinds back in place.

Everyone in the library turned toward the window. A few people gasped at the light that streamed in from outside. Most shielded their eyes. All I saw was the clear blue sky before the blinds dropped back in place. It was bright out, but once I blinked a couple of times and my eyes adjusted to the light, I couldn't see what the problem was. I must have been looking out at the wrong angle or in the wrong direction or something because whatever was out there seemed to be too much for everyone else. They threw papers, pens, and books into their backpacks, bags, or purses, and piled their other belongings into their arms. They rushed toward the exit, pushing one another in their hurry to escape, not bothering to check out the books they had shoved into their bags. Their fear freaked me out. What was out there? I threw my water bottles back into my bag and race-walked to the door with everyone else.

The librarian shrieked and ran toward the crazed swarm of people when the alarm at the door went off. "Wait! You have to check those out! You can't just take books without checking them out!"

No one paid any attention to her. "This is a library! What are you doing?" she yelled. She grabbed books from people as they pressed past her. The crowd pushed through the small lobby toward the automatic sliding glass doors. The front of the crowd stopped outside the doors, forcing the back of to slow. The people in the middle were pushed and shoved from ahead and behind. That's where I was: right in the middle.

Cell phones rang in a concert of different ring tones while people frantically talked to family or friends. I moved through the crowd, small enough to slip toward the front. I dodged the sharp corners of books, but got hit on the lip by someone's elbow. I tasted blood in my mouth and my lip began to swell. I blinked back tears, and the man who hit me looked at me blankly, his phone to his ear; he had no idea what he'd done, only that he'd bumped into someone.

I pushed past a woman in denim shorts and a tee shirt. Her hair was pulled back in a ponytail and she held a whining toddler in her arms. "Shhh! You're okay. We'll be home in a few minutes and you can watch a movie. How does that sound? Do you want to watch a movie?

The girl stopped crying and nodded happily. She started chanting a song I'd heard on TV when I hid under my bed sometimes.

The man who read the article aloud was at the front of the crowd. He shielded his eyes and kept blinking. He was talking on the phone to his wife or a girlfriend. "Yes, it's for real! And I want you to get home now! This is serious. Have you even looked outside?"

He paused to listen to her response. I tried to peer past him. What was it? What was out there?

He started talking into his phone again. "No, don't take the time to gather your stuff. I want you to leave now. Right now! It's going to be hard enough for you to drive home as it is. If it gets much worse, you may not be able to see well enough to make it home at all!"

I still didn't see anything, no matter where I looked, but all the bodies pressing in against me, pushing and shoving me, and moving me out the door blocked my view of almost everything. I started to hyperventilate.

Despite the shoving and jostling, the same man was still beside me somehow. He listened again at the tinny voice I could hear coming from his phone, and then he waved his arms in frustration, bumping the man next to him. "You don't understand. They're not saying it's a blindingly bright day because it's the middle of summer and the sun's out.

Something weird is going on. There's a lot of glare and it seems to be getting worse by the minute." He fought to find the words to describe what he saw. "Just go home. Right now. Okay?"

He must have been satisfied with the answer he got because he sighed with relief and nodded, then clicked his phone off. He squinted down at me when I was pushed into him. Sincerely, like he knew me, he said, "Good luck to you," before he squared his shoulders and walked into the parking lot. I watched him run to his car, rev the engine, and drive off.

A few others followed him. The anxious, murmuring crowd behind us pushed forward, encouraging others to move on, but some people remained rooted in place, afraid to move.

An older woman with frizzy white hair and a shapeless denim jumper talked hysterically on her phone. Her voice cut through the din of the crowd. "This is what Revelations is talking about! It says that the third angel poured out his bowl on the kingdom and the beast plunged them into darkness! That's exactly what it says! That's what's going to happen next! I just know it…"

I looked at her out of the corner of my eyes, confused. It wasn't dark out. I didn't understand, and I don't think anyone else who heard her did either. There was a momentary silence in the crowd. A few people rolled their eyes at one another.

Someone deeper in the crowd asked, "Does that sound right to you? Is that what the Bible says?"

A man snorted. "That's not what it says at all," he said. "She has it all twisted and backwards. As far as whether this is a judgment from God, I don't know. I'm no pastor."

I strained to hear the rest of the conversation, but the noise level increased again and I couldn't hear anymore.

I stood at the front of the crowd, a few steps away from the throng, rubbing my swollen lip and trying to catch my breath. I wanted to get home—fast—but I didn't want to draw attention to myself by leaving. Another part of me wanted to stay where there were other people, where someone else could make the decisions for once, but as I listened to the fear that buzzed around me like an angry swarm of bees, it got harder to breathe again. The silence and loneliness of my empty house and its locked doors seemed so much safer than where I was.

Two men had pushed their way through the crowd, and they stood next to me. I glanced up at them. One of them put on a baseball hat and sunglasses. The other held his hands above his eyes to shield them. "It's getting worse. No doubt about it, it's getting worse," the man in the hat said to the other guy. He had his hands up to his eyes, too, despite the sunglasses and hat.

"When I got here a few hours ago I thought it was extra bright today, but this is almost unbearable. It's so bright now that I almost can't even keep my eyes open. They just keep watering..."

I looked around at the others standing outside the sliding glass doors held open by all the bodies. Fear made the women's voices higher-pitched and the men's lower. The man in the hat wasn't the only one whose eyes were watering.

"I'm going now before it gets even worse," he yelled.

His decision got everyone else moving. People bumped and jostled into one another. I was pushed and nearly knocked over when people shoved past like a tidal wave sweeping into the parking lot.

The crowd flowed around me the same way it had at school on the last day, only this time instead of feeling disconnected and alone, I was terrified and alone. I pressed myself against the gate in a corner and stood there, trembling. The last few stragglers made it through the doors. They blinked into the sunlight, and then made for their cars, running through the parking lot as they peered upwards. I looked up to see what they were looking at, but there was nothing there—just nothing. The automatic doors slid open with a quiet swish one last time and the librarian came rushing out. She looked around nervously and blinked her eyes as furiously as everyone else had. She fumbled with the lock and then scurried toward the employee parking lot. She never even noticed me as she tripped her way to her car.

I was alone—really alone. Again. I stood outside the deserted library and looked up at the sky. A drumroll of thunder rumbled in the distance and the air felt heavy, like a monsoon was brewing, but there weren't any clouds yet. It was bright, but it still didn't seem different than any other day. The last few people in the parking lot found their cars. I watched them drive off like Laney had the first time she'd had a driving lesson with Mom. One of the cars hit the curb and drove up on the sidewalk before finding asphalt again. All of the drivers squinted and blinked behind their steering wheels.

I looked around and bit my lip and then winced. The raw spot tasted like blood and it hurt. A sudden sharp zing of anxiety made me want to throw up. What if it happened to me, too? What if whatever was happening to everyone else's eyes happened to mine, too? What would I do then? I breathed hard and fast, hyperventilating with panic again. I yanked my backpack onto my shoulders. The straps were twisted and they dug into my back, but I didn't try to fix them. I ran toward the corner to the crosswalk, glancing up at the sky every few steps.

I waited at the corner for the light. My heart raced faster with each breath. The light took forever to change. My stomach burned with fear, and terrified energy crawled through my skin and made my hands shake. I flapped my shirt to help the sweat evaporate a little and to give me an excuse to move—I needed to move! The crosswalk signal chimed and the "walk" sign flashed. I ran out onto the road. A red car came toward me. It weaved between the lanes, driving slowly. I ran faster, then sprinted—the car wasn't going to stop! I was close enough to hit the hood when the car screeched to a halt. The tires left a short black smear across the road, and the smell of burnt rubber sizzled in the air.

"Wait for the light, idiot!" the driver yelled. He started to roll down his window but the light must have been too bright for him because he rolled it back up. Before it closed completely, I heard him say something like, "…can't see a thing….stupid idiot is going to get killed…"

The man revved his engine like he was going to race off. Instead, the car lurched and he drove away slowly. He went right through the light like he hadn't realized it was red. I stared at him. I looked at the light to be sure it hadn't changed, but it was still red. I looked at the crosswalk light; it flashed with the white figure that meant I could walk. What was happening?

Beads of sweat dripped from my hair and hit the asphalt with soundless splats, evaporating almost instantly. The driver must have been drunk. That was it—he was drunk—he had to be. I started walking toward the other side of the street when I saw a car coming toward me from the opposite direction. It didn't slow down. It wasn't going to stop either! I was standing in the middle of the street when the car passed me. The driver peered out at me surprised, just a few feet away. He squinted and shielded his eyes as he drove, too. He swerved and yelled something I couldn't quite hear and then he was gone.

I didn't wait around to be nearly hit by another car. I ran the rest of the way across the crosswalk, and I kept running until I was deep in the neighborhood and far too hot. I only lived a few blocks away, but no one with any common sense ran during the hottest part of the day when the sun was so high in the sky; they warned about the risks of heat exhaustion and heat stroke on the news all the time, but I was too scared to slow down! I just wanted to go home.

Sweat made my back itch where my backpack pressed against my shirt, and more sweat dropped from my scalp and into my eyes, stinging them and making them water. My eyes blurred. Oh my God! I was going blind, too! My breath came out in ragged gasps but I kept running. I had to get home before I couldn't see at all!

A few cars veered slowly back and forth through the narrow streets of my neighborhood, but none of them were cars I recognized. They drove down the middle of the street and hit curbs. Some went up on the sidewalk and then thumped back down onto the road. Drivers squinted at houses and street signs as if they were trying to read addresses or identify the road they were on. Occasionally, a garage door went up and a car would slide inside. Then the door would close behind it. I blinked my eyes and rubbed at them. They burned and stung but didn't get worse. I wiped them with the edge of my shirt and realized I could see just fine after all. It was only sweat and tears that made my vision blurry.

***

I looked up at the sky one last time before I closed the door. I leaned against it, breathing hard, and then reality dropped away. This wasn't real! Of course it wasn't! It was a nightmare. It had to be. I was just dreaming. Or maybe this was the scene of a scary movie and my imagination had me trapped in the story. A mindless serial killer had murdered everyone and now he was after me! A scared noise came out of my mouth. I wouldn't be able to escape! I should just give up. I couldn't take it anymore!

I slid to the floor and wrapped my arms around my legs. I buried my face in my knees and gasped for air. I tried to think about anything other than horror movies and nightmares. I pictured Laney—my beautiful sister Laney. If she were here, she'd hold me until I stopped shaking, and if

I couldn't stop shaking, she'd make a bad joke that would make me laugh even though it wasn't funny. Or she would do whatever a doctor would do if someone was freaking out, and it would work. I would start to feel better.

I rocked back and forth trying to catch my breath, to just breathe, but it was so hard. Everything was so, so hard. I tried to pretend it was her hugging me tightly instead of the twisted straps of the backpack that dug into my shoulders. I kept my eyes squeezed shut. Laney wasn't here, but she wouldn't have wanted me to give up or be afraid.

"Be strong. Be strong," I whispered to myself. I opened my eyes a crack. The murderer from my imagination wasn't there. I was in my house and it was empty. And I could still see. I let out another deep, shaky breath. I was alone. But I was always alone, so what did that matter? I eased the backpack off my shoulders. The water bottles inside thunked against one another and I winced at the noise. In the kitchen, the refrigerator made a ticking noise. I *was* alone—wasn't I?

I kicked off my shoes. I was such a baby. Of course I was alone. I was always alone now. I unzipped my backpack and pulled out a water bottle and drank it down in a dozen long swallows. A spike of pain stabbed the middle of my forehead. I groaned and pressed the palm of my hand to my head. The pain eased up and I finished the water, more slowly this time. I finished another bottle and stayed tucked against the wall before I found the nerve to tip-toe into the kitchen, still thinking about serial killers and nightmares. I wiped my face with a rag on the counter. It smelled the way rags always do when it's been too long since they've been washed—musty and sour—but it felt good on my face. I opened the fridge and stood in front of it, letting the cold air drift over my body until goose bumps popped out on my skin.

DAY ONE: BEGINNING OF THE END

I didn't feel so afraid when I was inside my house, protected. I peeked out the front window, but there was nothing to see. No one was outside and only an occasional car passed, weaving its way down the road. But it was the middle of the day, in the middle of summer, and no one would ordinarily be out anyway. I looked up at the sky again. The storm clouds were closer, but they looked normal for monsoon weather. I dumped my backpack on the couch and fished out a squashed peanut butter and jelly sandwich from the front zipper.

I knelt in front of the TV and pushed the channel button. There hadn't been enough money for batteries for the remote in a long time, but without cable I only got a few channels anyway. The colorful bars and the buzzing ring of the emergency broadcast system played on one of them. A jolt of fear knotted my stomach again. I flipped through the other stations; they were all news, not the reruns of old sitcoms that usually played all summer long.

I only got half-way decent reception on one channel, so I left the TV there while I ate. A news anchor sat ramrod straight in his chair.

"…and so the speculation that the bright light from the sky is some kind of weapon is inaccurate. Reliable sources across the globe have verified that the light is, indeed, affecting the entire planet. Strangely enough, countries that are currently experiencing night time are also affected…"

I stole a glance out the window by the TV. I talked to the television like my dad used to when his favorite sports team wasn't doing very well. "It looks perfectly normal outside, people! What the heck is going on?"

I pushed the button on the TV and changed channels until I got to the one that came in next best. The President was speaking. "…again, I ask that you stay in your homes for the next twenty-four hours. Please keep your televisions and radios on. We will update you as we learn more about this phenomenon. Thank you."

The President held up his hand, ignoring a handful of reporters who shouted out questions.

"Mr. President, is this evidence of an alien presence?"

"Are you confident this is not some new kind of warfare?"

"Is this really happening across the entire globe?"

"Our foreign correspondents say that you are reacting much more quickly to this emergency than other leaders are. Is this true?"

"Why twenty-four hours? Do you anticipate that this will pass in that time frame?"

The President only answered one question. "Yes, I have declared a national emergency earlier than other nations have. We have been carefully monitoring this global crisis for the past few hours and we feel that, for the safety of all American citizens, it is prudent for us to act proactively rather than reactively given what little we know at this time."

He looked into the camera. "That's why it is imperative for everyone to return to their homes immediately and without delay."

He addressed all the other questions by saying, "No comment. No comment at this time."

The President walked out of the picture and the screen flashed to a glamorous-looking woman in a newsroom. Her hair was blonde and her hair was pulled back in a sleek up-do. She wore an expensive looking rose-colored blouse.

"We don't expect any more updates from the President at this time. Since the glare appears to interfere with outdoor photography and videography, we'd like to hear from you. What's happening out there, America? Call us at…"

A number flashed across the bottom of the screen, and the camera angle went wide to show three old-fashioned telephones set out across a long, folding banquet table. It made the newsroom looked like the setting for a telethon. An older woman with messy gray hair, a thick double chin, and the uniform of someone on a cleaning crew, settled heavily onto a folding chair behind one of the phones. A tall, elegant woman dressed in neat slacks and a low-cut blouse, who might have been another news anchor, sat at the opposite end of the table. A man in faded jeans and a tee shirt sat between the women. He pushed a pair of large headphones off his neck and reached over the table to hand them to another man who stepped forward from behind the cameras.

"Several members of our staff have volunteered to answer the phones for us. We should be ready to take calls in just a few moments, folks."

The phones began to ring before she finished speaking. The large woman waved her hand in the air. The loose skin on her upper arm moved with her. The anchor woman glanced off-screen to her left, then looked back at the camera and nodded.

"Our first caller is Mike from Washington. Go ahead, Mike. You're on!"

"This glare is the weirdest thing. I live in an apartment complex and I've met more neighbors in the past hour than I ever knew I had. But none of us can see much outside at all. It's like someone's shining the world's brightest floodlight right into our eyes. There's nothing but bright

light when you open the door or look out your window—
just glare. And it's getting so bad you can't see much inside
either, unless you cover the windows. You can't see past the
light. It's not like being out on a bright day where your eyes
get used to it. You just can't see anything but the bright,
bright light. It's like…it's like…"

The man was at a loss for words for a moment. "It's like
cave darkness, but in reverse. Have you ever been inside a
cave and experienced that? Your eyes are open, but you
can't see anything. Not a thing. That's what this is like.
Except it's bright. It's so bright you can't see anything. But
inside, as long as you block the glare out and turn on the
lights, well, then everything's fine…"

Caller after caller described the same thing. Some of
them told their stories with dead-sounding voices, like they
weren't really a part of them. Others were scared and upset.

The anchor woman kept taking calls. "Next up is Kathy
from Ohio. What do you have to say, Kathy?"

The woman on the other end was furious. "I'd like to
know what the President is going to do about this! I've got
three kids and I was planning on going grocery shopping
today. I'm out of milk. Who's going to feed my kids if I
can't get to the store? And what about school? My oldest is
in summer school. They can't just close the schools down
like this. My kid's teacher said that if he misses any more
days, he'll be held back next year. Someone needs to do
something!"

"I understand, caller, but tell me, what do you see out
there?"

"What do you mean, 'what do I see?' I see the same
thing everyone else sees, of course! The light comes in the
window and you can't see a thing anymore. I had to block
off the windows with newspaper. Then I had to put
masking tape around the paper so no light could come
through. We have all the lights on, and I want to know
who's going to pay my electric bill if I have to keep the

lights on all day and night!"

She sounded like a pouty little kid when she added, "Someone better do something about this. I mean it!"

The anchor woman tried to interrupt, but Kathy from Ohio was only getting started.

"...because when I open the door, BAM! There it is again! The bright light comes in, and I can't see outside at all. How am I supposed to get to the store when I can't see?"

"Yes, thank you caller," the anchor woman said. She nodded to someone off camera and Kathy was disconnected in the middle of another rant.

There were lots of calls from people trapped in their cars, too. One of the calmer callers summed it up when he said, "I pulled over when I couldn't see anymore. When I realized it wasn't going to get any better, I tried inching along but it seems like the road is gridlocked in front of me now. No matter how I turn the wheel, I'm blocked in.

"We've all been yelling to each other—me and the other people who are stuck in our cars. We're just trying to keep each other calm while we figure out what to do. Some people are freaking out. We've heard a lot of screaming from a car behind us a ways. Some woman is really flipping out. It got us all talking. We could survive a few days without food and water, but what then? That's the worst part. We don't know when this is going to end, and we can't see a thing. We—me and the people I've been talking to in the closest cars—decided to leave. We're going to start walking. It'll be better than sitting here, feeling helpless and trapped."

"Where will you go?"

The man gave a short, humorless chuckle. "That's a good question. I can see the GPS on my phone if I stick it under my suit jacket and block off all the light. It says that we're a couple miles from the nearest exit. I guess we'll all just try not to trip and break our legs until we get there. And let's hope people will let us into their homes or we can get inside a store or something until this is over and we can see again."

"Good luck to all of you," the anchor said as the man hung up.

For hours, the news station took more calls. I sat with my mouth open, staring at the TV. As hungry as I was, I even forgot about my peanut butter and jelly sandwich. It sat on the table next to me, getting stale.

When it started to get dark—at least it was dark to me—the news anchor, hoarse from talking for so long, said, "As you've been hearing for the past few hours, the story is the same across the country. The light appears to be impenetrable unless you're completely enclosed within a structure and can block it out; however, we've just received word that there may be a few individuals who can still see. We haven't substantiated this, and it may be nothing more than a rumor or possibly even a hoax, but if you're watching and you can see through the glare outside, we'd love to hear from you."

The number scrolled across the bottom of the screen again, and the phones continued to ring in the background. I sat on the edge of the couch, watching carefully as they were answered. A few words were exchanged every time a phone was picked up and then it was hung up, only to begin ringing again immediately.

"It looks like we're continuing to get calls from people blinded by the glare. If you can see outside, please call in. We want to hear from you."

I picked up Mom's cell phone and looked at it. I was afraid to draw attention to myself by calling. What if they asked to talk to my parents? I also didn't want to add any extra costs to the cell phone bill. I ran my tongue over my swollen lip, took a deep breath, and then started dialing.

I put the phone to my ear but instead of a ring, I got a funny tone and then an electronic voice said, "The number you have dialed has been disconnected. If you have reached this number in error, please hang up and try again."

I looked at the phone and double checked it against the number on the TV screen. I'd reversed two numbers. I looked up, my fingers hovering over the numbers, when the anchor woman said, "We have a call from a gentleman in New York who claims to be able to see! What's your name, caller? And can you really see? What's going on out there?"

"I'm Tom and yes, I can see just fine. My sister lives in Florida and she can see too, by the way. None of the rest of my siblings can, but she can. I don't know if that's important. Anyway, here in New York, it's pretty crazy. I live on the sixth floor so I have a pretty good view of things. All the stores around here closed down the second the President made the announcement. There's no road work going on either—you can bet all the construction crews took off the second they were told to go. But the streets are still insane. They're completely blocked with traffic. People have left their cars and cabs and they're feeling their way around. They look like zombies the way they're moving so slowly and have their arms out in front of them trying not to run into anything. I thought this was all some big crazy joke at first, but those people aren't acting down there! They can't see. They really can't see a thing! Even from up here I can hear them crying and screaming."

The newsroom was silent except for the muted ringing of the phones.

The anchor woman pushed a strand of hair from her face that had escaped her up-do as she searched for something to say.

"Wha...what do you plan to do, caller? You seem to be one of the very few lucky ones in the world who can still see right now. What will you do?"

The man took a deep breath. I held mine, waiting to hear his answer. The anchor woman seemed to hold hers as well. Reluctantly, Tom said, "I guess I'll wait it out like everyone else—oh, God!"

"What is it? What happened? What do you see?"

She looked into the camera when Tom didn't immediately answer and said, "If you're just joining us, we're on the phone with Tom from New York. Tom is the only person we've spoken to so far who is able to see through the glare.

"Tom, what do you see?"

"I can't believe this!" he said. "They're in groups down there now. They're breaking the windows of the stores. There's going to be a riot! They're breaking into the stores...except..."

"Except what? What's happening there on the streets of New York?"

Tom's voice was hushed when he finally spoke. "They're not rioting. No one's coming out with televisions or groceries or anything. People are stumbling around and slipping on broken glass from the windows, but they're just trying to get inside. The ones who are already inside are trying to help the others in, but no one can see. There's glass everywhere. Someone's going to get hurt, but they're trying to help each other..."

Tom started weeping. "They're helping one another. They can't see. Not one of them, and they're trying to help one another. They're moving fast...whenever they hear glass shatter, people are going that direction the best they can. Some of them are bleeding pretty badly from all the glass, but they're climbing inside and they're blocking off the broken windows. They've got the windows blocked off now! No one else can get in. Now the people still outside are moving toward the sound of glass breaking from farther down the street..."

He was quiet for a moment. "They're almost all gone from below me. They've nearly all moved on or gotten inside a store. The ones inside are still trying to block off the windows. No! Not just the windows that were broken, but all the windows—anything that's glass. It looks like they're covering it up with newspapers and magazines. This can't be happening, can it?"

The blonde woman shook her head and looked at the camera, talking to him through the screen. "What about you, Tom. Will you try to help them? Bring them groceries, formula for their babies, diapers?"

Tom's voice was nothing but a whisper when he answered. "They're already inside the stores where all those things are. Even if I started walking and found some stores they'd missed, what am I supposed to do? They broke in because they can't see. I can. Once this passes, I'd be thrown in jail for breaking and entering. I can't go around looting places just because no one can see me!"

"…and what if this doesn't pass, caller? What then?"

"How do I know? How many days have to pass before someone decides that it's not going to pass at all? Three days? A week? A month? Who decides when it's okay for me to start breaking into stores? And even if I did, what then? There's only one of me."

Tom was crying again. "There are thousands of people out there, and there's only one me…"

The anchor ignored his tears. "You bring up some important concerns." She swiveled in her chair and looked directly into the camera again. "What do you think, America? What should Tom and others like him do during this crisis?"

A woman named Diana was the first to call in and respond. Her voice quaked like my teachers' did when they expected students to behave better than they were. "Of course he should break into the stores. He should do whatever it takes to help everyone he can. He has a moral obligation to our society, and he'll be a hero when this is all over, anyway. No one will hold him responsible for breaking a few windows or taking a few things when he's saving lives! And he should march right down there and lead those people up into the other apartments in his building. At least then they'd have beds and bathrooms. Not helping is just not an option!"

Diana hung up before the anchor could respond and the next caller, a lawyer, didn't wait for an introduction before arguing his own point. "...not hold him responsible? Who is that loony lady kidding? This is a capitalistic country. The minute things are back to normal, that guy will lose his shirt in lawsuit after lawsuit. First the stores will hold him responsible for what he takes and any damage he does when breaking and entering their buildings. They'll also expect compensation for any damage he causes indirectly, like losses due to rodents that may have access to the interior of the building because he broke a window, for example. They'll hang him out to dry for damage he could have prevented, too, even if it has nothing to do with his actions. He'll be sued for not turning off the water main if he breaks into a store where a pipe has broken, for instance. And that's just the businesses! Anyone he helps can sue him for bringing them food that has expired and gone bad, or for providing them with a medication they have a bad reaction to, or even for not bringing them something they ask for. That guy would be a fool to help anyone except himself and his closest family and friends, and quite frankly, I'd even considering making them sign a release form if I were him."

A second man who claimed he could also see called in then. "Where are you and what's your take on all of this?" the anchor asked.

"Dude, I'm gonna surf!"

"What about helping other people?"

"Seriously? When I could be on the water? This is a stellar opportunity to have the waves all to myself! This light is a solar flare or space dust or something. It'll be over by tomorrow, just like the whole Y2K thing I heard about. I'm just gonna surf while I can! That's it, man. Just surf."

He interrupted the anchor woman as she was about to

speak. "Gotta go, dude. Surf's up!"

The next caller was a farmer from Nebraska who couldn't see. He agreed with the attorney who thought Tom from New York should take care of himself. His voice was low and he had a long drawn out way of speaking. I could almost imagine him sitting on the wide porch of an old farmhouse considering the situation and what it meant, except that if he was blind, he must be trapped inside like everyone else.

"I reckon it all comes down to how long this blindness lasts and how many people can see. Someone who can see could help others for a while. But there's a limit to what one man can do and how many others he can be responsible for. One or two? Sure. Five or six others? Maybe. More than that seems like a bit much if you ask me."

He paused for a moment and it sounded like he drew on a cigarette or maybe a pipe, before blowing the smoke out. "The longer it lasts, the fewer people one man can be responsible for. The food in the stores will last for a while, at least 'til things expire or the rats and roaches take over."

Then he asked the anchor woman a question. "Ma'am, what do you know about planting the fields and harvesting? Anything?"

She shook her head. "No, nothing."

"That's what I thought. How about digging a well and keeping your water supply safe? Do you know how to butcher a calf or a pig? What about canning? Can you make your own preserves like my wife used to?"

She shook her head again, and she looked like she might cry.

"Don't feel too bad, young lady. I doubt most of you city folk can do any of those things. Heck, there's a lot of folk around here who probably couldn't cut the head off a chicken if it came down to it. If this glare lasts long enough, and most all of us are blind in it, well then I figure we've had it."

The anchor woman blinked hard and nodded at something someone said off camera. Absently, she said, "Thank you, sir. You've certainly given us all something to think about."

The man was disconnected. The anchor forced a grim smile and said, "We're going to take a brief station break now. We'll return after these messages."

The screen changed to a mouth-watering shot of a cheesy pizza. Then the comforting jingle of a popular laundry detergent ad came on. A man flanked by two curvy blondes in skimpy bikinis talked about the newest model of some car in the next commercial, and that was followed by the preview for a new movie. When the news came back on, a different anchor had replaced the blonde lady, but all he did was take more calls. No one else who could see called in that night, and the others who called in were more upset.

I ate my sandwich even though the bread was stale from sitting out for so long. I watched the news for a few more hours and tried to ignore the rumble of thunder outside like I ignored the rumble in my stomach that hadn't gone away. A few flashes of lightening cut long white streaks through the dense clouds. Otherwise, even though people who called into the TV station said it was still dazzlingly bright out, it seemed as dark as any other night to me—maybe even darker than usual since the clouds blocked the moon and stars. The only light came from the streetlamp halfway down the block. It cast an orange shadow on the sidewalk. Despite the relative coolness brought by the storm that was rolling in, no one was out walking their dogs or jogging. Whatever was happening, it wasn't just my imagination. There wasn't enough imagination in the world for that.

DAY TWO: HABOOB

There was no rain that night after all, only a dust storm. The weather lady on TV used to call them haboobs. The wind shrieked and wailed until I partly woke up when an especially strong gust rattled the windows and pelted them with grit. I huddled in bed, shaking and terrified. I couldn't move—I was too afraid. Some kind of horrible beast was trying to claw its way through the windows! When I woke up enough to understand that it was just the storm, I stayed buried under my covers, dripping with sweat, but still afraid to expose any part of my body. I drifted back to sleep with thoughts of monsters and bill collectors swirling through my dreams. They turned into one another again and again as they chased me. The real nightmare—the glare that had everyone trapped and blinded—never broke through my half-awake, half-asleep nightmare.

When I woke up for real, close to ten, the sunlight that filtered through the blinds wasn't quite enough to banish the nightmare. It took a few moments before I remembered the news again. I knelt on my bed and pulled my blinds apart. They were kinked and bent and some of the slats had broken a long time ago. Another one broke off and fell behind my bed. The light outside was bright, but once I blinked the sleep from my eyes, everything came into focus. And then my shoulders slumped, and I almost wished I were blind like everyone else.

The sun was out, but a layer of dark clouds moved across the sky to remind me that it still hadn't rained. The sidewalk and driveway were covered with a thick layer of red Arizona dust; the inside of my window sill was gritty with it, too. Yellow flowers and small branches littered the ground around the oleander in the front, and the storm had pushed piles of red bougainvillea flowers into swirls against bushes and shrubs. I heard alarms echoing through the air when I put my ear to the window. They didn't sound like car alarms, but there were a lot of them. I pushed the window open an inch or two, but I couldn't figure out where they were coming from. The wind was blowing back and forth and the sound seemed to come from one direction and then another.

Across the street, at the nosy neighbors' house, a saguaro cactus was missing an arm. It lay a few feet away, on their driveway. A green City of Phoenix garbage can had been put out two days early, even though the people from the neighborhood association sometimes gave out nasty notes to prevent it. The can had blown down the road and its contents made a trail of garbage like a sick version of Hansel and Gretel's bread crumbs. A lot of things I couldn't identify had blown into my yard. I'd have to sweep the driveway and the sidewalk, scoop up the dead leaves and flowers, and pick up the trash and the broken twigs and branches in my yard. I sighed and stared at the clouds. I perked up when I saw that they were noticeably thicker and darker. Maybe I didn't have to rush out to clean up the yard right away after all. Maybe it would rain and the monsoon would wash away a lot of the dust and garbage. If I were really lucky, there might be just enough wind, from just the right direction, to blow most of the papers and leaves out of my yard, too. And if not, well, no one could blame me for waiting until after the rain came to pick up the yard, right? It's not like anyone else was out cleaning up theirs.

I felt like I was cheating a little by not cleaning up the yard when I hopped off the bed and walked into the kitchen. The refrigerator was always my first stop. I pulled it open and the smile dropped off my face. A carefully wrapped piece of cheese sat in one of the produce drawers and there were still some condiments in the door, but I didn't have much use for the crusty bottle of yellow mustard or the taller, sticky bottle of watery soy sauce. The last of my bread was on top of the fridge, but I knew without looking that there were only two more slices left, plus the skinny, crusty piece at the back. I'd finished off the last of my peanut butter and jelly the day before anyway. I also knew without looking that the pantry was as bare as the fridge. Only one lousy can of green beans would be sitting on the middle shelf if I bothered to open the door.

I slammed the refrigerator shut, rattling it. I'd have to go pick more cactus to eat even though it wasn't any more filling than green beans. I stomped to the family room and dropped on the couch to watch TV, blinking away tears. I caught the end of a clip of the President and somehow forgot about food as I watched.

He said, "Stay tuned, America. We are working around the clock to resolve this issue. Please keep your televisions on and stay in your homes until instructed otherwise."

After the clip, the news anchor said, "The White House has informed us that the President is preparing a press conference as we speak. As soon as we have more information, we'll let you know. In the meantime, we'll continue to take calls. What's going on out there, America?"

The calls were mostly the same as they had been the day before except that a few more people who said they could see called in, including a man in Arizona, like me. He lived up north though, in Flagstaff.

"Oh, I can see alright," he said. "Things don't look much different than usual where I'm at, though.

"What do you mean, caller? Things are normal there?

Can everyone see where you are?"

She sat up straighter in her seat, as if she'd made an important discovery.

"Oh, no. In town, things are as strange as what your other callers are describing. Everyone's found shelter. They've broken into some of the stores and restaurants— the ones close to the main road, anyway. And they've blocked off the windows and the doors. I guess it's like they're all saying it is. They can't see unless the glass is covered. But up here in the woods, where I live, there ain't nobody else for miles. Around here, all the forest critters are going about their business just like nothing happened. They can see just fine. That's what I'm trying to say. The animals are all going about their business just like they always have."

The anchor's voice sounded limp when she thanked the man and took a call from a woman in Wyoming who said she was eighty-six years old. The woman's voice shook when she talked, but she sounded lively for her age. She could see, but since she was in a wheelchair, she didn't figure it would do her much good. "That's what you call irony," she said with a cackle as she hung up.

A woman from Texas called in and said her five year old daughter and her husband could see but she couldn't. A man in South Dakota could see, too, and so could a woman in Tennessee. The woman's younger sister could see as well. It made me wonder if Laney would have been able to see, or if Mom could have. Or even Dad. It wasn't fair that they weren't there to find out!

The anchor woman asked everyone who could see the same question. "What are your plans?"
Their answers were the same ones I would have given if I had called in. What could we do? Like everyone else, we waited, glued to our televisions, for the world to go back to normal again.

DAY THREE: MY NEW NORMAL

Blue pinpricks of light flashed around my head when I sat up in bed. I'd eaten almost nothing the day before. I needed to get some food! Dad's social security check was supposed to come that day or the next, so maybe I'd be okay. As soon as it came I could go deposit it and get some money and buy food. I'd just have to wait until it came, that's all.

I wiped a tear away from my cheek as I watched TV and ate the last slice of bread in tiny bites, trying to make it last longer so it would fill my stomach more. There wasn't anything new on. The news anchor had changed again, but the new guy just took more calls and showed choppy videos of people in other countries who were trapped inside just like the people in America. Subtitles ran beneath the screen sometimes when someone spoke, but things were the same everywhere as they were in the States. Hardly anyone could see past the glare like me.

I kept peeking outside, hoping to hear the square white mail truck rumble past my house. I knew there wouldn't be any mail if no one could see to deliver it, but I couldn't get past the idea that the mail had to come because it wasn't Sunday and it wasn't a holiday. Neither rain nor snow nor dark of night...isn't that how the saying for the Post Office went? It was something like that anyway. In my growing desperation for food, the delivery of the mail and eating had become tied together, like a math equation. No mail delivery equaled no money. No money equaled no food. And I needed food.

The callers on the news were more upset than they'd been before. They were out of milk, or had sick kids, or were just scared. It had only been a couple of days, but people began calling in asking for help.

"My mother-in-law lives in Montgomery, Alabama, and she's almost out of blood pressure medication. Can someone help her? Please? She'll stroke out if she doesn't get more!"

Once in a while the news station would mix things up by reporting some statistics. "Out of the one hundred and six businesses and organizations we've attempted to contact, seventy-three percent do not answer the phone. Of the remaining twenty-seven percent, only one percent have a staff person on the premises. The other twenty-six percent of stores are occupied only by people who have broken in to escape the glare. The utility companies are the only organizations that are still staffed, although they are running on skeleton crews who volunteered to remain on duty.

"In related news, power company officials have warned that the brownouts we've been experiencing will only get worse as they attempt to regulate voltage outputs. The glare has caused record high electrical demands due to our need for a constant lighting source. They are advising us to unplug unnecessary items like computers and small kitchen appliances and to be prepared for temporary or permanent power outages."

Almost as if the anchor had planned it, the light I left on in the kitchen flickered. I got up and turned it off.

On TV, the man said, "...and now, let's return to our callers. America, where were you when the glare struck, and what are you doing now?"

A mother called in, sobbing so hysterically her words

were almost impossible to understand. "My daughter can't breathe! She's having an allergic reaction…"

The anchor man's horror was reflected in his face. "Hang up! Call nine-one-one!"

There was a fast, rasping sound in the background. Was that the girl's breathing? The sound got faster. The woman sobbed. "I did. There are no ambulances. Help us! Please, someone help us! She's only six!"

The rasping grew louder. There was no way the kid was getting enough air to live! There was a clunk and then the woman's voice sounded farther away and hollow. She must have dropped the phone. "Shhh…shhh…It's okay, honey. Just hang on! You're going to be okay…" The whooping, ragged breathing got faster and shallower. The woman's voice was high pitched and hysterical.

And then the rasping stopped. It just stopped. The woman screamed. "No! Oh, God, no! Breathe, Allie! Breathe! Someone help! Please, help us!"

The woman's hysterical cries continued until someone in the news room thought to disconnect the call.

The anchor man tried to speak, to move on to the next caller, but he couldn't do it. His voice cracked. He took a deep, shaky breath and shoved away from his desk. He ran off camera, pulling the microphone off his shirt, but not before it caught the sound of him crying.

The station switched to a commercial break.

***

The calls for help made me think of Amber. She was the only person I knew very well anymore, and for the first time, it occurred to me that her family might need some help. And more importantly, they might be so happy to see me that they'd probably invite me in for lunch, especially if I made a point to come by around noon. If I made my story sound just right, I might even be able to explain why Mom and Laney weren't around and why I couldn't get in touch with them.

The idea gave me some purpose, something to do. I ran a comb through my hair and brushed my teeth while I thought about what I'd say. I opened the front door to leave and stopped. Without the cleansing scrub of the heavy rain that still hadn't come, everything was still coated in a thick layer of red dust, and the air smelled as gritty as my window sill had. The few cars that were randomly parked on the street looked like they'd been there for months because of the dust and debris that covered them. The clouds were still thick and dark, and the air was heavier than it had been all summer. Crackling flashes of lightning lit up the sky here and there, but if there was a rumble of thunder, it was too distant to hear over the sound of the alarms that still rang through the air. I couldn't tell where they came from— nearby for sure—but not so close that I could hear them when I was inside.

I lifted the hair off the back of my neck as I walked to Amber's. I walked slower the closer I got to her house. I should have checked the news one last time before I left. What if everything had gone back to normal again while I brushed my teeth? What if I got to her house and everyone could see just fine? I looked up at the gray sky. How was I supposed to know if other people could see if my sight was normal? I almost turned around and went home, but I was so close and Amber was my friend. Why shouldn't I knock on her door?

I stood under the shadow created by the overhang of the roof, rethinking my plan. If they could see, I'd pretend I was glad and say it was silly of me to be worried about them. They might still invite me in for lunch. I might be the first person they'd seen in days, and we'd laugh about how scared everyone had been and we'd say, "Weren't we all lucky the glare didn't last forever after all?"

I nodded at the scene in my head. I was pretty sure

that's how it would play out, but lunch was lunch.

I knocked on the door. There was no answer. I knocked again and listened. I didn't hear any movement inside, so I rang the doorbell. Still nothing. Where could they be? Then I remembered. Didn't Amber say something about going somewhere during the summer? To her cousin's or her aunt's or something? That's right! She was spending most of the month at her aunt's house. I felt my shoulders sag. I'm not sure if I was more disappointed to find that I was still alone or to realize that the free meal I'd been hoping for had disappeared.

I used a stick to break off a cactus pad in their yard, and I carried it in my shirt so it wouldn't poke me while I walked home. I tried to ignore how weak and lightheaded I felt. It was my new normal, after all.

STOP, THIEF

I woke up to thunder and lightning again, and the sky was darker than I'd ever seen it. Normally, I liked stormy weather. Bright skies and sunshine day after day can get kind of boring, but I was too hungry to care much about a little variety in the weather. My food was gone. I'd eaten the last half of the green beans before bed. My stomach never stopped growling; it's not like green beans have many calories. I drank the salty, sickly green water and filled the can with more water, hoping to get an extra calorie or two from it, but all the water did was make me feel nauseous and sloshy. I cooked up the cactus pad I'd picked too, but it was tough and stringy. I'd eaten all the young, tender ones in the neighborhood already. I choked the last bits of it down, but I don't think they have many calories, either.

The news was nothing but background noise now. Another clip of the President aired, but it was even briefer than the last one and the news channels showed it every few minutes, as if they were afraid someone might have missed it. A few more people who could see outside called in, but they didn't see anything different than I saw when I peeked out my windows every few hours; there were no cars on the roads, but there were more birds and small animals. People who lived close to stores said the shops were all closed or had been broken into. There seemed to be very few people trapped at their own workplaces, and the people who had been stuck in their cars had mostly tried to walk to safety. There were fewer and fewer calls from them.

"Maybe they're conserving their cell phone batteries," one reporter suggested.

***

I don't remember making the decision to walk to the bank. I just found myself walking up the street with that stupid math equation running through my head like the words on a reader board: Money equals food. I was much more lightheaded and it was hard to tell whether the lights that danced around my head were flashes of lightning in the gray sky or if they were a side effect from being so hungry. I wasn't sure whether the ringing sound I heard was the sound of more alarms or another sign that I was starving, either. I was so preoccupied with the thought of food that I didn't notice the car wreck until it was right in front of me.

I'd come across only one small accident in my neighborhood, and it was a couple of streets away from my house. A car had run into a bank of mailboxes on the side of the road and the driver had just left the car there. There had also been a few cars parked very crookedly in driveways and by the side of the road—some that were up on the curb and even a couple that were in the middle of someone's yard—but I hadn't seen any other accidents. It was different on 48th Street. As the main road that ran through Ahwatukee, 48th Street had two lanes on each side and a turn lane in the middle. The street was always busy, and for the first time I saw what it must have been like for the people who couldn't make it home when the glare got bad. Cars were crumpled into light posts and smashed together bumper to bumper, as if a giant had tried to turn them into a train set. They were mostly in the outside lanes and on the sides of the road, but some had swerved out into the other lanes and even into the middle. Some doors were ajar as if their owners had just meant to step away for a moment. I didn't see any people, at least not at first.

I made the mistake of peering into a red car that had been in an accident. Dried blood made black polka dots around the bald spot on the top of a man's head. His face was buried in a partially deflated airbag that cushioned him from the steering wheel. White powder from the airbag dusted the inside of the car and the man's body.

His skin looked strange and waxy. And his head was misshapen somehow. The longer I stared at his powder-covered body, the more convinced I became that he would turn his head and stare back at me. He would have a piece of glass jutting out of his eyeball, and blood would be dripping down his face. Or maybe he would moan like a zombie and gnash his teeth at me. I shivered despite the sweat that streamed down my face. I stumbled away from the car and ran through the maze of cars until I came to another wreck at the intersection that was too close to ignore.

A water delivery truck blocked the sidewalk where it was jammed against the signal pole. A small blue car was sandwiched between it and a square white mail truck. Mail had spilled out the back of the mail truck. What if Dad's check was there? I started to pick up envelopes—all the white ones with windows in the front that looked like the kind his check came in. But there were so many and they'd blown everywhere! I'd never find his check. I didn't even know if this was the right mail truck, anyway. I tried to count the days. How long ago did the glare start? My heart sank. This couldn't be my mail truck. Or if it was, it didn't have Dad's check. His check should have come yesterday or today. The glare had begun before that.

I flipped through the envelopes in my hand anyway. Maybe the check had come early for a change. Maybe this was the right truck. And maybe, of all the envelopes that had fallen out of it, his check was one of them…

My heart raced each time I flipped to the next check—this one might be the one! I dropped the ones that didn't matter to the ground. There were only a few more left. It had to be one of those, didn't it?

I let the last envelope fall from my hand and I watched it flutter to the asphalt. Why did I always get my hopes up like that? What was wrong with me?

The back end of the blue car was crumpled like a piece of newspaper by the mail truck. No wonder all the mail had gone spilling out the back of it. Everything inside must have been flung backwards when the mailman hit the car. The car's windshield was lined with a spider web of cracks, and the inside was coated with blotches and splotches of dark blood. There was a lot more blood here than in the car with the zombie man inside. I could see the shape of a body through the hazy windshield, and I looked away so I wouldn't see more. The mail truck was empty but there was a sticky black mess on the floor mat and a handprint-shaped smear on the gray seat.

My eyes followed the heavy trail of black splats that wound away from the truck. The stream of blood wove left and right and then back to the truck again before meandering to a small patch of summer grass by the sidewalk. I sucked in my breath and tried not to scream. A pair of yellow-eyed coyotes crouched when they heard me. Their ears pricked forward. Their eyes never moved from mine, but they continued to feed on the bloody remains in front of them. Their bodies were stiff, like they were waiting to see what I would do.

The rain began to fall then. Fat drops dripped from the sky. The coyotes kept gorging themselves. I eased away from them, walking carefully backwards and watching them as intently as they watched me. Their ears pricked forward each time a whimper escaped my throat—when one of them bit into a hunk of flesh that was all that was left of a man's hairy thigh, when I heard the loud pop of a shoulder being dislocated, and another when I banged into a car and fell to the ground.

I scrambled to my feet. I didn't want them to eat me, too! I stopped thinking and ran. I didn't know where I was going, only that I had to get away from there. My flip-flop blew out and a zing of pain shot up my ankle when I tripped over it. I stumbled to a stop and bent over, trying to catch my breath and stop the lights that circled my head, making me weave. I put my hands on my knees to hold myself up. My back arched and I threw up.

Long strands of mucous and a gush of bitter water shot out of my mouth. There was nothing solid left inside me. A little bit of puke splashed onto my ankle. I spit out the sour taste and dry-heaved as rain dripped down my back. My brain felt empty, as drained as my body. The zombie man and the coyotes were behind me somewhere. I stood back up slowly and began walking again, dragging one foot to keep my flip-flop on, like I was a zombie too. Did it matter if the coyotes got me? Or if the man really *was* a zombie who wanted to eat my brains? I was almost dead anyway.

***

The rain came down harder; heavy drops plopped onto my head, my arms, my shoulders. They rolled down my skin in long drips that felt like bugs skittering down my body. I kept walking.

Tap. Tap. Tap. Tap. I was under the flat metal roof that covered the drive-through ATM at the bank. I looked up, confused. How did I get there? Had I walked that far already? I pulled Mom's debit card out of my pocket like a mindless robot. The machine sucked it in. My stomach jumped as it always did when I went to the bank, and it jolted me back to life. What if the machine didn't return the card? What then? But it whirred and the welcome screen appeared. I wiped away the scratchy, damp dust from the screen so I could read it, and I punched in Mom's secret number. I needed money to buy food, but without something to deposit, I wouldn't be able to pay the bills that sat on the table at home. I wasn't thinking well enough to realize that if I couldn't get a check in the mail, I wouldn't be receiving any bills. I was too hungry to think that clearly. Besides, there were people-eating coyotes out there! I stared at the amount on the screen, trying to clear my head. There wasn't enough money! And there were people-eating coyotes out there!

What should I do? I could cancel water...maybe that would be okay. I could get water from a water fountain or maybe a neighbor's hose. But then I wouldn't be able to bathe and it would Arouse Suspicion very quickly when I started to stink. Besides, trash pick-up was part of the water bill and a pile of garbage outside would definitely Arouse Suspicion. What about electricity? I considered it, but only briefly. Without electricity, I couldn't cook food or keep it cold. The phone? Maybe Mom's phone! I hardly used it, but what if Laney tried to call? What if she tried to call and she couldn't get ahold of me because the number was disconnected? My shoulders shook with silent sobs. Laney wouldn't call. She was dead. Deader than the zombie man in the red car. Deader than the guy in the blue car and deader than the bloody mailman the coyotes were eating. She had to be. She would never have abandoned me otherwise. And if I wasn't strong like her, I was going to die, too.

So that was it. The phone had to go. I withdrew ten dollars but my hands shook when I took the money and tucked it into my pocket. I took it out again and clutched it in my hand. What if there were more coyotes and I had to run again, though? What if I dropped the money? I stuffed it back in my pocket and kept patting it as I walked to make sure it didn't fall out. I cut across a strip mall parking lot to avoid the intersection with the zombie man and the coyote.

The grocery store was the other direction, but it was too far. I was too dizzy to keep walking, and the stores in the strip mall should have had some kind of snacks and drinks up by the registers. The ringing in my ears grew louder. I thought I might be about to pass out until I realized that the sound was coming from the stores.

The three stores closest to the street had been broken into. Windows were shattered out of them and boarded off from the inside. Just like one of the callers on the news had said, the windows that hadn't been broken were blocked off, too. The windows of the educational supply store were covered with poster board and colorful butcher paper, and the windows and doors of the baby superstore were blocked off with the thin cardboard packaging from breast pumps and baby monitors and diaper boxes. I stood in front of the doors like a real zombie. There had to be people inside, but when I stepped closer and reached for the door, I heard the sounds of screaming and shouting. I leaned in closer to hear over the sound of the alarms.

"We can't stay in here forever!" a man yelled.

"And what are we supposed to do? Where are we supposed to go?" someone else yelled back. "At least here there are snacks and drinks. You think there will be more next door? Isn't that a teacher's store? Or maybe you think the office supply store will be better?"

I didn't wait to hear more. I took a quick step back. My foot crunched on glass.

Someone inside said, "Did you hear that?"

I froze. How could they hear me over the alarm? That was impossible, wasn't it?

"Hear what? I didn't hear anything."

"Shhh! Someone's out there. I heard something!"

A man yelled out to me. "If someone's out there, go away. We can't take any more people. Don't come in here!"

I didn't answer.

He yelled again. "You hear me? I know you're out there!

Stay away. We'll protect ourselves if we have to. There are a lot more of us in here than you think!"

I tip-toed backwards, easing my broken flip-flop down with each step so it wouldn't make a sound. Chunks and shards of glass reflected images of the clouds that hung overhead and I wove through them like they were landmines. I walked away as quickly as I could until the blue lights started swimming in front of my eyes again. I looked for more coyotes, worried about them again, but there were only quail bobbing along in a line and a few lizards darting from one scraggly bush to another as they sought shelter from the rain.

I sat down on the curb of a small island in the parking lot until my head stopped spinning. Then, because there was nothing else to do but keep going, I got up and walked some more. I went farther away from the coyotes and the stores that had been broken into. There was a convenience store and a couple of restaurants in that direction. Maybe those doors would be unlocked or someone would be working inside—someone who would let me in to buy something.

***

No one had broken into the convenience store. It must have been too far from the main road for people to get to easily. I stepped onto the mat in front of the automatic doors, waiting for them to open, but they didn't. I stepped on the mat again, harder. It was as if I'd gotten so light that even with my water-logged clothes I wasn't heavy enough to trigger the doors to open. I stared at them stupidly.

Of course nothing happened! What did I expect? For some dumb teenager to be working there when every other store in the country was closed? I was such an idiot! The lightheadedness increased for a moment. I swayed, but the dizziness passed. I couldn't do it anymore. I just couldn't. It didn't matter if someone got Suspicious. My mom was dead. Laney was dead—she had to be. And if I didn't get some food soon, I would be dead, too.

I put my hands up to the glass doors and looked inside. The glass was cool under my palms. The air conditioning must be running on high. It would feel so good in there. And there was so much food just sitting there! Shelves and shelves of it. And I had money. That's the thing! I had money. I could pay! Desperation and anger burned in my chest. It wasn't fair.

I screamed up at the dark clouds that spit rain at me, plastering my hair to my face and making my clothes stick to my body. "It's not fair! I hate this!"

I picked up a milk crate that sat beside the door, forgotten in the last employee's rush to leave and lock up. I threw it at the door and screamed again. The glass shook when the crate hit it. I kicked the crate and it bounced against the door again, then tumbled back and slammed me in the shin.

The fire in my heart was replaced with agony. I dropped to the steaming wet sidewalk and rubbed the growing welt. Blood and water sheeted through my fingers and down my leg. I rocked back and forth on the ground as helplessness washed over me. I picked up the crate and hit it against the glass door, again and again, but it was half-hearted. I wanted the anger back. I needed it—somehow I knew I needed it. I stood up, favoring one leg and then the other; my ankle ached from twisting it when my flip-flop blew out, and my other shin throbbed. I slammed the milk crate against the door with all my strength and I screamed in anger and pain.

The door shattered. Large shards of glass hit the concrete. I froze in shock. Had I really done that? An alarm inside screeched and it was much louder than the other alarms had been. I took off in a terrified and lopsided gallop. My heart thudded in my throat as I skidded and slid on the wet pavement. I got all the way to a nearby restaurant before I could force myself to stop. My breath came in ragged gasps and I collapsed onto the ground again. I crawled to the corner, ignoring the small shards of gravel that dug into my knees. I peered back at the store.

The alarm continued to shriek, but no police cars raced toward me. No manager chased after me with a gun. No one stared out at me from the stores across the way. No one was coming. There was no one there. I wanted to go home, but food was so near, so close, and I didn't have many choices left.

I walked back to the store, my eyes darting back and forth as I waited for someone to come out and scream at me. I stopped and stared when I saw a slinking movement not far from where I'd just been. Dogs. It was just a couple of dogs, but I couldn't quite shake the image of the coyotes I'd seen at the intersection. I shuddered and ducked inside the hole I'd made in the door. Glass crinkled under my flip-flops.

The store was empty, but I still wasn't sure exactly what I was going to do. The wet rubber of my soles squeaked against the tile and the cold air made me shiver. I leaned against the counter that held the cash register and slid to the floor, holding my head in my shaking hands. The angry, high-pitched drone of the alarm didn't help the growing throb in my temples.

I stared at the deli display in front of me for a long time before my eyes focused and I understood what I was seeing. I stood up, but I had to hold onto the counter until the tunnel of darkness that almost made me crumple back to the floor eased back again. I reached for a sandwich and then pulled my hand away. I looked around, feeling guilty. What if someone saw me?

"Just do it," I whispered to myself. I licked my lips. They felt parched and dry, despite the rain and sweat that still dripped from my hair. My mouth felt like it was stuffed with cotton. My head felt that way, too: overstuffed like an old man's armchair. My brains were going to leak out of my ears. They would come out white and fluffy, like stuffing from a pillow. No wonder my head hurt.

I snuck a sandwich off the shelf, pulling it away quickly. But no one stopped me. I peeled the plastic wrap off and sat back down with my back to the counter again. I bolted the sandwich down, not really tasting it, just trying to get food in my stomach. My eyes darted from the door I'd broken to the back room of the store. I checked the mirrors near the ceiling that let me look down the aisles. I still expected someone to yell at me or stop me, but no one did.

I finished the sandwich. I wanted another one but my shrunken stomach was too full. It felt like the overstuffed armchair, too. I was nauseous, but this time it was because my stomach wasn't used to having so much food in it. I got up again, more slowly this time so I wouldn't feel so faint. I took a soda from the case along the wall, still shivering in the cold air that blew out on my wet skin. I passed an aisle with small, overpriced packages of odds and ends. I ripped a packet of pain relievers open and swallowed them down dry. I took earplugs, too, and stuffed the puffy pink cylinders into my ears. They took the edge off the sound of the alarm and eased the throb of my headache, at least a little.

And then I robbed the place.

I took all the sandwiches from the deli display. Their expiration dates were that day so I thought maybe the police would take that into account if they caught me. I filled plastic bags that bore the store's red logo with pepperoni sticks, pretzels, a loaf of bread, and a tiny jar of peanut butter. For a moment I wished I'd made the long walk to the grocery store instead. I could have gotten a lot more for the ten dollars in my pocket than I did in the convenience store, but it was so much farther away. I bit my lip as I looked in the bags I'd filled. I'd taken more than ten dollars in groceries, but I hadn't taken enough to last me very long, and since I was there anyway...

I wouldn't be able to carry much, but I added some chips to the bag with the jar, and put a couple of cans of bean dip in the other bag. I put the bags down to pull the money from my pocket and hesitated. Should I just leave it on the counter? What if someone came in and took it? No one would believe me if I swore I'd left money, even if it wasn't enough to pay for what I took. I put the money back in my pocket. I was a thief anyway. I was probably a vandal now, too, since I'd broken the door. I shook my head. I was already a criminal so what did it matter if I took more, if I took everything I needed instead of just a few things?

I stepped away from the jagged shards of glass that stuck up from the door like the teeth of a deep-sea fish and dumped the bags on the counter so I could start over. I filled them with as much as I thought I could carry, and then I stuffed the pockets of my jean shorts with candy bars, making sure nothing would fall out of the hole in my front pocket. They would be a melted mess by the time I got home, even in the rain, but it didn't matter. I would put them in the fridge to solidify them again and I would lick the chocolate off the inside of the wrappers. I found an aisle with nutrition bars, the ones that sort of taste like candy bars but are supposed to be healthier. I tucked them into the waistband of my jeans and filled another bag with more candy and beef jerky and some little bags of nuts—stuff that wouldn't go bad in the heat before I got home. I weighed the bags in my arms, testing them to see how heavy they were. I stepped out the door again and looked around, just in case there were more coyotes or maybe some police officers aiming their guns at me. No one seemed to care about what I had done, though, despite the angry cry of the alarm that droned on and on.

PRESS CONFERENCE

It's funny how a sandwich can change your life.

The walk back was long and my hands cramped from the weight of the bags. My shoulders ached too, and the blue lights still danced in front of my eyes, but the sandwich took a small bite from the terror that had been eating through my body, at least about starving. I might go to jail or juvie, or get eaten by a coyote, but I wouldn't starve to death. That was something, right?

I stopped and rested in the rain four or five times to ease the aching in my hands and arms and to eat—a smooshy, melty candy bar the first time and some chips the second time. The third time, I chugged another can of soda, and then a spike of pain in my belly made me heave up everything I'd eaten. Did I have food poisoning? A zing of panic buzzed through my brain. The sandwich I'd eaten in the store was almost expired. Was it bad? What if I had e-coli or something? I rinsed my mouth with the few sips of soda that were left in the can and spit out the sour taste of puke. The sugar made my teeth feel furry. I concentrated hard on the way my stomach felt, but it didn't feel sick, just empty again.

I went home a different way to avoid the car wrecks and the stores with people trapped inside. The walk was longer, but I just couldn't pass by all that death again. I reached the entrance to my neighborhood and dropped to the wet grass. Even though I'd just thrown up and my mouth tasted terrible, my stomach demanded more food so I ate another sandwich. Then I leaned back, just for a moment, and let the warm rain wash over me. My stomach felt bloated, like I'd just eaten a huge Thanksgiving dinner. It should have been too uncomfortable and scary to sit there. It was wet and sticky and hot, and somewhere nearby there might have been more coyotes, but I didn't quite have the energy to move. It felt safe being so close to my house, so I didn't get up, and as I sat there I began to notice things I'd missed when I was so busy watching for coyotes and zombies.

I heard the leaves in a nearby shrub rustle when a lizard raced out from under it and into the street. A flock of pigeons, with their creepy red eyes, cooed and pecked at the skin-colored pods that had fallen from a mesquite tree. I watched a family of quail bob across the top of a block wall despite the rain, and in the distance, the muted sound of store alarms still screamed to be heard. There were dogs barking too. All of the sounds seemed magnified by the ones that were missing. There were no engines starting, no whisper of car tires, no screeching of brakes, or doors slamming, or sounds of people laughing and talking. For a moment I thought I heard the drifting sound of music, but when I sat up and strained to listen, it was gone.

I used to think that Ahwatukee looked like a ghost town during the summer. Once it got over 100 degrees, all the people disappeared. They stayed sealed up in their cool homes unless they had to leave for work or run errands. Sometimes at dusk or before the sun came up you'd see the hard-core athletes out running or people walking their dogs. But during the day, unless it was raining, you'd hardly ever see anyone.

Now though, Ahwatukee really was a ghost town. Near the main road, I should have seen cars driving back and forth all over the place. The strip malls and gym should have been busy. The movie theater and all the restaurants should have been packed. People should have been shrieking in pretend horror at being caught in the rain as they ran the short distances from their cars to the stores and back again. But they weren't.

Would it always be like this? Was Ahwatukee going to be one of those deserted towns where tumbleweed rolled down the streets and doors squeaked as they swayed open and shut? I was so tired that my eyes wanted to close, but I was beginning to get nervous—too nervous to stay where I was. I had food in my stomach, and I needed to sleep and let my body recover from nearly starving. I needed to think about what the zombie man and the coyotes and becoming a criminal meant. But I couldn't do it there, not unless I wanted to be coyote food myself.

***

I didn't bother to take a shower when I got home. I was soaked with rain and sweat, so I just stripped off everything but my tattered bra and underwear. Even those were damp, but I didn't have the energy to change. I turned on the fan in the family room and ate two more of the deli sandwiches—a turkey with mayo and a ham and cheese. The tomatoes were soggy, but food was food. The sandwiches had more calories than green bean water, and that's what was important, not taste. I opened another bag of chips. My stomach processed the food just as fast as I could get it inside of me now. It seemed to have a mind of its own, and I imagined it saying to my other organs, "Well, what do you know? There's chow! Bring it on, baby! Bring it on!"

I eyed the stuff from the bags I dumped out on the coffee table and pulled the lid off the bean dip before I turned on the TV. I hadn't missed much. The news station was still taking calls. I dug lumpy scoops of bean dip out with my chips before the caller's comments sank in.

"…I doubt the President will even bother with a press conference now," she said.

The anchor man shook his head. "Of course he will. This is an emergency of global proportions…"

"No," said the woman. Her name and title ran across the bottom of my TV and her picture flashed across the screen. She must have emailed it to the news station. She was some kind of political expert. "Just think about it. This isn't like a riot or a national disaster where people are out looting or threatening one another with guns. All over the country we're all very nicely sequestered in our own homes by this blinding light. There's no better place for three hundred million Americans than that…"

The anchor man held up a finger and put his other hand to the earpiece in his ear. The woman caller was disconnected in mid-sentence and there was a flurry of activity in the newsroom. He said something to someone off camera for a moment and then nodded his head briskly. He turned back to the camera. "This is it, America. This is what we've been waiting for!"

The screen flickered like there was an issue with the connection and then the President came on. He had already begun speaking. "…and so I'd like to introduce Dr. Fieldberg. He'll be speaking to us via a webcam from his research lab at MIT in Cambridge, Massachusetts. He and his colleagues have been working around the clock in an effort to understand the cause of what people across the globe are calling 'the glare' or 'the blindness.'"

The picture of an ordinary-looking man with thinning gray hair appeared on the screen behind the President. The camera angle went wide when the President stepped to the side of the screen. The same reporters who had been trapped at the White House since the last time they interviewed the President, sat in rows of wooden chairs. The President stood between two big men at the corner of the stage so the reporters and the cameramen could see the screen, too. The men on either side of the President wore wireless devices in their ears. Unlike the sloppy reporters, their black suits were spotless. The President stood with his hands crossed in front of his body, his attention focused on the screen.

"Eh-hem. Yes. Well, I'll get right to the point," the scientist said. "To the best of our knowledge, the cause of the glare appears to be a wavelength of light our planet has never been exposed to before. Our preliminary research indicates that the visible spectrum—that is, the light our eyes use to see—is still there, just as it has always been. This new wavelength appears to block our body's ability to utilize our usual source of light. In essence, the glare over-stimulates the rods and cones in our retinas and possibly even scrambles some nervous system signals, thereby effectively blinding us."

One of the reporters yelled out, "Speak English!"

His frustration was echoed by the handful of other tired looking cameramen and reporters in the room.

The scientist cleared his throat again. "What that means, in layman's terms, is simply that our planet is being exposed to a wavelength of light we are not adapted to using. We cannot see x-rays, or radio waves, or microwaves, for instance. It just happens that rather than being invisible to the naked eye, this wavelength effectively blinds us, or at least most of us. You see?"

The audience in the White House stared at the image of the man on the large screen. He looked back, shook his head at the dumb-founded faces that stared back at him, and went into lecture mode.

"Let's see if I can clarify. As you've probably noticed, as long as you're in an enclosed area with the light from outside blocked out, normal light fixtures are enough to light up a room and allow you to see. That's because this particular wavelength is easily blocked from the room by the walls, a layer of newspaper, or a piece of cardboard. We're extraordinarily lucky in that respect, by the way. Radio waves and x-rays, for instance, aren't stopped so easily. Except for their wavelength and energy per quantum, radio waves and light waves are virtually identical. If this wavelength had properties more like radio waves, we would be blind indoors as well as out."

"What about our cameras? Why don't they work outside?" someone called from off screen.

The scientist rolled his eyes like he couldn't believe someone would ask such a stupid question. "Obviously they aren't designed for this wavelength, just as they aren't designed to pick up UV light, or x-rays, or gamma rays. It will take years to develop an analogous technology for a wavelength we've only just discovered."

A woman yelled out, interrupting him. Her front teeth were smeared with lipstick; she probably tried to neaten up in the ladies room before the press conference. "And why can some people still see but not the rest of us?"

"It's a simple matter of Darwinian evolution, of course. Like every other species, our genetic material contains random variations or mutations that may or may not be obvious or observable, and may or may not even be present on the genes themselves. Genes only comprise about two percent of the human genome, after all. The remaining non-coding regions of our chromosomes are largely a mystery to us. When there is a change in the environment, as we are currently experiencing, those mutations—wherever they may be—sometimes end up being beneficial to our survival. The individuals who are able to see through the glare are simply the very lucky winners of an evolutionary lottery."

The reporters scribbled notes on their notepads. The same woman asked another question. "You said the entire planet was being exposed to this wavelength. Are you trying to tell us this came from outer space? Really?"

"This particular wavelength appears to be millions, if

not billions, of years old and has only now reached us from another galaxy. It may be from a distant star or from some other source entirely, so yes, it came from outer space."

"You've got to be kidding," someone muttered. "...and you didn't see this coming?"

Dr. Fieldberg waved his arms in the air. "Of course we didn't see this coming. Our solar system is constantly bombarded with asteroids, meteorites, and clouds of gas, in addition to various electromagnetic emissions. What's more, there's no single telescope that is capable of detecting the entire spectrum. Once one type of telescope identifies a particular phenomenon, it's often too late to view it from another type of telescope, at least for short-lived emissions like gamma-rays. It's ridiculous and ignorant to think we could have predicted this!"

Spit flew from his mouth and he sputtered with excitement. "We're constantly making new discoveries about the electromagnetic spectrum and our galaxy as a whole; it's unfathomable that we could possibly identify every single phenomenon that pelts our solar system. Why, the visible spectrum itself wasn't even discovered until the early 1900s. We've never seen anything like this particular type of emission..."

The first reporter cut him off. "Okay, so let's say we believe you. You didn't see this coming. But you know about it now. When will we be able to go outside again? When will this emission, or whatever you're calling it, pass? When will we be able to see again?"

The scientist licked his lips and his eyes shifted back and forth. "Well, that's the thing now, isn't it? You see..."

The President took a long stride across the floor and stepped in front of the podium. He looked back at the screen. "Thank you, Dr. Fieldberg. I will answer any further questions."

Dr. Fieldberg disappeared and a picture of the Presidential Seal took his place. The reporter stood up. "So?

When will we be able to see again? When will we be able to go home?"

The President looked at the grumbling reporters. He stood silently with his hands on either side of the podium until the talking ceased. He squared his jaw and looked directly into the camera.

"Ladies and gentlemen of the United States. Today we are facing an unprecedented emergency of global proportions, one that could change the future of all of humanity."

My stomach suddenly felt funny, sort of like it did the time I went on a roller coaster with Dad when I was barely tall enough to get on the ride.

The woman with the smeared lipstick started crying quietly and a cameraman in the background began to shake. His camera shook with him until he pulled his hands away.

The President raised his voice. "All is not lost, America! All is not lost!"

"We have received confirmed reports that a very small percentage of the population has remained unaffected by this disaster. They may, in fact, be watching this press conference at this very moment, wondering what's going on since the outside world probably looks perfectly normal to them."

He looked up from his notes and stared directly at the camera again. My stomach lurched again. He was talking to me. "If you are one of the lucky few, then the fate of your family, your friends and your neighbors, the fate of your colleagues, your acquaintances and yes, the fate of your country and all of mankind, lies squarely upon your shoulders. You are free while we are separated from our loved ones by the glare. You are free while we are trapped in our cars on the side of the road or made prisoner in our own homes. To you I say this: break into the nearest supermarket or your neighborhood convenience store. Ransack the corner drugstore if you must. But please, feed your neighbors! Bring them food and supplies and medication. You have just become the heroes and the saviors of this new world."

The President stopped abruptly, overcome with emotion. He swallowed hard and fought to regain control. The reporters stared at him, expecting him to continue. When he did not, they shot more questions at him.

"Does this mean the glare isn't going to end?"

"So that's it? You're not going to do anything about this?"

"How many people can still see?"

"Are you sure this is happening everywhere else, too?"

"What about animals? Can they still see like some callers have indicated?"

"Did your people really not know this was coming?"

"How do you think this will affect the economy?"

"What do we do now?"

"Could this have been prevented?"

The President held up his hand and the questions stopped. "Now that we know the source of the glare, we have verified that it will not pass. Not in our lifetimes, anyway."

The reporters stood and waved their arms in the air, shouting out questions. The President raised one finger to warn them that he had more to say. He waited until they were seated and silent again. "I promise you, we will do everything in our power to find a solution to this problem. As I stated before, the finest minds in the country are working around the clock. Even as we speak, our scientists are exploring every possible resolution with dogged determination, from special glasses that will block out the glare to the possibility of surgery or gene therapy to allow us to see."

A reporter near the front shouted out, "How will you distribute these glasses, and who will get the surgery first?"

The reporters leapt to their feet again and yelled over

one another.

"What criteria will you use to choose who gets to see first?"

"Will it be a lottery? Will everyone have equal standing?"

"Yeah! Will people in jail have as much a chance to see again as law-abiding citizens?"

"How do we know you won't select people based on your own agenda?"

The President shook his head. He started to speak, but his first few words were lost in the commotion. It was only when the reporters realized they couldn't hear him that they quieted down, although they still mumbled.

"...said that we're exploring every possible solution, not that we've found one."

"Wait! So you *don't* have a cure?"

The President raised an eyebrow at the woman who yelled out. She sat down in her chair again and glared back at him.

"That is correct. We have not, as of yet, developed a solution. That is why I am begging those of you who can see, as few as you are, to help your neighbors. You have my word that you will not be held liable for any damage you cause while we are still experiencing this state of emergency."

He raised his hand to prevent the next question. "The same goes for those of you who own stores or other places of business that are ransacked during this time. You are feeding the country. You will not become destitute as a result. I promise you this."

I glanced down at the food spread out in front of me. My head spun with relief. I wasn't going to go to jail!

When I looked up at the screen again, the President was staring right back at me. He grabbed the sides of the podium again. His knuckles were white. "The glare will not end, but we *will* persevere! We will never stop searching for a solution. Never!"

He waited for silence again, and the next time he spoke he sounded like one of the narrators on TV who try to keep you from changing the channel during a commercial. "And now, America, I simply ask that you stay tuned for more updates."

He turned and walked smartly out of the room, flanked by security. Cameras panned the room as the reporters stood and yelled questions at him. The cameraman who had started shaking earlier was sitting on the floor with his back against a chair. His skin had a sort of green tinge to it like he was going to be sick. His chair slid back a few more inches with every breath he took. Several others sat with their heads between their knees, breathing deeply. One man was flipping through pictures of his family in his wallet. In another corner, a woman wept hysterically. Her knees were drawn to her chest, showing polka-dotted panties that seemed almost silly with the rest of her professional, but rumpled outfit.

One of the reporters covered his face with his hands for a moment to hide the tears he couldn't stop. He cleared his throat and turned to the camera. "That's it folks. We're finished." He looked off camera and drew his fingers across his throat. "Shut it off, Paul," he said. "We're through here."

The screen went blank for a moment before the local station came back on. An anchor woman's hand fluttered at her chest as if she were having a hard time breathing. Her face was pale, and her voice trembled as much as her hands. "We'll be back after these messages from our sponsors."

I got a goofy grin on my face as I stared at the TV. The police weren't going to arrest me for breaking into the convenience store! That meant I could go back there or go anywhere else I wanted. I could get more food—all the food I needed—and I wouldn't get in trouble for it!

I started to make a mental list of all the things I needed that I could just go and take. I would get food, of course.

117

Lots and lots of food. Enough to last for years so that when the glare ended—I was sure it would end—I'd have plenty to eat forever. Laney would find a way to come back by then too, so I'd be able to take care of her. I'd get us toilet paper—tons of it! No more unrolling it by the yard and stuffing it in my backpack when I sat in the stall at the library! Shampoo—I wouldn't have to water it down or only wash my hair every couple of days. I could wash it every day if I wanted! I ran my hands through my wet hair. And I could use conditioner again, too. What about paper towels and tissue? Those had been luxuries, but now I could wipe up a spill without having to wash the towel later. Now I could blow my nose on something soft...wow! I could get some stuff to clean the counters and the tub and the floor, too. Laney and I had tried to keep things clean, but we made do with water because that's all we had. Oooh! That reminded me! Kitchen sponges! The only one I had was falling apart. Every time I washed a dish, little bits of yellow sponge peeled away and crumbled off the rough green scrubby side.

My thoughts darted from one idea to the next as I looked around. I'd get some extra deodorant and hand soap and socks, too. I really needed new socks. And shoes! I looked down at my feet and wiggled my toes. I had a blister from walking home in my blown-out flip-flop. I could get some new shirts and shorts, and I could get some pretty nail polish and maybe some earrings and sunglasses and some scrunchies for my hair! Maybe I could even find one of those belt buckles everyone loved. And I could get a new coat for when it got cold and some extra blankets for my bed! I ran to the list on the fridge and in big bold letters, I wrote: THE GLARE.

I took an old, half-used notebook and a pen to bed with me that night and I fell asleep writing a list of all the things I wanted to get. I didn't know what the blindness meant for the future, and at that moment I didn't care. All I knew was that I wouldn't have to worry about anything ever again!

It turns out that wasn't quite true. Survival is about so much more than just finding food to eat, but that night I slept better than I had in a long time. I had the good dream again, too. From the shore, Laney cheered me on like she had done in real life but somehow, in the dream, I knew she wasn't talking about learning to swim when she yelled, "You can do it! You can do this!"

WHEELS

I didn't go anywhere the next day or even the following one. The storm got worse and lighting sizzled in the air while thunder cracked and boomed above the dark clouds. It didn't matter. I had food so I ate. And ate and ate. And I kept working on my list of the things I wanted to get before the glare ended.

When I woke up the next day, the storm had shifted. The stifling, thick air and heavy gray clouds were gone. The only clouds that were left were fluffy and white. They scooted through the sky as if they had things to do like I did, but without the heavy cloud cover to block the sun, it was already scorching hot out. I knew exactly what I wanted to do and where I wanted to go. Target was only about as far as the convenience store, but in a slightly different direction. I found Dad's old hammer in the garage and remembered to shove the earplugs I'd stolen from the convenience store into my pocket before I left the house.

It didn't occur to me that someone might have already broken into Target until I got there, but none of the doors were broken and nothing covered them up. I stomped on the mat in front of one of them; it didn't open. It didn't matter.

I threw Dad's hammer at the pane of glass on the right side of one of the doors. The door broke much more easily than I thought it would, and glass shattered and splintered into the air. I twisted away to keep from being nicked by the sharp pieces. Had I been that weak from hunger when I broke into the convenience store? Or was it just the difference between throwing a plastic crate and a hammer? Maybe next time I wouldn't throw the hammer quite so hard. The alarm sounded nearly the same as the other one had. I looked around. Maybe now people would stick their heads out of a shop, or someone who was trapped in a nearby car would roll down a window and yell, "Stop, thief!" but no one did. There was no one nearby—not even a coyote—but then, it was a lot hotter than it had been before, so maybe all the coyotes were resting in the shade somewhere—like the way lions of the Serengeti did when their stomachs were full of antelope. Except that it wasn't antelope the coyotes had been eating, and this wasn't Africa anyway.

I took the earplugs out of my pocket and stuffed them into my ears, dulling the alarm to a bearable buzz. I grabbed one of the oversized, cartoonish plastic carts that looked like it belonged in a comic book, and wheeled it through the aisles. If everything went back to normal soon, I'd probably still go to jail. I wasn't helping anyone else, like the President told me to do. I was only helping myself. But I did need to eat, and I had outgrown most of my clothes. I couldn't keep living this way until I was old enough to get a job. I just couldn't. And if I was going to jail anyway, what did it matter if I took a few more bags of groceries or some clothes?

But what if the things that the lawyer on TV said were true? What if, after everything went back to normal, people who took stuff got thrown in jail? What if people tried to sue me for breaking into their stores? They'd find out I was all alone! I started to get myself worked up, convinced that I *would* go to jail and that it *was* just a matter of time before things went back to normal. Then the police would check the cameras at Target and at the convenience store. They would show pictures of me on the news and ask people to call in if they had any leads.

My friends would say, "She was so sweet and quiet. I can't believe she would do something like this."

And their parents would say, "She was always so polite when she came over, but you know, now that I think about it, food was always missing after she left. I can't believe we didn't suspect she was stealing from us."

Then I thought about the press conference. The fear dissolved and I stopped feeling so guilty. The President had *said* to break in. He had *said* to rob the stores. Even though I took more than food and it was all for myself, I really did need the things I wanted to take. Most of them, anyway. But I couldn't get in trouble if the President said to do it, right?

Stop! I needed to stop worrying about it. Maybe I would get in trouble or maybe not. But I was going to do everything I could to survive right now, and I was tired of always being just one meal away from starvation. Plus, I hated eating cactus. I really did.

I put food in my cart, but I also took clothes and shoes and earrings. I wandered through the toiletries department and took toothpaste and one of those sonic toothbrushes; I hadn't been to the dentist in a very long time and they were supposed to be the best. Weren't the commercials always saying that two out of three dentists recommended those toothbrushes to their patients? Or was that a certain kind of gum? Anyway, I put the most expensive one into my cart.

It's funny now to look at some of the rules we used to follow. If I hadn't heard the President tell people like me to break into stores and take what we needed, I don't know how long it would have been before I got up the nerve to do it again after breaking into the convenience store. Even though I was starving and there was no one to come after me, I had only done it out of desperation. A part of me had hoped I'd get caught so I wouldn't have to keep pretending anymore. Juvie might be jail for kids, but there was a roof, and air conditioning, and regular meals, and other people. Compared to the way I'd been living, that didn't sound too horrible.

There were so many things we did before the glare that were just a part of the way things worked that I never thought to do them differently. Take the cart I was pushing around. I didn't live very far from the store, but I planned to bag my stuff up and carry as much as I could. I'd make extra trips if I had to. But why? I could have just wheeled the cart out of the store and pushed it home. But that never occurred to me; carts weren't supposed to leave the store. If you took them out of the parking lot, you could get in trouble. I could break into a store and take what I wanted because the President said so. But he never said anything about taking the carts, too. Following the rules was how you avoided trouble, and it was how Laney and I kept from Arousing Suspicion. No one noticed the rule-followers.

I accidentally found another way to get my stuff home that day that helped me much more than stealing a cart anyway. I went through every aisle, browsing the shelves and taking whatever I wanted. I saved the toy section for last. I was thirteen, so most of the toys were too young for me, but there were crafts and puzzles and books back there, too. The sports section began where the toy department ended. I started to skip it; I wasn't into volleyball or soccer or tennis or any of those things. We couldn't afford for me to be after Dad died—and besides, who would I have played with?

I turned into the first aisle of the sporting goods department anyway. I don't know why. Maybe only because I could. I pulled the cart to a fast stop when I came around the corner. Bicycles lined the back wall. There were big black ones with thick tires for riding on mountain trails, tiny pink ones with flowers on the seat and training wheels for little girls learning to ride, expensive ones with thin tires for grown-ups who wanted to tool around the block, and one that was perfect for me.

I ran my hand across the bikes as I passed. They were all so shiny and new and very expensive. The one I liked best was bright blue, the color my dad's eyes had been. It wasn't very fancy. It didn't have many gears or anything, just a simple water bottle holder on the frame, but it looked like it might be my size. The tires bounced when I pulled it over the hump of the rack that kept it in place. I straddled it and grinned as I pushed off with one foot. I pedaled down the aisle and swerved a little until I got my speed up and then I laughed like a crazy person. I couldn't help it. A bike! I had a new bike!

I rode it back to my cart and then stopped. How was I going to carry home all the stuff in my cart and ride the bike, too? What I needed was something I could pull. I found the answer in the aisle with all the bike accessories. The store had three different kinds of bike trailers on display. There was a small one that was meant for a little dog or very small child, a medium-sized one, and a very large one that had two seat belts inside. The big one was bright yellow with black trim and it zipped all the way up so that kids—or my stuff—could be zipped inside and stay dry if it rained. It didn't even take me very long to figure out how to attach it to my bike. It was perfect!

I loaded all the stuff from my cart into the bike trailer and tricked out my new bike with some other cool stuff from the bike aisle. I got myself a helmet (one that matched the bike) and a squishy cover that tied onto my seat so my butt wouldn't get sore from riding. I found a water bottle that fit perfectly in the holder, and I attached a basket that didn't look too toddlerish onto my handlebars, just because I thought it might be handy.

The bike trailer didn't hold as much as the cart. I filled the bottom with some canned goods and other heavy stuff and crammed smaller, lighter things like clothes and toothpaste into the crevices. I put my helmet on and rode slowly to the front door through the large, main aisles. It was harder to pedal pulling the full trailer, but it was still easier than lugging lots of heavy bags around.

The alarm was still screeching when I twisted the small knob and unlocked the broken door and pushed it open. The alarm went on and on, dulled to an irritating whine by the earplugs, but no one ran after me and shouted, "Stop, thief!" No one came after me with guns drawn. And this time I didn't expect them to.

***

I was nearly home when I passed a small pack of dogs panting in the shade of a tree. Two of them barked at me. The others were gnawing on something. I stared at them— the thing they were chewing on was covered in denim. Were the dogs really eating a person like the coyotes had? I didn't want to know! I looked away. I thought I saw a pair of coyotes slink behind a car on the road too, but it could have been my imagination. It *had* to be my imagination. Coyotes were supposed to be solitary. But I'd seen those two eating that man the day I robbed the convenience store. So maybe they weren't always solitary after all.

I relaxed a little when I reached the entrance to my neighborhood. I was daydreaming about what I was going to eat after I got home when I saw the man. I was so surprised, I whizzed right past him before I could stop. I pedaled backwards to brake the bike but the trailer fishtailed behind me. It almost turned over before I got my feet under me. The bike and the trailer came to a shuddering stop.

I turned and stared at him. I knew him! There was no mistaking the man who lived across the street—it was the old man who had spied on me and Laney with his wife. He tried to look in my direction, but he couldn't see through the glare.

"Hello…is someone there?" He sounded nervous, and

the mean part of me was glad he was afraid. Seeing his fear sucked the fear away from me like it had been vacuumed off of me and pushed into his body. The pain in my stomach that stabbed at me faded away. It served him right for scaring Laney and me for so long! He called out again and I almost answered, feeling a little ashamed for avoiding him—until he screamed at me.

"If someone's there, speak up! You hear me? Speak up!"

I snapped my jaw shut and wheeled my bike straight home. He tried to follow the quiet whisper of my tires, but once I was a few houses away from him and he couldn't hear the tires anymore, he lost track of me. I unlocked my door and began to unload stuff from the trailer and into the house as quietly as I could. I watched him as I worked.

He carried a ball of pink yarn that he unraveled as he stumbled around. Every so often he gave it a tug to make sure it was still secure at the other end where it was tied to the door of his house. For a second—just for a second—I thought about sneaking out with a pair of scissors and cutting the yarn. Maybe he'd wander away the way a balloon drifts away when a kid lets go of it. On second thought, no. He'd probably start screaming for his wife to open the door and she'd yell his name and he'd go to the sound of her voice. It'd be like a real-life game of Marco Polo.

I watched him make his way down to the next house, four doors away from his own. I felt another pang of guilt for not helping, but I didn't call out to him.

He stopped to tug on the yarn again, and he squeezed it as if he were gauging how much was left. He shuffled his feet as he walked, and when he veered off the sidewalk and his shoes crunched on the gravel in the yard, he over-corrected his path and nearly went off the curb. He had to bend over and feel for the curb to line himself up in the middle of the sidewalk again. He kept moving until the sidewalk turned into a driveway. He followed the edge of the driveway until it led to the front door. His feet hit the single step that made up the stoop of the house, and he almost fell, but then he caught himself and cursed again.

He kept his hands out in front of him and when he found the door, he patted it, feeling for the handle. His shoulders relaxed, and I thought I could hear him crying softly. But I still did nothing but watch from the safety of my house.

He pounded on the door with his knuckles and then felt around for the doorbell. He pressed once, then waited, listening. The door opened a crack. The face that peered out was too far away for me to tell if the person could see, but the windows of the house were blocked off so probably the man inside was blind, too. There was a brief conversation, then the door closed again. The old man began to sob, loud enough now that I could hear him clearly. He turned around and felt for the step with his foot. He sat down on it and wept into his hands. When he cried himself out, he wiped his face on the pink yarn that he still held tightly in his hands. Then he stood up and began rolling the yarn back up as he made his way back to his own house.

I watched until he got inside and shut the door. I stood staring at his house for a long time. I turned to go back inside when I thought I heard that same music from the day I broke into the convenience store. I turned my head back and forth—where was it coming from? If the store alarms weren't ringing, maybe I could have heard it better. I listened harder, but there was nothing but the sounds of the alarms now. Laney always said I had an overactive imagination. I must have just been hearing things.

I went back inside to watch TV, but the only thing on two of the channels I got was reruns. The other two channels kept broadcasting the President's press conference over and over again.

The last thing the news anchor said before I turned the TV off that night was, "Please continue to stay inside and stay tuned for more information."

TATTOO MAN

I began to see people in the neighborhood every time I went out. They were all blinded by the glare, and most of them used yarn or rope like the man across the street had. One end would be tied to a door knob or would lead inside a house so they could find their way back. I saw a man use a garden hose the same way. He cussed with each step. He got as far as his neighbor's driveway before he ran out of hose. He stood there, yelling and screaming words I'd never even heard before, not even from Rich. When he stopped yelling, he shuffled back to his house, using the hose as a guide. He felt his way from the side of the house where the hose was attached to the faucet and then used the wall to get back to his front door.

Another time, I saw a woman who tied a bunch of clothes and sheets together to make a long, fat rope. Most of the people knocked on doors, looking for help, and hoping they would find someone. And sometimes they came to my door.

I never knew what to do. Should I pretend that no one was home? Or should I answer the door and pretend to be blind? If I pretended that I wasn't there, someone might try to break in like they were starting to do at other houses. But if they thought I was alone, they might try to come in and take the food I finally had, so I was back to Avoiding

Suspicion.

I opened the door a crack when a man pounded on it. It was almost always men. I tried to sound panicky and afraid. I *was* panicky and afraid. That's why I always pretended like my house was full of people: "I can't see! None of my family can—not my dad or my brothers or my mom or my sister. None of us can see. Can you help us?" I said. It was hard to sound like I wanted their help while I braced the door with my foot and got ready to slam and lock it if they tried to get inside.

It was awful watching the hope drop off their faces, too. Some of them—grown men who thought I couldn't see them like they couldn't see me—crumpled to the ground. After I closed the door, I watched them wander away using their yarn or rope, and I made sure they were far away before I left the house again.

The first time I saw someone break into a house was when I was on my way back to Target one day. It was my favorite place to go because it had everything: food, clothes—everything. First the man pounded on the door and stabbed at the doorbell with his thumb. He had a piece of rope tied around his waist and an ax in one hand. Crumpled plastic grocery bags hung out of his back pockets like giant tissues. The rope led back to the house next to the one he was at. I straddled my bike and watched him try to get inside—and why shouldn't he? If his neighbor wasn't home, it wasn't like stealing, at least not anymore. Besides, if the stores were fair game for me, I figured that his neighbor's house was fair game for him. When no one answered the door, the man rattled the door knob and then pounded on the door. "Mark? Annie? You guys home? It's me, Dave—from next door. I'm comin' in if you don't come to the door. We need food. If you're in there, just tell me and I'll try someone else's house."

He put his ear to the door and listened. He pounded on the door one more time, but no one answered it. I was in the middle of the street watching him; but with his back to me I couldn't tell if he was relieved that his neighbors weren't home or not.

He felt for the door knob again and then swung his ax at it. He missed, but the ax made a thunking sound when it hit the doorframe. He swung again and this time the ax clanged against the door handle. He swung again, even harder, and then did it again once more. The clanging noise was louder—he was getting the hang of it. His next swing broke the door handle off entirely, and it dropped to the stoop and made a ringing sound like a pair of cymbals. He carefully placed the ax on the ground and felt for the door. The handle was gone, but the door was still locked somehow. He pushed his shoulder into the door and it budged, just a little. He did it again, ramming the door with his body. The door swung in and he fell into the house, cursing.

When I rode past the house later in the afternoon on my way back from Target, the man was carrying bags full of cans and boxes back to his house. He froze when he heard me sail past on my bike, like he thought I might not see him if he didn't move. Actually, now that I think about it, he was probably on to something; if he didn't make any noise, another blind person wouldn't know he was there.

I didn't help him or any of the other people I saw. I cried as I watched them from my window, or when I passed them on the street. My heart ached with guilt and pity, especially when I noticed how they were losing weight at the same rate I was gaining it, but I didn't help any of them. The people on TV were right. I couldn't help everyone. I could barely take care of myself. How was I supposed to help all those people? I did start to think more about what the President said, though.

His words chased each other in a vicious cycle in my mind, like a snake swallowing its own tail. "Take what you need…help your neighbors. Take what you need…help your neighbors." I didn't have a problem with the taking part anymore. I made several trips to Target, the convenience store, and one of the grocery stores that hadn't been broken into by people trying to escape the glare. It was fun, and I couldn't get enough stuff. I stocked up on all the things I needed, like toilet paper and canned goods and bottled water. I filled the pantry and the fridge until they were so full I had to pile things by the front door. I emptied the shelves of all the mac and cheese they had, but only the good kind, the kind where you cut the top off the foil pouch and squeeze the cheese on top of the pasta before you mix it all together. I had bags and bags of candy bars, and the freezer was full of ice cream. I cleared the store shelves of all the rice and pasta I could find, too—the boxes that already had seasoning in them so you just added water and boiled them for a while. Mac and cheese, pasta, and rice were about all I knew how to cook, but it was pretty great to have something besides cactus and green beans to eat. Every day, I took more stuff: cereal, juice pouches, soda, and whatever else I wanted.

The taking part was easy and fun. But I hadn't done the second part. I hadn't helped anyone else. I tried to argue myself out of feeling guilty. I'd gone to Amber's house, hadn't I? I'd tried to help her family. It wasn't my fault they weren't home. And why should I help anyone else, anyway? No one had helped me and Laney. No one had helped Mom when she started drinking. No one had even cared when Dad died.

The quiet part of my mind whispered things back at me. *The teachers at your school gave your mom a really big gift card to the grocery store when your dad died, and people left gift baskets at the doorstep for months afterwards. And what about the lunch lady at school who sometimes gave you an extra carton of milk because she said you were too thin? How about Mr. Black at the bagel store? And what about Brian and Mary?*

Brian and Mary. They had helped me. They'd been

Suspicious, I was sure of it. But they had still given me yard work to do and overpaid me for it. And Mary had given me cookies and all that food. I swallowed hard, remembering how relieved and grateful I'd been when I opened that bag.

I *would* help someone else. It was the right thing to do. But I wasn't going to help everyone. The caller on the news was right. I wouldn't be able to help everyone. And I definitely wasn't going to help any of my own neighbors, the people who complained about the weeds in our yard and Mom's old car sitting out for too long. But I *would* help Brian and Mary. And maybe the other people on their street were as nice as they were. That was it. I had decided. I would help Brian and Mary and their neighbors, but not mine. And not today.

***

I didn't do anything—not at first—but each day I thought a little more about helping people. No one had tried to break into my house yet, but every once in a while I'd hear the sound of windows shattering or an alarm going off when someone tried to break into a house nearby. I started sleeping under my bed again. Getting out of the neighborhood on my bike was trickier every day, too. There were more people out, and I had to ease my way around them sometimes so they wouldn't know I was there.

Two men, one with the shadow of whiskers on his jaw and one with a tattoo on his arm and a big dimple in the middle of his chin, were standing about fifteen feet apart, talking. They more or less faced each other. Tattoo Man had a gun in his hand and the other man carried a baseball bat. Whisker Man looked relieved to come across another human being. "We could team up. What if you and your family come over to my house? We could pool our resources, that kind of thing."

Tattoo Man squinted, trying to look at the other guy.

His face was suddenly suspicious. "I don't even know you. How do I know you're not going to kill us?"

"What? Why would I do that? Are you nuts?"

Tattoo Man smirked into the glare. "Why? For our food. Not that we have any," he added quickly.

The older man shook his head and looked bewildered. "That's preposterous! If we work together maybe we'll be able to figure out how to get to a store or find help. We wouldn't be alone, either. Surely you've been hearing all the break-ins. We could take turns standing guard!"

I concentrated really hard on pedaling past them as quietly as I could, but they were in the middle of the road and no matter which way I went, I would have been within a few feet of them.

Tattoo Man cocked his head. "Did you hear that?"

"I don't hear anything…"

"Shhhh! Who's there? Is someone out there?"

It was like being at the store all over again. The trailer on the back of my bike rattled as I went over a crack in the asphalt.

"Someone's there!" he shouted. He ran toward me with his hands stretched out in front of him. I stood up on my pedals and pushed hard. The trailer rattled again. Tattoo Man ran after me—or tried to. He grabbed the air behind my bike and missed the trailer by only a few inches before I sped away, breathing hard.

Tattoo Man stumbled and dropped to his knees. "Someone's there. I heard them. Did you hear them?"

"I heard you shouting and yelling, that's all."

I looked back in time to see Tattoo Man spin around toward the sound of the other man's voice. "Or maybe that's what you want me to think. Maybe there's someone else out here and they're with you. Maybe you're the decoy. You're trying to distract me so your friend can sneak up behind me!"

He flung his arms around like he was sure someone was

behind him.

Whisker Man tried to interrupt him.

Tattoo Man held his gun up even though the other man couldn't see it. "It won't work. I'm warning you. I can take care of myself, buddy. You and your friends better keep your distance if you know what's good for you!"

"I'm not with anyone else! I don't know what you're talking about!" Then the expression on his face changed and he hefted his red aluminum baseball bat up in front of his body and took a small swing. "Maybe you're trying to trick me! Maybe *you're* the decoy and *you're* trying to distract me while someone sneaks up behind *me*!"

They started screaming at one another. "Get back! Don't come any closer! I have a weapon!"

"Yeah, well so do I! You just go back the way you came. You stay away from here! You hear me? Stay away! This is my territory. I mean it!"

Tattoo Man aimed his gun in the general direction of the other man's voice and pulled the trigger. The bang of the gun echoed down the street. Whisker Man dropped to the ground. I tucked my body close to the handle bars of my bike and pushed the pedals as hard as I could. I didn't look back to see if the man got up or not, but for the first time I saw the bigger picture, the one that didn't just involve me having enough food and clothes. If I was going to help anyone, I probably needed to do it soon.

HELP HAS ARRIVED

Maybe this wasn't such a great idea. I almost turned around and left. Instead, I took a deep breath, raised my hand, and rapped on the door before I lost my nerve. If I hadn't immediately heard shuffling footsteps echoing closer and closer on the other side of the door, I probably would have turned and left even though the windows were blocked off so I knew someone was inside.

The door opened a few inches. A tiny, wrinkly woman stared out at me—or she tried to, anyway. Her eyes were squeezed shut and when she tried to open them to look at me, I caught a glimpse of filmy brown eyes before she shut them again. "Who's there?" the woman croaked.

I waved hesitantly. "Hi. I'm one of your neighbors..." I started to say, using the speech I'd rehearsed. I didn't get to say anything else because smoke billowed out of the house and I couldn't breathe without choking.

The woman's face was pointed in my direction, but it was clear she couldn't see me no matter how hard she tried to open her eyes. The glare was just too bright. She wheezed and struggled to catch her breath. "I don't know what you want, but I can't see a blasted thing out there, so I can't help you."

The door started to close. I knocked again and it opened immediately. "I said I can't help. Now git!"

135

"No! You don't understand. I don't need your help. The thing is, I can see. I wondered…well, I wondered if you needed *my* help."

The woman opened the door a bit more. "You can see, eh? Why don't you come in where I can see you, then?"

I knew she was probably harmless. I thought I could have knocked her over just by bumping into her, and I wasn't exactly big myself. But something in my imagination turned her into the old witch who tricked Hansel and Gretel into her cottage made of candy. I took a step backwards.

"Uh, no. No, thanks. I'm going to the store, though. Is there anything you need?"

The woman opened the door wider, more eager than she was before. "Cigarettes. If this is what it's come to, ain't no good trying to quit now. Bring me cigarettes."

My voice was faint when I answered. "What about food? Do you need food or anything?"

The woman cackled. "Food? Ha! I have food. Just bring me cigarettes. The doctors have been telling me for years that smoking will kill me, and by God, that's how I aim to die!" Then she slammed the door in my face.

I fled. It was the middle of the afternoon before I could convince myself to try the other houses on Brian and Mary's street.

***

The next house was empty. So was the one next to it. Their windows weren't blocked off, but I rang their doorbells anyway—just in case. The old lady who smoked scared me, but if she was the only one I had to take care of, it might not be so bad. It sounded like all she wanted was cigarettes, and they weren't very big or heavy. She would be easy to help. Besides, she smoked so much she'd probably die in a few days anyway.

Someone answered the door at the third house, the one

next to Brian and Mary's, and the woman began sobbing when she heard my voice.

"Oh God! I thought no one would come," she said through the door as she unlocked it. "Come in! Please come in!"

I stepped in and she fumbled with the door. When it was closed and the cracks were taped off and she could see again, she stared at me. "But…but you're just a kid!"

She slid down the wall and buried her hands in her face, crying again. A toddler came into the hall on a small riding toy. Long red, blue, and yellow ribbons hung from the handle bars, and they swished every time the little boy pushed the toy forward with his chubby feet.

"I…I'm sorry," I said. "I'll go…"

I turned and reached for the door knob. The woman grabbed my arm desperately. "No! No. Please don't go! I guess I was hoping this was an elaborate trick or a hoax or something. I thought that if it was real that maybe they'd find a way to help us see after all. I thought there would be special glasses or something, like the President said. I thought you must be someone from the army or the government," she babbled. "But this is all real, isn't it? Nothing's going to change!"

She shook her head as tears dripped down her cheeks. "Don't go. Please don't go. Stay, okay?"

She scooped the little boy up. I rubbed my arm where she'd grabbed it, but I nodded and followed her into her living room. Her name was Susan, and her little boy's name was Jeremy and they looked a lot alike. She had long black hair and big brown eyes. His hair was thick and messy, but just as shiny and dark as hers. Thick black lashes framed his green eyes and he waved at me while he made toddler noises. I didn't ask her where he husband was, but I promised that I'd bring her food and diapers and I'd stay longer when I came back. When I left, I took out the garbage. The Cigarette Lady's house smelled like smoke, but

Susan's smelled like poopy diapers and baby powder.

***

I skipped Brian and Mary's house and went to the house on the other side of theirs. Why was I so worried about seeing them? They couldn't be more Suspicious of me than they already were, could they? Anyway, they might not even be home. I stared at their house as I walked by—they were home. They had to be. Their windows were all blocked off with newspaper and tape. But what if they didn't answer? Or what if they didn't want anything to do with me? Maybe it was stupid, but I just wasn't ready to find out. The house next to theirs was empty like most of them had been. I kind of remembered my mom saying there were a lot of houses in this part of the neighborhood that were owned by snowbirds, the older people who only spent winters in Arizona. Maybe that's why there weren't as many blocked-off windows as there were on my street.

There was only one other house in the row and people were in it. A man came to the door when I knocked. He was older than Susan, but not as old as my mom had been. And unlike Susan's house, which looked comfortable and safe even if it did smell like poopy diapers, his looked like no one lived in it. There was furniture in it and all the things you need in a house, but it looked like the picture from a magazine, not an actual house that someone lived in.

The man was just as disappointed that I was only a kid as Susan had been. "Well, beggars can't be choosers, now can they?" he said when I told him that I wanted to help, like the President said I should. He didn't sound very happy about it, though.

His girlfriend, Rebecca, cried the whole time I was there. It wasn't a cry like Susan's where it had exploded out of her and she had to force it down just to breathe. I understood that cry. Susan cried because she was scared and alone. Rebecca sobbed like a little kid who only cried because her mom saw her fall, not because she was really hurt.

Jonathan wrote a list for me, and he looked up at Rebecca as she sat sobbing into her hands next to him at the kitchen counter. I could hear the disgust in his voice when he said, "Go into the other room if you're going to keep crying. I'm sick of hearing you whine all the time. I wish you would have gone home when the glare struck. Then I wouldn't have to listen to you!"

He folded the list and handed it to me. "The sooner you come back with this stuff, the better," he told me. "We're out of everything and I need a drink."

I opened the list and scanned it, worried he might ask for more than I could carry, or that he wanted stuff I couldn't get by going to Target, the convenience store, or the grocery store. He had some food on the list: frozen chicken, milk, and cereal—easy stuff like that—but the last half of the list was mostly words I didn't know.

I tried to sound the words out, but they looked foreign or something. "I...I don't know what this says."

Jonathan rolled his eyes and made another sound of disgust in the back of his throat. He snatched the list out of my hands and tapped some of the words. "It's wine. And those are gourmet cheeses. You *can* read well enough to match the words, can't you?"

I wasn't stupid! I was thirteen. How was I supposed to know about weird cheese and expensive wine? I didn't like Jonathan or his weepy girlfriend, and I wished I had never knocked on their door.

***

Brian and Mary's house was the only one I hadn't been to yet. I wiped my palms on my shorts. They were suddenly very sweaty.

Brian's voice sounded wary on the other side of the door. "Who's there?"

"It's me, Jenna," I said. I thought maybe they wouldn't remember my name, so I added, "I live around the corner. I picked weeds for you…"

The deadbolt on the door clicked, and the door opened a crack. Brian tried to look out but he was as blind as the rest of them. It was easy to tell because he blinked so much, just trying to keep his eyes open in the bright light. My heart sank. Somehow I'd been hoping they could see—like maybe they were so nice that of course they'd be able to see, because then things would be a little more fair. But nothing had been fair in my life for a very long time. I should have known better.

"Are you alone?" he asked. I nodded, a lump building in my throat. Then, realizing he couldn't see me, I said, "Yeah. I'm alone. Can…can I come in?"

He seemed to weigh his options for a moment. Maybe he was deciding whether I really was alone, like the Tattoo Man.

He stepped aside and opened the door wider. I slipped in and pushed the door closed with my back. He locked it and smoothed back tape that covered the frame of the door. Nearly every light was on, just like at everyone else's house.

"You can see?"

I nodded. He looked at me, studying my face, my clothes, my hair. Then he called out, "Mary! You can come out. It's our young friend from around the corner. It's Jenna!"

I heard some scraping from one of the back rooms and then Mary came down the hall. Her hair was messed up the way mine got when I hid under my bed, but she smiled and she looked like she was glad to see me. Meatball bounded in front of her, nearly tripping her. His shaggy fur flopped in front of his eyes, and he leaped toward me. I dropped to my knees when he pranced within petting range. His back end wagged like crazy before he dropped to the ground and rolled over so I could rub his tummy.

"Oh, Jenna! We've been wondering how you were! We're so glad you're okay. How is your family? Was your mom home when things went bad? How about your sister?" Mary wrapped her arms around me and gave me a quick, tight hug before I could answer her questions. She smelled like vanilla.

"Well, that's the thing," I said when she stepped back. She and Brian both looked at me with concern.

"See, my mom, she…well…"

I licked my lips. I had told the same story to the other people on the street, but I had to be more careful with Brian and Mary. I didn't realize it when I was knocking at their neighbors' doors, but that's why I had saved their house for last. Brian and Mary knew me just a little bit, and I really wanted them to believe what I told them so they wouldn't ask any more questions I couldn't answer. I would have to explain where my mom and sister were and why I was home alone. I wanted to have a story ready that wouldn't Arouse Suspicion, but I also wanted the story to make sense so I would never have to be afraid of getting caught again—so that the part that was the most real now, the part where I lived at home, alone, wouldn't be a secret or a lie. Only the part about *why* I was alone and *how long* I'd been alone would be a secret, and no one would ever have to know those things.

I took a deep breath and then told them the story I'd been practicing. "See, my mom went on a trip with some friends. She went to Washington, DC." Washington seemed far enough away that she'd never be able to get back home.

"Laney's friend, Sammie, asked if Laney could go out of town for the night with her family." The story sounded ridiculous but I kept going. "She called our mom and Mom said she could go if one of *my* friends spent the night with me so I wouldn't be alone. My friend, Amber, was supposed to come over, but her mom changed her mind after Laney already left."

The way I ended my story felt weak and lame. "So I'm alone," I finished.

In a rush to cover up the story that now sounded terribly Suspicious, I said. "Do you need anything? 'Cos I can see, obviously, and the President said that people who can see should help their neighbors…"

Brian and Mary exchanged glances and I had the same worry I had with them before, that I'd messed up somehow, that they knew I was lying. Brian especially. Mary pulled me toward her and hugged me again.

"You must have been terrified for the past few days. Thank God you could see, though! At least you weren't trapped in your house like the rest of us."

Brian cut in before Mary could go on. In his gruff voice, the one he used when he told me I needed to take some cookies home, he said, "Let's get you home so you can pack up. I'll walk back with you if you can stand leading a blind old man with a gimpy leg and a bad back around the block. Mary will fix up the extra bedroom and you'll stay with us."

I froze. I hadn't expected that. No one else even thought to ask how *I* was. No one else wondered if I was scared or worried living all by myself. What could I say? Should I do it? Briefly, I imagined living with the Bransons. It would be like…like…like having a family again. Having grownups who cared about you and who wanted you to be safe. Having people around to talk to. Not being alone when you woke up in the middle of the night, terrified by the bad dream you'd just had, or a strange sound that had woken you up. Having someone take care of you when you were sick. Knowing that someone *cared*.

I swallowed hard. I wanted to stay, but I was afraid, too. If I lived with them, if I loved them like a family, it would be harder to keep the secret from them, the real secret. If I slipped up and they figured out that Mom was dead, they might think Laney and I had murdered her since we never called the police. They wouldn't want to live with a murderer, would they? Of course not. No one would. Even if I wasn't one. And then I'd be alone again.

"No," I said as I stepped away from Mary. "It's okay. It's not so bad being alone."

They looked at each other again. Very quietly, Mary said, "The offer stands, Jenna. It doesn't matter if it's tomorrow or in a week or in six months. If you want to stay with us, you just bring your stuff over. Okay?"

I nodded and swallowed hard. I wouldn't cry. I wouldn't!

Brian watched me. He was Suspicious, but he tried to hide it with a joke. "So you aren't looking for a friendly place to stay, huh? I'm curious, then. Why did you come by? Surely you weren't looking to do more yard work?"

I laughed. He *was* Suspicious. But he wasn't going to push me. "I saw the President on TV the other day. There aren't very many of us who can see, and if we can, we should try to help our neighbors. So here I am. I wanted to know if you need anything."

"Ah, yes. The President. That was quite a speech he gave. He really put a lot of responsibility on very few people, didn't he? I wonder just how many of you there are, anyway. He never did give us any estimates. I heard a few people who called in to the news stations claiming they could see, but there weren't many. Have you seen anyone else out?"

We were in their family room. Brian dropped into a well-worn recliner, and I sat across from him on the edge of the couch. Mary was in the kitchen. The layout of their house was similar to mine. Their house was bigger, and their kitchen looked into the family room instead of having a little nook where the dining room table was. Their house was well taken care of, too, not like mine. There was tile in the kitchen instead of old, peeling linoleum, the carpets were clean, and the walls didn't have any holes from Rich's fists.

"You'll eat cookies if I make them, won't you?" Mary asked over the counter.

Brian answered for me. "If she doesn't, you know I will, diabetes or not." He winked at me.

Mary made a noise that sounded something like, "Hrumph," but cabinets kept opening and shutting and the oven beeped, so she couldn't have been too mad.

The lights dimmed and flickered for a moment, and the air conditioner whirred louder, like it wanted to stop working. That was happening more often, I noticed. We all stared up at the lights until they were bright again.

Brian asked me again. "So? Have you seen anyone else out? You seem to be wearing new clothes, and you don't look quite as, uh…lean as the last time I saw you. I'm guessing you've taken the President at his word and taken some things you needed? Are you the reason I hear security alarms all over the place when I stick my head out the door?"

I sucked in my breath. He knew. Maybe not all of it, but some. But he didn't sound mad or disappointed, just matter-of-fact. I wondered if he and Mary had known I wasn't getting much to eat before. Maybe he thought Mom didn't make very much money. That must be why they had overpaid me and sent me home with cookies…of course! I felt my face turn pink when I understood: of course they'd known. That's why Mary had come after me and given me all that food. None of it was close to expiring. They could see that I was hungry. I'd practically been a walking skeleton.

I stuttered, trying to come up with an answer that fit my new knowledge. "Yes. No. I mean yes, I took some things I needed." I tried not to sound defensive when I added, "I had to. I didn't have any food left. But most of the alarms are from the stores where people broke in to escape the glare."

Mary leaned on the counter and interrupted me before I could say more than I wanted to. "Of course you had to. You used more common sense than some adults would have under the same circumstances."

"Don't interrupt the girl," Brian said. "I want to know how many others can see."

Mary rolled her eyes at me, but she smiled. "Yes, dear."

It was funny. Sometimes he talked to her the way Jonathan had talked to his girlfriend, but it didn't come out the same, somehow. Jonathan wasn't a nice person. I knew it the same way I knew that Brian *was*. Mary, too. And I knew that Brian loved his wife. He wasn't being rude when he ordered her to stop talking. It was like their secret language. The words sounded tough, but there wasn't any meanness behind them. I had only been at Jonathan's house once, and for only a few minutes, but I could tell he didn't care about Rebecca. He really meant it when he told her to shut up.

"So?" Brian asked. "Have you seen others?"

This was one of the tricky parts. How did I tell them about the people I'd seen in my neighborhood without having to explain that I wasn't helping them? I was going to tell him that there were people on my street with guns and I was afraid to go to their houses so I came to Brian and Mary's street instead. It was better if I didn't have to complicate the lie, though. Since Brian only asked if I'd seen others, not where I'd seen them, I answered his question in a general way.

"I went to some of the other houses on your street," I said. "People only answered the door at three houses. None of them could see outside. I've seen people out in other neighborhoods, too, looking for help. None of them can see, either. And when I went to the convenience store—the one sort of by the movie theater—and to Target and the grocery store, I only saw people in the neighborhoods using rope or yarn to keep from getting lost. I can hear people inside some of the stores that have been broken into. But they're not trying to take stuff. All the glass is blocked off from the inside. They've all been stuck in there from the day the glare happened. I haven't seen anyone else who can see. There are a lot of cars on the side of the road and some accidents. There are dead people in some of them, and there are animals out everywhere now, and the coyotes have been eating some of the dead people, too…"

I gulped for air. I hadn't meant for everything to come rushing out like that. I had kept it together when I talked to the Cigarette Lady and to Susan, Jonathan, and Rebecca. What was wrong with me?

Mary came out of the kitchen and sat on the arm of Brian's chair. They both stared at me.

"Well, go on, young lady. There's more, isn't there? Spit it out. We might as well know," Brian said.

I hesitated. I was afraid. They seemed okay with me stealing food and clothes since the President said to take what I needed, so maybe it was okay to tell them more.

"I broke into the convenience store and Target and the grocery store. The alarms rang and rang and rang at all of them, but the police never came. No one ever came."

Brian wrapped an arm around Mary's waist and they looked at each other. Her eyes filled with tears but she didn't sob like Susan had or weep like Rebecca. Meatball stayed with me. Whenever I stopped petting him, he pushed his fuzzy head under my hand and whined for attention.

"So, it's true, then," Mary murmured to Brian. "This really is the end. Our food will only last so long. I'm sure you're right about the electricity and the water, too…"

The lights flickered overhead again.

"Yes, but it's a good thing you talked me out of the place I wanted to buy out in the desert."

"It had solar power and a cistern, Brian! At least we would have had a chance there."

"Hmph. Did you forget about all the skylights for the

natural light the real estate agent went on and on about? We would have been blind the first day. I would have never been able to reach them to cover them up. The ceilings were vaulted, remember? We would have been blind inside and out. The solar power would have been nice, though."

The regret melted from her face. "Well, we've had a good life together, haven't we? It's not the worst way things could end."

It made me anxious to hear them talk as if I weren't there, especially like that. Usually when adults talked, I tried to stay out of the conversation. Normally, I steered clear of anything that might draw attention to myself, like butting into an adult's conversation, but I liked Brian and Mary so much! More importantly, I trusted them. Not with all my secrets, maybe, but more than I trusted anyone else.

"But it's not the end! That's why I'm here! I'm doing what the President said. I'm going to help you! I'll bring you food and water and whatever else you need. I'm only helping people at three other houses! I never even knocked on any of the doors on my own street! There are only..." I stopped and counted mentally. "There are only eight of us including me to worry about, and there's enough food to last forever," I said, thinking of all the stores in Ahwatukee.

"There are tons of grocery stores and convenience stores and drug stores and two department stores and a zillion restaurants that probably have those giant cans of food..."

I rambled on, listing all the stores I could think of nearby. It was true that a good many of them were too far for me to bike to, and a lot of them probably had people in them, but there were still tons of stores!

They looked at me and then at each other. They seemed surprised, like they hadn't considered that they might need me, only that I might need them. How strange.

Finally, Mary spoke. "Jenna, hon. Would you do us a favor? Would you mind leaving for a bit? Brian and I need to talk about a few things in private. Maybe you could come back in a few hours?"

They believed me. They had to! "No, it's getting late. I'll come back tomorrow, okay? In the afternoon. Everything will be fine. You'll see! I'll even bring some food and stuff with me. I already told the Cigarette Lady—I mean the old lady—at the end of the street that I'd bring her some cigarettes, and Susan and Jeremy need some food, and Jonathan and Rebecca need some stuff, too…"

Brian and Mary walked me to the door with their arms around each other. I heard their voices on the other side when the door clicked closed behind me and the lock clunked into place, but I couldn't quite make out their words, only the sound of their voices. They were worried. But that was silly, wasn't it? They had me to take care of them now. Why should they be worried?

DELIVERY GIRL

The Cigarette Lady's real name was Martha. I got that much out of her when I stacked cartons of cigarettes up in the hall, right inside the front door.

"Aren't you even going to take them into the kitchen for me?" she croaked. She probably had cancer in her throat— that's how hoarse she sounded.

"Uh, I'd better not." I said. "I have to go back to the store and get stuff for the others."

It was a lie. I had everything in my bike trailer already, and I was sure she was harmless. She had to be, right? But the little kid part of me was still afraid she might try to fatten me up and eat me. It made me kind of glad I was still on the skinny side, even though I practically never stopped eating.

"Just as well. You'd probably want to chat or something. I'll put a note on the door when I need something else. You just make sure you don't come by at some ungodly hour. And my shows are on between one and three, so don't come then. They're all reruns now, but I don't want to be interrupted. Don't bother me then…"

"Uh-huh," I agreed, trying to escape. "I have to go. A note would be fine. Bye!"

I was only in her house for a few minutes, and I already stank. I thought about going home to take a shower, but I wanted to take Jonathan and Rebecca the stuff they asked for so I could get it over with. I would take a shower afterwards, before I went to Susan's house. Little Jeremy was so cute and she was very nice, too, just as nice as Brian and Mary.

***

"You stink." Jonathan said, shutting the door behind me. "Don't you know that smoking is bad for you? It's a disgusting habit."

My mouth opened and shut like a goldfish's. "I'm only thirteen and I don't smoke! I was delivering stuff to Martha and *she* smokes!" I was helping him and he didn't even care! He hadn't said thank you to me—not even once!

He spoke to me like I was some little troublemaker he had to set straight. "Well, you're going to have to deliver our stuff before you go over there from now on. You stink, and I don't like the smell in my house."

I snapped my mouth shut and brought in more bottles of wine and the food he'd asked for. I let the bottles of wine clink together so hard that he winced. I wished one of them would break and spill wine all over his light beige carpet, but it didn't. I let the bottles clang together again, just in case they were one bump away from breaking. Still nothing. Dang it!

I put everything inside the door like I'd done at Martha's house, and I didn't speak to him again. I started to close the door behind me when I was done unloading but he called out. "Wait! Wait a sec."

I shut the door again and relaxed a little. He was going to apologize.

"Here's more stuff we need."

I stared at him open-mouthed again when he handed me another folded list.

"What?"

I shook my head. "Nothing."

I slammed the door and left him standing in the hall. I hoped I cracked his door or the frame or something.

***

That's how I spent the next few days. Martha and Jonathan couldn't be bothered to talk to me much, but I didn't mind. Sometimes Rebecca tried to talk to me, but it always went something like this:

Her: Have you seen any more people?

Me: Just the ones like you guys. The ones who can't see and need help.

Her: What are we going to do? How are we going to survive?

Me: What do you mean? I'm bringing you everything you need, aren't I?

Her: But you're just a child. I can't believe our lives are dependent on a child!

Then she would fling herself onto the couch and weep with big sobs that made her shoulders shudder. If I was lucky, she would run into the bedroom and slam the door. Then I wouldn't have to pat her back and try to console her. She talked to me like I was a useless little kid, but when I patted her back, she would fling her arms around my neck and cry like *she* was the little kid. She wasn't ever mean like Jonathan, but I still didn't like her much.

Jonathan and Martha taped their lists to their front doors each night. In the morning I picked them up and got what they wanted. I left as soon as I woke up, and I always took a spray bottle in the basket of my bike so I could spritz myself down if I got too hot. I took a couple of extra bottles of water to drink, too. Brian had been telling me about the dangers of dehydration, and he made me promise to always carry lots of water with me.

There were more animals out than before. It was

starting to make me nervous. I always saw a few coyotes and dogs—they didn't like my bike and trailer, but every day they were braver—Brian called them brazen. I filled the bike trailer as full as I could and delivered stuff before I went home: TV dinners and cigarettes for Martha and fancy, expensive food like caviar, stinky cheese, weird-looking crackers, and lots and lots of wine for Jonathan and Rebecca. I rang their doorbells, put their things inside their doors when they opened them, and left. They never thanked me. They just told me to come back in the morning for another list.

I delivered Susan's things and the stuff Brian and Mary asked for after I showered. They asked for food too, and Brian also had me bring a bunch of stuff from the camping section of Target: battery-operated lanterns with special LED bulbs, flashlights and candles, candle holders, a camping stove, a manual can-opener, and propane. When I asked him why he wanted all that stuff, he tapped his temple and said, "The electricity won't hold out forever, kiddo. It's all about survival."

He also had me bring ink for his printer and a bunch of computer paper which seemed kind of weird, but at least it wasn't wine and gross, smelly cheese. Whenever I'd come by, he or Mary would be in their small home office, using their printer. They were distracted, but they always invited me in, and they always thanked me again and again for helping them.

I gave Susan and Mary each other's phone numbers and they'd been chatting but couldn't place each other despite being neighbors. I even led Brian and Mary to Susan's house so they could visit. Before the glare, Susan was always working or tutoring—she was a teacher—or picking Jeremy up from daycare, and since Brian and Mary were retired, their paths hadn't crossed. Once I introduced them, they liked each other very much. It wasn't long before Susan and Jeremy moved into Brian and Mary's extra bedroom. I thought maybe Mary had only wanted more company since she gave Susan the room she said I could have any time I wanted it, but after I carried all of Susan's things over, Mary took my hand and said, "There's still plenty of room for you, Jenna. There will always be plenty of room for you here."

***

"It was so nice of you to get those toys for Jeremy," Susan said when I came over one day.

I rolled my eyes at her and laughed. "It's not like I paid for them or anything."

"Still, it was nice. Thank you."

Brian sat with his arm around Mary's shoulder. "So how was it out there today?" He asked that every day. "Did you go anywhere new?"

I nodded and swallowed a big gulp of ice cold soda. "I did. I went to the other drugstore for you, the one that didn't have people trapped inside. The alarms always freak me out but I figured out how to turn this one off. You were right, there was a code up by the register and keys for the pharmacy, too. I took all their diabetes medicine for you."

Brian smiled but it looked a little strained. He never said anything, but I knew from taking so much of it and reading the expiration dates that the medicine I stole for him expired after a year, and since there wasn't anyone making more of it...

It was silent for a moment, and then he shrugged and gave a short laugh. "We've all got to die some time, don't we? And hopefully, thanks to you, that won't be anytime soon."

The rest of us laughed, but it was uncomfortable laughter.

Brian sat up and leaned forward, pulling his arm away from Mary.

"We have something to talk to you about, Jenna. It's important."

I looked at Susan and Mary. Their smiles were nearly grimaces, and they wouldn't meet my eye. Worry made my stomach churn.

"Here's the thing, Jenna. We're all grateful for what you're doing for us. Well, the three of us are, anyway. The others don't sound so appreciative, so I hope you'll consider what we have to say more than what they may tell you."

I nodded as I twisted my fingers through Meatball's fur. What was it? What did they want to tell me? They weren't going to tell me to go away, were they? They couldn't!

"I think we're all aware that this can't last forever." He motioned toward the boxes of stuff that sat in the hallway.

Is that all they were worried about? The knot it my stomach loosened. "What do you mean?" I said. "It's not hard. I told you. There's tons of stuff in the stores!"

Brian glanced down at Jeremy who was playing with the light up piano I'd brought him. Then he looked at Susan. She gave him a shaky smile so he continued. "We'll take what you can give us, Jenna. One of the things I learned in the military is that part of survival is never giving up hope. But this is about your survival too, and it's only right that you understand."

He looked at Mary and Susan again. They nodded at him to continue. "We've talked about it, and we know this won't last forever. There may come a time when you have to move on and leave us, and we won't hold that against you. We just want you to know that."

I tried to protest but Susan interrupted. Tears dripped down her face. They beaded up on the cushion of the couch and magnified the fibers until they sunk in. She gulped hard, but nodded. "If it weren't for him," she said, pointing her chin at Jeremy, "I might have killed myself by now. I'm not very brave, but I can't give up when he's depending on me, you know?"

Mary got up and sat beside Susan. She patted Susan on the back, crying herself. Susan tried to smile through her tears. "It's funny. Before this happened, I would have done anything for a break from him. Since his dad didn't stick around after Jeremy was born, all I ever did was go to work, pick him up from daycare, then try to get him fed and in bed as fast as I could, just to have a few minutes to myself. Now, I can't bear the thought of being away from him. I know things are going to get bad. I know food will run out or go bad and the electricity will go out sooner or later. We're having more and more brownouts every day. It can't last much longer. Who knows how long the batteries and candles you brought will last when the electricity does go out. And we don't have a doctor if one of us gets hurt or sick, but I'm still grateful that I'm not one of the billions of people who are trapped in their houses without any help at all. I don't know what I would have done if you hadn't come to my door."

Trembling, she said, "If I have to, I'll kill him, then myself." She looked up at Brian. "Brian said he knows how we can do it painlessly if we need to."

Brian's face was grim when he nodded, and she swallowed hard again. Susan raised her chin the way Laney always did when she was being strong and said, "But until I know there's no chance for us, I'm not going to give up hope. I just can't do that to him."

Mary held her hand across her mouth to choke back her sobs, and Susan wept in her hands. Brian went over to Mary and buried his face in her hair, crying himself. I cried, too. Meatball whined at us, but Jeremy looked up and grinned, showing a few perfect, pearly little baby teeth. He clapped his hands and laughed.

Susan smiled at him. "I know, buddy! What are we doing? Why are the silly grownups all crying like babies?"

She dropped to the floor and wrapped her arms around him, burying her face in his neck and blowing a loud raspberry into it. He giggled again, and the rest of us laughed through our own tears.

Mary jumped up from the couch. "That's enough of that," she said, dashing tears away. "Who's ready for dinner?"

Brian was the first to sit down at the table, but the rest of us were close behind him. I looked around as we ate. It would be so easy to pretend that Brian and Mary were my parents and that Susan was my sister. Jeremy would be my little brother or maybe a nephew. Our dog, Meatball, sat under Brian's chair and waited for Brian to slip him the extra vegetables Mary pushed onto his plate.

No! They weren't my family, no matter how much I liked them and no matter how much I wished they were. My family was dead, and these people all had each other. Mary and Brian had each other. Susan had Jeremy. Even Jonathan and Rebecca had one another. Martha, well, Martha didn't have anyone, but she did have her cigarettes, and that's all that mattered to her anyway.

I didn't really pay much attention when we watched TV after dinner. Brian disappeared into his office again, and Mary and Susan fussed over Jeremy as they got him ready for his new bed, a blue and white portable crib I found at Target. Mary offered me the couch. "The offer still stands, Jenna. You should stay, too."

I couldn't look at her when I answered. "No thanks," I mumbled.

"I wish you'd stay," I heard her say as the door clicked to a close behind me.

It was just starting to get dark and the clouds were back. They were heavy and low but I barely noticed them as I rode home on my bike. Long streaks and shafts of jagged lightening flashed and sparked behind the clouds and sometimes exploded in sheets, lighting up the sky. I pedaled faster. My bike was metal. I could probably get electrocuted by riding around in the middle of a thunder storm.

The smell of garbage left to rot in the heat hit me in waves when the wind blew, and I had to swerve a couple of times to avoid the rats that skittered back and forth across the street, searching for the tastiest morsels in the bags that people had thrown out their doors. They chewed holes in the bags and pulled things out. Sometimes they crawled all the way inside the bags, and the bags would move as they squirmed around inside. It was a good thing the neighborhood association people were as blind as everyone else, or there would be a lot of people getting warnings taped to their doors, for sure.

I stepped inside my house just as the first drops of rain fell from the full clouds. I tried watching TV for a while, but it was just the same old reruns I'd been watching all summer. Sometimes a line of text would appear across the bottom of the screen: "Stay tuned for more updates." But there weren't ever any more updates.

The monsoon that hit that night was a big one, and water flooded the streets and drainage fields with inches and inches of water. The water swept the garbage down the streets where it collected around corners and against the curbs. Thunder boomed all night long, and the house shuddered. I slipped under my bed and even though the thunder kept waking me up, I slept a lot better than I normally did. No one would try to break into the house tonight, not in the middle of that wild storm.

I didn't know exactly when the power went out, but it never came back on.

POWER FAILURE

Without electricity, there was no air conditioning, no fans, no ice, and no cool drinks. We had massive feasts at Brian and Mary's house for days, trying to eat up the food in the fridge and then the freezer before it could go bad. But there was too much of it, and I had to haul it outside with the rest of the sticking garbage. The rats were getting braver. They were everywhere, and cockroaches as long as my finger swarmed the trash, too.

Besides the smell, the only reason being inside was better than being outside was because inside meant shade and protection from the bugs. With no electricity to run the pool pumps all night, it only took a few days for all the swimming pools in the neighborhood to fill with algae, and the pools became stinky breeding ponds for mosquitos. Brian said that he once Googled a satellite view of our neighborhood, and he remembered that every third or fourth house had a pool. I didn't have to see pictures to know he was right. Swarms of mosquitoes hung over each pool like squirmy gray clouds, and I could see them over the brick walls of each house as I rode past.

They swarmed me when I went outside. It was as if I had a neon sign blinking over my head that said, "Yoo-hoo! It's time to eat!" I got so many itchy welts on my body that I looked like I was covered in blisters. I started coating myself with bug spray; I sprayed my head and rub it into my face and on my ears. My hair was stringy and greasy, and when I went outside, dust stuck to the bug spray, and then I was gritty and sticky until I showered again.

I saw fewer people outside each day. Were the mosquitos driving them inside? Unless they were campers, they probably didn't have mosquito repellant. Would they even know what had bitten them if they came out and got swarmed? Or maybe they were just dead. Brian told me about the rule of threes. He said that you can live about three minutes without air and three hours without shelter if the weather is bad. You can live for about three days without water and about three weeks without food. "But," he told me, "Those are just estimates. If the weather's really bad and you don't have enough water—especially here where it's so hot—three days is the upper limit of survival."

"And," he said, "Most foods contain some water, so if you've got enough food, you might last longer than three days even if you don't have anything to drink." I guess the water from the can of green beans I'd had before the glare struck might have helped me after all.

So where were all the people? Were they just sitting inside, hoping the glare would end, eating their own cans of green beans and drinking the sickly green water like I had? Or had they done what Susan said and killed their families and themselves so they wouldn't have to suffer anymore? Would people really do that? Laney and I had been starving, but we hadn't ever considered killing ourselves because of it. But I got a whiff of a funny smell when I passed certain houses. It was a lot like rotten garbage, only different, somehow. Sometimes when I went outside, I counted bags of garbage. There weren't as many new ones as before, and the rats seemed to like the older ones better. I understood that. Sometimes Laney and I had licked the insides of our bowls when we made mac and cheese to get every last bit out. We'd been too hungry to throw anything out. Our garbage wouldn't have attracted many rats, either.

When I was done collecting supplies for the day, I hung out at Brian and Mary's house. I tried to lead Jonathan and Rebecca over once, but Rebecca freaked out.

"Just hold onto me and you'll be fine," I said. I stood between Jonathan and Rebecca with my arms linked in theirs.

"You won't let go, will you?" Rebecca asked.

"For Pete's sake! She said they only live a couple of houses away! We could find our way back by following the sidewalk," Jonathan said before I could answer.

I opened the door and led them out into the sun.

"Good Lord, it's hotter outside than it is inside," Jonathan muttered.

Rebecca started weeping. "I can't believe I'll never see the sunset again or see a flower bloom or..."

Jonathan groaned. "Just shut up, would you? My God! All you think about is yourself! Has it ever occurred to you that other people might be worse off than you?"

I nodded even though neither of them could see me. I thought about the zombie men in the wrecked cars, and the starving people trapped in their houses, and the ones the coyotes had eaten.

"It's not like I'm any better off than you are," Jonathan continued. "What about my career? I spent all those years kissing butt to get where I am now, and it's gone. All of it. Just like that! At least before the electricity went out there was the Internet and music and a glass of chilled wine to look forward to. What's left now? Nothing but listening to you whine and complain about how miserable you are and how horrible everything is. Wah. Wah. Wah!"

Rebecca didn't seem to hear anything he said. Her long painted fingernails dug into my arm. We got as far as the end of the driveway before she started hyperventilating. "Oh, my God! I can't do this! I can't do it!"

Jonathan tried to reach around me to smack her, but

since he couldn't see her, he just slapped at the air.

"Take me back! I want to go back!" she cried, pulling me backwards.

"Okay, okay," I said. I turned around and led them back to their own door. Jonathan cursed and swore the entire time, and when I opened the door for them, they stumbled in and he slammed it shut, almost hitting me. I could hear Rebecca crying and him screaming at her as I walked away.

PANIC ATTACK

The grocery store was the last place I wanted to go, but everyone needed something from there. It smelled even worse than the garbage on the streets or the swampy swimming pools, but the things on my list were easiest to get from there. The sun made the asphalt shimmy with heat as if the road was covered in water. I wondered if that's what a mirage was—just an optical illusion from the heat that made people think they saw water. Or was there really even such a thing as a mirage? Maybe it was just a word someone made up for cartoons and TV shows. Did people in the desert really think they saw water in the distance?

I pedaled slowly up the street, procrastinating and watching for animals. Things were changing faster every day. Pigeons had taken over all the parking lots. Small flocks of them pecked at the asphalt and then flew off in a loud rush of wings. I saw snakes—big brown rattlers and other kinds I couldn't identify—slither across the pavement every time I went out. Once, I nearly rode over what I thought was a stick, but when I passed it, the "stick" rattled its tail and sprung up at me. I screamed and swerved away from it. After that I watched the road more carefully, especially in the early morning. The snakes liked to lie out in the sun then, and that's when I liked to go out, too. It was a little bit cooler in the morning.

There were a lot of animals, but it seemed like the rats had taken over. I saw them run along the block walls and dart under bushes when I passed. Some were so fat from all the garbage they were eating that they looked more like gray snowballs with whiskers than rats. There were lots more bugs than before, too, and not just mosquitos. Spider webs stretched across open car windows and were draped across the branches of bushes that were losing their tidy shapes. There were small brown ones and greenish ones. I saw black widows, too. Before the glare, I'd only see their stringy, crazy-looking webs in corners and dark places, but with all the mosquitos for food and no people to tear their webs down, I saw them everywhere. There were black ones with red hourglass shapes as well as brown ones with orange hourglasses.

I saw lizards that were short and spikey and some that were thick and fat and covered with orange spots. I saw long centipedes—or maybe they were millipedes—and scorpions, and tons of dragonflies. There were also hummingbirds, brown toads, and quail. Once, I watched a tarantula creep across the sidewalk. Its long, hairy, jointed legs moved up and down like a wind-up toy. Had there always been so many animals? It's not like whole generations of them could have been born since the glare started. So where did they all come from? Were they always there, slinking around us, practically invisible to us because we just didn't pay attention?

There were dogs everywhere, too, usually wandering around in small packs, and there were coyotes, and little families of javelinas. At dusk, bats flew through the air, swooping around after all the mosquitos. When they saw me, the little animals like the lizards and toads and rats scuttled away. At first, the bigger animals like the coyotes and javelinas slinked away, too. But each day, they seemed less afraid of me. Instead of running, they'd just freeze and watch me until I passed.

A sprinkler head on the left side of Ray Road had been knocked free, and a thin stream of water sprayed into the air. I stopped my bike in the middle of the stream to cool off. Brian said it probably wouldn't be long before water would stop coming out of the faucets or would become contaminated and we'd have to start boiling it. I saw three rabbits eating the grass in front of a store as I stood there, straddling my bike in the stream of water. The small patch of green summer grass was nearly high enough to hide everything except the tips of their ears, and I counted eight more bunnies before I'd gone a block farther.

I heard the dogs before I saw them. I swerved away, intent on turning around, but I jerked the handlebars of my bike too quickly and the bike shuddered. I skidded on the loose gravel that covered the side of the road. I put my foot down just in time to keep myself from falling over, but it was too late. They heard me!

I'd surprised them. They all froze and one of them, a muscular dog with faint streaks of white in its brown coat, growled at me. Its lips curled back from its teeth and its ears went flat against its head. Most of the other dogs crouched down and growled at me, too. I stared back at them. Should I turn the bike around? The trailer made it hard to turn sharply and I couldn't do it fast. But if I dropped the bike and ran, they'd catch me for sure…

A filthy Chihuahua darted away from the pack and ran at me, barking in a high pitched yip. I yelled at it. "No! Bad dog! Bad dog!"

The dog skidded toward me, trying to stop, but it was too close. It brushed against my bare leg and then raced back to the other dogs like it had been dared to run up to me. I started turning my bike, screaming the whole time. "Bad dog!"

My voice meant something to the dogs, or to a few of them, anyway. A big black dog that might have been a lab, and a smaller, gray dog with an angry-looking gash across its snout, both dropped to the ground and whined. I could hear my own heart beating as I dragged my bike around. The striped dog growled at the two dogs on the ground and snapped its jaws. The smaller dog yelped and rolled over, exposing its stomach. The dog with the streaked coat stood over it, growling.

I didn't wait to see what would happen next. I put my feet on my pedals and pushed hard. The pack started after me. I kept screaming, "No! No! Bad dogs! Bad dogs!"

The bike trailer slowed me down, but it scared some of the dogs, too. I couldn't hear anything but my heart beating in my ears. Were they still there? I looked back—they'd changed direction! They were stirring up dust and biting and snapping at one another, but they were going the other way!

I looked forward just in time to swerve away from two cars that were almost parallel to each other in the street. I was going to crash! I pulled the handlebars hard to the left. I mostly missed one of the cars, but my knuckles scraped against the side view mirror, ripping up flaps of skin. Blood welled up on them and made trails that flew up my arm and dripped down my hand. I wrenched the handlebars to the right to keep from crashing into the other car. I was going too fast to stop! My tires wobbled. I was going to crash and the cars were too close—the trailer was going to get stuck and I was going to go flying over the handlebars! I tried to peddle backwards to brake the bike but I was afraid I'd hit my knees, too. All I could do was just hang on—why hadn't I worn my helmet? I knew better than to go riding without it! I saw the giant spider web full of wriggling bugs before I rode into it, but there was nothing I could do.

I screamed. The spider web wrapped itself around my neck and shoulders and then I was through the cars. I shook my arms in the air trying to get the bugs and the web off of me. The bike wobbled and fell to the ground, trapping me beneath it. I pushed it off and scrambled up. There were bugs all over me! I could feel them everywhere! They were in my hair and on my neck and inside my shirt! Something moved on my neck. I grabbed at it. It squirmed in my hands—the spider! I screamed again and flung it away. I ripped my shirt off and slapped at my head and my hair until I was sure all the bugs were gone. And then I slapped at my skin some more. Sweat dripped down my neck and blood ran up my arm—all the way to my armpit—every time I lifted my hand.

I picked my shirt up off the ground with my thumb and finger and carefully turned it right-side-out again. The dried bodies of bugs dropped off my shirt and bounced on the asphalt. I studied my shirt for more bugs. A few small, beetle-like things clung to it, wrapped up like little mummies. I flicked them off with a shudder. When I was sure my shirt was clean and there were no more bugs on me anywhere, I put it back on and looked around for the first time.

In my rush to get away from the dogs, I'd ridden toward the intersection I'd been avoiding ever since the day I saw the zombie man and the man-eating coyote.

I didn't want to look at the cars with the bodies in them, and I really didn't want to see the bloody remains the coyotes had been eating! It was dumb of me to let the spider web freak me out like that. What if the coyotes were still there? Or what if there were more dogs, instead? And what if there were other dangerous animals I just hadn't seen yet—something besides spiders and rats or the javelinas that Brian said could kill people, too? What then? Laney would have never been that stupid! If she'd run into a spider web like that, she would have just kept riding her bike until it was safe to stop.

I shook my head. No. That wasn't true. She was brave and strong and things like blood and puke didn't bother her, but she would have freaked out even more that I had. I didn't like spiders and bugs, but she hated them.

I looked around. The body on the corner was gone, or

at least most of it was. A group of fat rats were clustered around the rest of the fabric, and I thought I saw white shards of something. Bone? Was that a bone—a person's bone? I swallowed hard and looked away. The splotches of blood on the road were so dark from the sun and the heat that they didn't look like blood anymore, just drops of black ink. I tried to keep my eyes down as I passed the car with the zombie man, but I couldn't seem to help myself. I had to look twice to make sure it was the same body when I came up to it. The body wasn't lying against the steering wheel the same way as before! Maybe it *was* a zombie—a real one! My heart started beating too fast. What if it turned its head and looked at me?

And then I remembered the unit on Egypt we did at school. The Egyptians mummified their dead. They did it with some kind of salt or sand or something. But my teacher told us how bodies could mummify naturally, too. In Scotland, where there are peat bogs, bodies can be mummified by the acid in the bogs. There are ice mummies too, and a lot of natural mummies are found in deserts. If the air is hot and dry, and there aren't any insects or predators to eat it, a body can become a mummy naturally.

I snuck a peek at the man again. He wasn't a zombie. He was becoming a mummy! Somehow that didn't seem as scary as a zombie. He was protected from the monsoons and the rats and coyotes in his car, so he was just mummifying, that's all. He looked bonier than before, and his skin was darker, like it was turning to leather, which I guess it kind of was. I could see the side of his face, and his lips were starting to pull back from his teeth. The smell that leaked from the car was like puke and diarrhea and something else mixed in. It was the same smell I'd gotten whiffs of when I drove past certain houses. It was just much stronger. I pulled my shirt over my nose and tried not to breathe in the smell, but I stood there for a long time, staring at the man who had become a mummy. I put my hand up on his window; my knuckles throbbed and the blood had dried on my hand and arm. My bloody arm made me look like I belonged in the mummy's world instead of this one. Or maybe this *was* the mummy's world now after all. "I'm sorry you had to die like that," I whispered.

That was the last time I was scared of a corpse.

GUN SLINGER

"Hold it like this," Brian said. "Go ahead. Don't be afraid of it, just be respectful of it."

I took the gun in my hand. It was heavier than I expected.

"Spread your legs, but bend them a little and put your arms out. Always hold a gun with two hands to steady it if you can. And keep your other fingers away from the trigger. It snaps back fast, and it's pretty painful if the trigger catches your fingers or thumb."

We stood in the Branson's living room. Brian was teaching me how to hold a gun. Mary and Susan were learning, too, but the lessons were mostly for me. He moved my hands a tiny bit and raised my arms a little higher. I tried to remember all the things he said to do.

"Okay. You're ready. Now shoot!"

I pulled the trigger on the gun. It wasn't loaded, so it only made a snapping sound. Next to me, Brian screamed in my ear, "Bang!"

I jumped and dropped the gun. It skittered away on the tile floor and came to a stop next to Jeremy. He reached for it, but Susan scooped him up before he could touch it.

"No, no! That's dangerous! Ouchie! That will hurt you!" she said.

"What'd you do that for?" I asked Brian. "You scared

me!"

He chuckled and patted my back. "That was the point, kiddo. You can learn to aim and stand properly and all of that, but shooting a loaded gun is an entirely different matter."

He picked up the gun and aimed it at the wall. "In the movies, when you see this," he said as he pulled the trigger and jerked the barrel of the gun upwards, "it's because that's what happens when you really do fire a gun. The gun will kick back or jump a little in your hands. The bigger the gun, the bigger the kick. The noise and the kick are going to scare you the first few times, so it's better if you know to expect it."

We practiced for three days, loading and unloading the gun, oiling it, cleaning it, and pretend-shooting it until he decided I was ready.

Brian kept his eyes tightly shut when we walked down the street to the drainage field by his house, but the light still made his eyes water.

"I guess I should have listened to Mary and worn the blindfold she made."

He covered his eyes with a hand. "You go ahead and tell her I said so when we get back home. She'll get a kick out of telling me, 'I told you so.'"

I led him by the elbow down the steep hill to the grassy field and over to a patch of shade under a mesquite tree. The cool air that settled in the field felt wonderful even if there were more mosquitoes there.

"What does the field look like now?" he asked as he slapped at one that tickled the back of his neck despite the thick coating of bug spray we both wore.

I looked around and tried to remember what it used to look like, just a few weeks ago. "Uh, there are a lot of mosquitos and tons of those gnats that swirl around in the air, too."

I waved my hand above my head to try to move a

swarm of them away. It fell apart and then molded together again above our heads. "The grass is really high since it hasn't been cut, and there are some broken sprinkler heads by the basketball court. There's a tree Laney and I used to climb when our dad would bring us here when we were little—a big branch is broken off now. There are tons of bunnies everywhere, too. Mostly they like the shade."

The rabbits all looked identical, like they were all clones of one another. They had really long ears, and their fur was the color of used-up sandpaper—a sort of dull reddish-brown. Their feet were tipped with white and their tails were white tufts of fluff.

"Nothing else? No people?"

"No, no people. Not anymore. Maybe they're coming out at night when it's cooler," I suggested, trying not to think about the odor that was getting worse in the neighborhoods.

Brian nodded, but he didn't sound convinced when he said, "Maybe."

Then he nodded and said, "Alright, young lady. Go set up that target."

I counted out twenty steps and put the target down. We'd taken a big cardboard box from his garage and turned it into a sandwich board. Susan had drawn a target on it with fat markers.

My hand shook as I loaded the gun. I'd done it so many times that I dreamt about it at night, but this time I was going to shoot for real.

"Loaded?"

"Yeah."

"Check your stance. How is it?"

I looked down at my legs and moved them so they were as wide apart as my shoulders.

"They're good, I think."

"Okay, you know how to hold the gun. Watch those fingers, remember?"

171

I doubled-checked to make sure I only had one finger on the trigger.

"Then aim and fire. You're ready for this. Let's go!"

I lined the sights up and pulled the trigger. I screamed like a wimpy little kid when the gun jumped in my hands and the bang echoed in the field.

Brian laughed. "You still alive? No broken fingers?"

I shook a little when I answered. "Yeah. I'm okay, I think."

"Alright, then! Put the gun down and let's go check out that target! Can you tell? Did you hit it? Now, don't be disappointed if you missed entirely. It's your first time, after all."

But I did hit it. Not a bulls-eye or anything, but I hit the top edge, shooting a circle out of it. Brian felt it and nodded, impressed.

"Good job, Jenna! You pulled up a bit but that's not bad, especially for your first time. If you start to see a pattern of misses like this, then you'll know to correct a little and aim lower."

We stayed there for hours, practicing, and we came back the next day, too.

The following day he made me shoot a bunny.

"But I don't want to!" I wailed. "I don't want to kill a rabbit! I don't want to kill anything!"

He felt for my shoulders and grabbed them so I had to face him. I stared at the striped tie Mary had made into a blindfold for him to block out the light. "What do you think we're doing this for, Jenna? For fun? Is this fun?"

It kind of was, but that didn't seem like the right answer just then. "No! I just don't want to kill anything!"

"What are you going to do when the canned goods expire, Jenna? How are you going to eat then? Canned goods will last a year or two at most. Dried food, a little longer. You know that. You've seen Mary and Susan rotate the stuff you bring for us to make sure we open the cans with the earliest expiration dates first."

His voice got harder the longer he talked. "You're keeping us alive, girl, and we all know it. But there are things you need to know if you're going to stay alive yourself. One of those things is being able to shoot to kill. We're having rabbit stew for dinner tonight, and we're not leaving here until you shoot a rabbit. You need to be stronger than this, so stop crying and shoot."

I wanted to throw the gun down and have a temper tantrum like Jeremy did when he got too hot and tired. It wasn't fair for Brian to ask me to do this! It wasn't fair that my dad was dead and my mom was dead and Laney probably was, too! It wasn't fair that I had to take care of other people—I was only thirteen! I wanted to scream at him. I shouldn't have to learn how to shoot a gun or be responsible for everyone else! I shouldn't have to do anything except go to school and do my homework and hang out with my friends.

Instead, I thought about Laney. If Laney were still alive, she would kill as many rabbits as she needed to, to make sure we could eat. Maybe she wouldn't ride bravely through a spider web full of bugs, but she would kill rabbits for us. I wiped my eyes on my sleeve so Laney would be proud of me, and I took aim at one of the nearest rabbits.

The gun went off with a bang. I wasn't even close. The rabbits scattered like they did every time I shot the gun. But they always came back after a few minutes. They did this time, too.

I didn't need to tell Brian I missed. "Try again," he said.

I took aim again and held the gun steady with both hands. I stepped toward a rabbit, just a few tiny steps. Tears blurred my eyes. I blinked them back and pulled the trigger. BANG!

"I did it!"

I looked at the rabbit. "Oh, no! I did it!"

Brian ignored my tears. "Great job, kiddo. Now you're

going to pick it up, and we're going to take it home, and I'm going to teach you how to skin it, gut it, and cook it…"

I walked over to the rabbit. "Oh, no. Oh, no!"

I hadn't killed the rabbit after all. I'd only shot it enough to hurt it. It tried to hop away, but its mangled back leg dangled from its body, and it couldn't get away. When I reached for it, its black eyes darted back and forth in terror and pain.

I crumpled into the tall grass and touched the bunny's soft fur. It panted as it tried to creep away, but it was too injured. "I'm sorry bunny! I'm so sorry. I didn't mean it. I didn't mean to hurt you!"

Brian stumbled toward the sound of my voice and jerked me up. "What happened?"

"It's not dead," I said between gulping sobs. "I only shot it in the leg. It's not dead!" My voice rose higher and higher as I tried to explain.

"Then you pick up the gun, and you put that poor creature out of misery," he said. His voice was hard and sharp.

I gulped and leveled the gun at the bunny again. I wouldn't have done it except that it was in so much pain, and I'd caused it. *I'd* made it hurt like that. I pulled the trigger and even though I shook and my eyes were closed, I was close enough this time to hit it.

"Well? Did you kill it?"

I lowered the gun and looked. And then I burst into hysterical sobs. The second shot had been too close. The ground was covered with blood and gore. I'd blown the rabbit's head off.

I gave up on trying to be strong, and let myself cry as we walked home. We were a few houses down from Brian and Mary's when Brian shushed me. I snuffled, but I didn't really try to stop my tears. He did it again, more insistently.

"Shh! Be quiet, Jenna. Do you hear that?"

I choked back a sob and listened. I heard it too, the

thumping sound of music somewhere nearby. I was suddenly afraid.

I carried the bloody remains of the rabbit in one outstretched hand and pulled Brian along faster. We needed to get away—fast! "C'mon. Let's go. Hurry!"

It was the first time the music was loud enough that I knew it wasn't just my imagination. I knew it meant that someone else could see, someone who knew how to drive, but the music terrified me, and I didn't know why. I only knew I wanted to get back to the house, fast.

"Maybe we should see who it is," Brian started to say.

Panic made my voice high pitched, even though my nose was stuffy from crying. "No! Let's go. Let's just go. Please?"

He was quiet for a moment, thinking or listening. "Okay. Let's go home."

The music had faded away by the time we got to the house. When Brian asked me why I was so scared, I couldn't explain. "It just scared me. I don't know why."

He nodded. "Well, I've always told Mary to go with her gut when she doesn't feel safe, so I guess I can't tell you anything different."

I felt a little better until he made me skin and gut what was left of the rabbit. I cried most of the rest of the night, and Brian wouldn't let Mary or Susan near me. "Leave her alone," he growled when they tried to give me a hug.

I cut the meat into bloody chunks and then boiled it in water with some canned vegetables and bouillon cubes. It was tough and chewy, and I only ate as much as Brian made me. Before he let me leave to go home, he took me into Susan's room and sat me down on the bed. He made me look him in the eyes. I refused at first. I didn't care if I seemed like a spoiled brat or a big baby. I hated him for making me kill that rabbit. As soon as he let me leave, I was going home and I was never coming back. Not ever!

He stayed crouched down in front of me with his hand

on his bad knee until I stared back at him with all the hate showing in my face. Then he smiled at me.

Gently, he said, "You did good today, Jenna. The first time is always the hardest. You've got to mean it when you shoot another living creature. Sometimes it helps if you tell yourself it was you or him."

"But it wasn't me or him! It was only a rabbit!" I screamed at him. "I didn't have to kill it!"

"No," he said. "You didn't have to kill that particular rabbit, but you needed to kill something in order to learn how to do it. You have to be able to do it without hesitation. Shooting at targets isn't the same. This isn't a game. You've got to be able to kill your own food, and if it comes down to it, you've got to be able to protect yourself too, Jenna. Those packs of dogs and the coyotes you've seen won't always be scared of you when you yell at them. And it won't be long before firing a gun in the air won't frighten them, either. They'll tear you to shreds instead and eat you. And Jenna, if you die, we all die. Me, Mary, Susan, Jeremy, and those other three too. It's that simple. Our survival depends on you. I'm going to do everything I can to make sure you survive, even if you hate me for it. Do you understand that?"

I nodded but I wouldn't look at him.

I felt empty inside when I rode my bike home, the gun carelessly tossed in the basket between the handlebars. I wasn't even really that angry anymore. Just sad and very, very tired. But after that, I started carrying the gun with me wherever I went.

HOT DOG

Brian was right about the gun. I came across another pack of dogs the next time I went to the grocery store, or maybe it was the same pack as before, and it had just grown larger. I screamed at the dogs, but this time the sound of my voice didn't make them hesitate. They stirred up a cloud of the dust that coated the road as they slunk toward me. I put a foot on one of the pedals of my bike. I'd gotten away from them on my bike once before. Could I do it again? Then I thought about what Brian had said. I straddled my bike and pulled the gun out from under the extra water bottles in my basket. I held it in both hands, steadying it, just like Brian taught me. I aimed into the pack of dogs, put my finger on the trigger...and froze. Those dogs were someone's pets. What if the glare ended and all that someone had left was their dog, and I killed it? I raised the gun into the air and pulled the trigger. The dogs scattered, yelping at the sound. They regrouped, and then ran off together, all except one dog that hunkered toward the ground and whined at me.

A cloud of dust followed the other dogs as they ran off, but Brian was right. Next time, the noise might not be enough. Next time I might need to have more guts.

I aimed the gun at the dog that was left, but it didn't look aggressive, not like the other dogs. It kept its body against the ground and crawled toward me, like it was doing a trick someone had taught it. I tapped the kickstand with my foot and propped my bike up in the shade of a tree. The dog whined and kept coming toward me. Its tail wagged fast and low. I kept the gun in my hand, just in case, but when the dog got to me, it flopped over on its back—it was a girl—and she twisted her head around to look at me. Her tail wagged the whole time and she looked like she was grinning at me. I put the gun back in my basket and slowly crouched down. The dog flipped back over and cowered toward the ground. I moved more slowly and put my hand out so she could smell it. She sniffed and moved even closer. "That's a good dog," I whispered. "Good girl!" She wagged her tail harder so I reached out and petted her. That was all the encouragement she needed. She jumped up on me, putting her front paws on my chest. Her tail wagged so hard that her whole rear end moved back and forth, and she covered me with kisses while I petted her and hugged her like she was my dog and we'd been separated for years. I buried my face in her fur after she practically climbed into my lap. She stunk really bad, and I started crying. Why? I was happy—not sad—that the dog was friendly. Why should that make me cry?

I blinked back my tears, mad at myself for being so stupid and looked at the dog more closely. She was panting pretty hard, and her ribs stuck out under her fur. There were hard round things, some about the size of marbles, between her toes and around her ears. I thought they were tumors at first, but when I spread her fur away from her skin, I could have sworn one of them moved, just a little. Were they ticks? I'd never seen a tick before so I wasn't sure. There were eight or nine big ones and a lot of tinier ones that were about the size and shape of sunflower seeds, but darker.

I sat there petting the dog while I thought about what I was going to do. I still needed to go to the grocery store, but what was I going to do with the dog? I didn't want to leave her. If she rejoined the pack, she might not come to me the next time. I took a water bottle out of my basket and sipped it while I thought things out. The dog whined at me and pawed the air. "What's wrong girl? What do you want?" I didn't have any food with me, just water. Oh! The water had stopped working a couple days before, and it hadn't rained in a while either. "Are you thirsty? Do you want a drink?" I poured water into my cupped hand and put my hand down by the dog's mouth. She didn't know what to do. "C'mon girl! It's okay! Have a drink!" She flicked her tongue into my hand and then started lapping up the water. She licked my hand until every last drop was gone and then she sat down in front of me and whined again, wagging her tail a little bit. Her poor tail! The tip of it was gone, and it was scabbed over. The last inch had no hair at all. It sort of looked like a rat's scaly tail.

Despite all of this, the dog seemed happy. She hadn't moved as I looked her over again, but when I stopped petting her, she whined. I could almost hear her say, "What now?"

I scratched her behind her ears, being careful to avoid the tumor-tick things. I laughed. "C'mon, dog. Why don't you just come with me."

I climbed back on my bike and pushed off. I looked behind me—she hadn't moved. I patted my thigh.

"C'mon girl! Let's go!"

She whined again as if to say, "You really mean it? I can come with you? Oh boy, oh boy!"

She got up and trotted along side of me, limping slightly.

The grocery store was even worse than it had been the last time. I covered my nose and mouth with my shirt. The smell coming from the produce section on the left side of the store was ripe, wet, and moldy. The smell from the back, where the meat department was, was even worse. It was a lot like the smell of the mummified zombie man, and it almost made me puke. It smelled like the ammonia my mom used to use to clean with sometimes—and rotten eggs and the sour, sick smell of poop and puke even though there was only beef, chicken, pork, and seafood going really, really bad.

The dog whined when I pushed the doors open and the smell hit us full force. She didn't want to go into the stench, either. "I know, girl. We'll be done soon."

I shouldn't have opened my mouth. The smell stuck in my throat and coated the inside of my mouth like grease. The dog followed me as I threw things into a cart: more special-label wine for Jonathan and Rebecca, diapers and wipes and cream for Jeremy's diaper rash. Dried rice and beans and trail mix for Brian, and of course, cigarettes for Martha. I breathed in shallow gasps, trying not to take full breaths. I was going to be sick if I didn't hurry! I wanted to get more soda for myself, but I didn't want it badly enough to stay in the store any longer.

I went to the dairy section last. Brian said that some hard cheeses might still be okay as long as they hadn't gotten too warm. I held my breath when we passed the meat section, and I couldn't help but sneak a peek. The plastic-wrapped meat trays were swollen, and the meat was strange and disgusting colors: brown and green, and sometimes a shimmery orange. I gagged and pushed the cart past as fast as I could.

I opened the door of the dairy case but it was just as warm inside as it was everywhere else in the store, and new smells slipped out: curdled milk, sour cottage cheese, and moldy sour cream. The dairy products had been spoiling for a while now, but most of the smells had been contained in the sealed cartons. Not anymore. The smell was thick and sour, and a lot of the containers had burst or were bulging and swollen. Some of them had fuzzy starbursts of green and blue mold growing along their seams.

I closed the door again, and the motion forced more of the stinky dairy air into my face. I turned away from the cart and puked—the smell was so awful! The dog sniffed the puddle I'd made on the floor. "No, girl," I said, trying to nudge her away. She whined at me. There were a few more things I had wanted for myself, but I didn't care about any of it anymore. I jogged with the cart even though it meant I had to breathe faster and harder. I was going to puke again if I stayed in the store any longer. I ran down the pet aisle. For the first time, the dog didn't stay with me. She sniffed at the bottom shelf where the largest bags of dog food were.

"I know, I know! Here, look!" I said, shaking a box of dog treats I grabbed off a shelf. "Let's go!" I wish I hadn't spoken because I could taste the thick smell in the air on my tongue, but the dog seemed to understand what the box was and that we were finished. She bounded ahead of me and out the doors. She raced to an island of long grass while I pulled the broken doors closed and pushed the cart to the corner of the store where my bike sat. I'd forgotten about the gun when I went inside. It was still sitting in the basket, gleaming in the sun. Good thing Brian didn't know. He'd lecture me forever about it! What if an animal had gotten inside the store and I'd needed it?

I sat on the curb and breathed in long, shaky breaths to settle my stomach while I watched the dog. Even though she was already filthy, she tried to get the stench of the store off herself. With her skinny butt in the air, she rubbed the sides of her face against the ground, then flopped down on her back and wriggled in the grass. When I laughed, she froze and looked at me. Her tongue hung out the side of her mouth, and she looked like she was laughing too.

She leapt over to me and licked my face. I scratched her behind the ears and patted her sides. Her fur felt thick with dirt and grime, and my hands smelled like dog, but I didn't care.

"We'll get you some more food on the way home," I promised, talking to her like she was a little kid. "We'll go to the pet store. They'll have everything you need. I bet you'd like a little something now, though, huh?"

I should have gotten her that stuff in the grocery store, but it had smelled so bad. What if there were people in the pet store? It was closer to the freeway, and that's where most of the stores were that I'd seen people in. Maybe I should just go back inside and at least get her a small bag of dog food.

I pulled the treats from the box and gave her a handful and some water from my last water bottle. I still felt a little queasy. I probably should have had some water myself since it was so hot, but I thought I'd be okay until we got home.

The dog thumped her tail while she ate the biscuits. She watched me as I moved things from the cart to my bike trailer. I tried to think of all the things a dog would need. Dog food, of course. And more treats. I thought about the marble-shaped things on her body and remembered the commercials I'd seen for that flea and tick medicine that you put between a dog's shoulders every couple of months. She definitely needed some of that stuff and a bath, too. That would be tricky with no running water. Brian wouldn't want me to use any of the gallons and gallons of water I'd been bringing home to wash her with, but she really did stink.

Maybe I should risk it and go to the pet store. It couldn't smell as bad as the grocery store, and it would have everything the dog needed, for sure. I could always come back if I had to. Or I could go to Target. They had pet food too, didn't they? But the pet store would have more stuff. There would be toys and some bones and collars. I could get her one with fake jewels or something. That might be kind of fun. And a leash in case I ever needed it...

I was still thinking about the things she needed when we got to the pet store. The dog trotted happily by my side, and for the first time in a couple of weeks, I wasn't worried about other animals.

***

There was no one inside the pet store. None of the windows and doors were broken, and nothing covered them up. I wouldn't have to go back to the grocery store! I unzipped the bike trailer and made a face; the smell from the grocery store had soaked into some of the packages, and the heat brought the smell out. I held my breath as I dug to the bottom of the trailer for my hammer. I used to keep it in my basket until I started carrying the gun around with me. It was battered and dinged and tinged with a few spots of rust on the claw end. I could have picked up a new one anywhere, but it had been Dad's, so I'd kept it.

The dog walked toward the door as if she knew we were going in. I had to call her back and grab her filthy collar to get her to stay with me while I threw the hammer. I'd broken into enough stores by then that I knew exactly how hard to throw it to break a door. I turned away as it shattered, just in case a piece of glass came flying back at me. I felt the dog cringe from the noise of the breaking glass. There was no alarm. Either the store didn't have battery backup or it had died a long time ago. The dog tried to pull away, but I held her tight.

"It's okay, girl." She thumped her tail and whined. She wasn't so sure.

I reached inside the broken glass and unlocked the door and pushed it open. The smell made me step back. The pet store sold small animals and fish. How could I have forgotten that? I guess I was too busy thinking about dog supplies. It didn't smell quite as bad as the grocery store, but close. It smelled like the ocean and a barnyard, all at once. The aquariums were on the right side of the store, against the wall. Even from the front door I could see that the tanks were green with algae. The colorful oval shapes of dead fish floated at the top of many of them, but a few bigger fish still moved through murky green water. Maybe they'd eaten the smaller fish in their tanks.

Directly in front of the doors, just past the cash registers, were the small animal cages. Most of the animals were dead, but some were still alive, even after this long. I stepped closer and saw why. Someone had taken the time to put extra water bottles and piles of food in some of the cages. The water bottles were mostly empty but there were still food pellets left in some cages—not much, but a few pellets, here and there. Whoever had filled the cages with food and water must have dumped in scoop after scoop. There wasn't much food left, but there was plenty of poo. The bedding in the cages was soaked with pee that smelled like ammonia and stung my nose.

The dog sniffed at a low cage of hamsters. She watched one skinny survivor dive into a hidey hole. It suddenly occurred to me that she'd probably been eating the rabbits and rats and pigeons I saw all over the place. The hamster probably looked like food to her.

"C'mon girl," I said. "Let's get you that food." Her ears perked up and she followed me down the dog food aisle. I let her sniff at the bags, and she seemed most interested in one that looked like the same kind that she'd stopped at in the grocery store. Maybe it was the same brand her owners used to buy. I tore the string at the front of the bag and let the kibble spill onto the floor. She danced around in a circle, skidding on the tile. What a crazy dog!

"Go on, silly! Eat! I know you're hungry!"

She woofed once, and then started chowing down like she'd never seen food before. I watched her for a minute. Is that what I'd looked like when I ate that first sandwich in the convenience store? I bet it was.

"Good girl," I said. "You keep eating, okay?"

She looked up at me and thumped her tail, but didn't stop eating.

I hadn't helped any people except for the ones who lived in the three houses on Brian's street, but I saved all the animals I could at the pet store that day. I couldn't do much for the fish. I sprinkled food in the tanks of the ones that hadn't died, but I couldn't do anything else. Not unless I did what Brian made me do to the rabbit when he told me to put it out of its misery. Maybe I should have broken all the tanks and let the water drain out so those few fish would die faster, but I didn't. I just couldn't.

I got a box from behind one of the cash registers, the kind they put your hamster in so you can take it home after you buy it. I used it to trap the few animals that were still alive. The two gerbils and hamster were the easiest. The guinea pigs were all dead. Some rats were alive, but they were harder to catch. They were big enough that they made me nervous. Plus, they were rats! Some of the ones I'd seen outside were kind of dangerous looking! But I got them all—all the animals that were still alive—and I took them all outside and released them. I poured bags and bags of food pellets out there for them, too. Maybe they'd survive. Maybe not. But at least now they had a chance.

I released a couple of birds from the small glass-walled bird-room, too. I didn't try to catch them though. I just rolled their cages outside and opened them. Only one flew out when I opened their doors. The others just sat in their cages, making whirring, peeping noises. I sprinkled birdseed in the grass and at the bottom of the cages.

The dog followed me in and out of the store the first few times. Then she lay down by the cash registers on the tile. Her stomach looked full and round. She glanced up at me every time I stepped out the doors, then she relaxed and put her head back down when I came back in.

I took a cart and filled it with all the stuff on my mental list of dog supplies and then repacked the bike trailer to put the dog food at the bottom so it wouldn't squish the stuff from the grocery store. I zipped the trailer shut. It bulged and the tires looked a little flat from the weight. There was a bunch of stuff I couldn't fit into the trailer, so I hung bags from the handle bars.

I didn't even have to call the dog when I was done. She seemed to know I was ready to go, and she plodded along beside me in the heat. I had to pedal hard to pull the full trailer, and the bags on the handle bars swung back and forth. They made the front end of the bike hard to control so I had to go slowly. It was probably good I couldn't go very fast, though. About half way home, the dog had diarrhea in the street, but it didn't seem to bother her that much. She squatted and strained and then trotted to catch up to me. "You're okay," I told her each time she had to stop. "You just ate too much. When you're starving like that, it sometimes takes your body a while to get used to having food again." Her limp was more noticeable when she ran, and she didn't like it if I got too far away so I waited for her each time.

I had the dog by the collar when I got to Brian and Mary's house.

"Hey, Brian! Where are you?" I called.

He came around the corner and blinked at the light that came through the door. "What's up kiddo? You okay? And what's that smell?"

"It's a dog! That one pack I told you about is getting really aggressive, but this dog stayed behind after I scared the others off. Can I bring her in?"

He waved his hand in front of his nose. "You'd better take her around back and give her a bath first. Mary will kill you if you stink up this house. I'll put some jugs of water by the back door for you."

I guess he didn't care about saving water that much after all.

***

The dog flopped down on the rug and rubbed her face against it like she'd done in the grass. The whole house smelled like wet dog. What if Mary didn't want the dog in her house? She always kept it so clean and it always smelled good, even now that there was no electricity. I guess I didn't have to spend so much time there. If Mary didn't want the dog inside, I could just drop stuff off and go back to my house. But I liked being there. I didn't want to be alone all the time. But when Meatball, who was half the size of the new dog, started tugging on her ear and made her roll over and bare her scratched-up tummy to him, Mary laughed like the rest of us. I wouldn't have to be alone! Mary didn't mind the dog at all.

Brian eased himself down on the floor and started petting the dog so he could get a closer look at her. Her tummy was scratched up, and the rest of her body wasn't in much better condition. The pad on one of her feet was torn up—that's why she'd been limping—and there was a gash on her rump that I hadn't noticed before. The edges of it were warm and red and there was a little pus in one corner.

"Hey, Mary, do we still have that antibiotic cream? Grab it for me, would you? And get the tweezers, too, and some rubbing alcohol if we have any."

The dog stayed on her back and only whimpered once when he prodded her wounds. "Good dog. Yes, you're a good dog, aren't you?"

Meatball tried to wedge himself between Brian and the dog. Brian ignored him until Meatball put his front paws on Brian's legs and stuck his wet nose in his face and whined. Brian grabbed Meatball's head and ruffled his fur. "Jealous, are you? Don't worry, Meatball. She's not going to replace you! This is Jenna's dog."

I let out my breath even though I hadn't realized I was holding it. My dog? My dog. The dog was mine!

Mary came back in with her hands full, and Brian asked me, "Have you ever removed a tick before?"

I shook my head. I hadn't even been sure that's what the hard, round things were. He took the tweezers and wiped them down with the alcohol. "You always want to sterilize the tweezers each time you use them. If you don't have alcohol, you stick them in a flame for a few seconds or in boiling water, okay? That goes for anything you do for a person, too, even if you're just pulling out a splinter."

He peered at me over the top edge of his reading glasses until he was sure I understood.

He tried to lean over the dog to get at a cluster of ticks, but Meatball got in the way again. "C'mon, Meatball," Mary called. He whined and licked Brian's face and then ran to Mary. She pulled him up on her lap to keep him out of the way.

Brian spread my new dog's wet, black fur away from the ticks and pointed out their tiny, spider-like legs, which didn't seem strong enough to hold their swollen bodies. He took the tweezers and firmly grasped the biggest one. He explained what he was doing as he worked. "The trick is to grab the tick as close to the dog's skin as you can. You want to pull it straight out without twisting it or jerking it because if the mouth parts aren't removed, they can cause an infection."

The tick's tiny legs waved in the air like it was trying to fight him. The tick came out, and Brian dropped it in an empty soda can with a splash of rubbing alcohol in it.

The dog was half asleep and only thumped her tail occasionally. Brian handed me the tweezers. "Now you try."

"But, I…"

He shrugged. "She's your dog."

My dog! He really meant it. I really had a dog of my own! I took the tweezers and leaned over the next tick. Brian walked me through the steps just like he had when he taught me to shoot, and just like he was doing in the driving lessons he'd started giving me.

"Make sure you don't grab the tick by the big, round part. You've got to grab it closer to the head. You want to be holding it firmly enough that you have a good grasp on it. If you squeeze the abdomen, bacteria from inside the tick can get forced out."

Great. If I didn't pull it out right, I'd make my dog sick. If I squeezed too hard, I'd make my dog sick.

"Let's go, kiddo. You learn by doing. You can do it."

That's pretty much what Brian said every time he taught me something scary. I didn't even want to think about my next driving lesson. So far he only had me practicing with cans of vegetables under my feet to represent the brakes and the gas pedal, and a plate in my hands that I pretended was the steering wheel.

I pulled the tick out. Brian looked at it carefully. "Looks like you got all of it. If you do break off the mouth parts, you'll need to try to pick them out with the tweezers or clean the area with alcohol and antibiotic cream if you just can't get it out."

I asked Brian about her paw. "Do we need to bandage it up or something?"

A big flap hung from the bottom of the pad and oozed a little bit of blood. The dog rolled onto her back again when he took her paw and examined it closer.

"No use putting a bandage on a dog's paw unless you're going to get a cone for her head. She'll just chew it off. I'd just put some cream on it if I were you. She'll probably lick it off, but maybe she's tired enough to ignore it for a while. She seems pretty beat. Most likely, she just needs to stay off of it for a few days."

Sometimes I thought Brian knew everything.

I spent the rest of the night examining every inch of my dog and carefully covering each scrape and cut with antibiotic cream, and removing every tick I could find by the light of the battery-operated lanterns that lit the room. If Laney had been there, she would have done it for me, even if the dog was mine; she always used to be the one to pull splinters out of my fingers, even when Mom and Dad were still alive. Mary glanced at Brian and said, "It looks like Jenna made a friend."

He nodded. Susan sat on the edge of the couch, holding Jeremy as he squirmed and reached for the dog. It wasn't until after I was done and Susan saw how the dog had let me pick the ticks off of her without nipping at me or trying to get away that she let Jeremy pet her. "What are you going to name her?" Susan asked.

I ran my hand through the dog's soft, clean fur and thought for a moment. "Molly. Her name is Molly."

Jeremy reached for a fist-full of fur and tried to say it. "Olly! Olly!"

Susan leaned forward to pick him up again, but Molly just whined and licked him across the face.

***

After Jeremy's bedtime, Brian, Mary, Susan, and I talked about the same things we talked about every night before I went home: what I saw that day, mostly. But we also talked about Jonathan, Rebecca, and Martha. Sometimes Brian told us stories about his days in the military, or he played with Jeremy while Mary taught Susan and me how to crochet or knit. Susan made me work on school stuff, too. "An education is important, even now," she told me. It was stifling hot with no air, but the lanterns that lit the room always made it feel like we were sitting around a campfire.

The first time Brian talked about being in the Air Force, he said, "I'm certainly not giving away any national secrets, and if this young lady is going to be responsible for all our lives, I suppose it's in our best interest to make sure she knows as much as she can about survival."

He winked at me and then said, "I started out thinking I'd be a Navy Seal. It was the excitement and the intrigue that attracted me, just like it attracts pretty much every other boy who was my age, I'm sure. I had an uncle who was an Air Force recruiter, though, so it was the Air Force rather than the Navy for me. I ended up becoming a SERE

Specialist. SERE stands for Survival, Evasion, Resistance, and Escape."

I never told him, but when Brian described the things he learned in his training, I sometimes thought that Laney and I had spent the time after Mom was killed being our own kind of survival experts. We had stolen and scrounged food to feed ourselves—we'd even eaten those nasty cactus pads—and we had lied to keep from being found out, all so no one could separate us. So we'd been survival and evasion experts, even if we didn't know anything about resistance. As far as escaping, sometimes I was sure Laney was dead, but sometimes I thought maybe—just maybe—she was trapped someplace or sick and she was only one secret tunnel away from escaping and coming home.

"I spent the first three years of my career as a Field Training Instructor before I went on my first mission," Brian said.

"Then I went on a few dozen other missions before I blew my knee out and hurt my back. That ended my career in the field. The Air Force retrained me, and I went into the Visual Information end of things. I helped make training films, created the recruiting videos, and website for the SERE program. I might not have the expertise of a Navy Seal, but I do know a few things about survival. There are some things you just don't forget."

Sometimes he explained different survival techniques he'd learned. That night he just told us funny stories about all the weird and gross things he'd eaten during his trainings and on his missions. "I could teach you to cook maggots and ants if you want, although if you're desperate enough to eat them, you usually just pop them in your mouth raw. I admit I could never stomach eating raw maggots—they're just writhing little bundles of goo. Carpenter ants aren't so bad though. They taste kind of like lemon chicken if you cook them right. And I still think you should have collected a bunch of those cicadas from the tree the day you killed that javelina. They probably would have tasted better than the javelina did!"

There had been a small group of javelinas that liked to rest in the shade of the mesquite tree in the field where Brian taught me to shoot. I'd gotten pretty good at shooting rabbits, and I could skin and gut them all by myself. It wasn't even that gross to have rabbit guts on my hands anymore, except when the rabbit had a stomach full of parasites; that still grossed me out a little. But otherwise, it wasn't so bad.

Brian had said it was time for me to try bigger game, something that would feed more people for longer. We didn't need the food—there was still plenty of canned chicken and tuna in all the stores. He just wanted to make sure I could hunt for real when all the canned goods expired.

He'd been nervous when he told me what to do. "Make sure you're up in that tree, and you stay there until you're sure that the javelina is dead and that its friends aren't coming back. Those things are just as dangerous as any predator. Do you understand me?"

I understood. Rabbits only fought back in my nightmares. Javelinas were much bigger and a lot scarier.

When I climbed the gnarly mesquite tree with my gun that morning, I wasn't angry like I'd been when Brian made me shoot that first rabbit—I was just a little nervous, that's all. When the sun got higher, the javelinas trotted into the shade right under me, just like I'd seen them do most days. They sniffed around the tree and seemed a little worried, but they never even looked up at me. Brian said that sometimes golden eagles ate young javelinas, so I wondered if maybe they thought the top of the tree protected them from eagles. Or were they just so dumb that they couldn't figure out to look up in the tree for the human they smelled? The cicadas that had stopped buzzing when I climbed the tree started making their buzzing noise again. They only stopped if I moved too quickly, like when one of them dropped onto the branch near my arm. I flinched and all of the bugs around me went silent. A moment later, the cicadas in the other tree stopped making their buzzing noise, too. Beneath me, the javelinas sniffed the air again and moved closer together, like they knew something bad was about to happen. Looking down at them was the closest I'd ever been to one before; I'd always stayed as far from them as I could because even from a distance, they looked dangerous.

Brian had said they weren't really pigs even though they looked a lot like them. He said they were peccaries, whatever those were. The biggest one beneath me was shorter than Molly, but a lot thicker. They had snouts like pigs and they were covered with bristly, black and gray hair. The big one had a spikey mane and big yellow teeth that looked sort of like over-grown vampire fangs except that they came up from the bottom jaw *and* down from the top one. The two smaller javelinas didn't have the same big teeth or the mane, but they looked mostly the same otherwise. And they all stank. Really, really bad—kind of like one of Jeremy's poopy diapers.

I breathed as quietly as I could and tried to ignore the itchy beads of sweat that dripped from my forehead as I watched the cicada by my arm. It was almost as long as my pinky finger and much fatter. It looked like a fly on steroids, and I watched its bulging red eyeballs dart around. I hadn't moved again, but it still hadn't started moving its abdomen to make that irritating, buzzing noise again. I looked down. The javelinas were still nervous. What if they left? Then I'd have to come back and try again, and I really didn't want to. I got into position as quietly as I could, about five feet above the biggest javelina's head. The cicadas in the other tree started to make noise again, a few at a time, but the ones in my tree were still silent. I steadied the gun with both hands and took careful aim. I held it out until my arms started to shake. The cicada around me started to buzz again, one at a time. The javelinas relaxed. Out of the corner of my eye I saw the cicada by my arm start vibrating its fat abdomen, too. I pulled the trigger and the sound of the gun made the javelinas below me scatter, which turned out to be lucky since I fell out of the tree. Why was I so stupid? I'd forgotten to take into account the way the gun kicked, and how it would affect my balance when I pulled the trigger!

I tumbled out of the tree, scraping my arms and legs and even the side of my face on the bark. Twigs jabbed into me and I squeezed my eyes shut—I didn't want to get one of my eyeballs poked out! I landed with a loud thud. I couldn't breathe! I was dying. I was paralyzed, and I couldn't breathe! My lungs made a loud whooping sound as I sucked air in—I was breathing again but it hurt! I twisted around. Where were the javelinas? Most of them were already across the field, but the one I'd aimed at was only a few feet away, staring at me! It made a weird sort of woofing sound and clacked its teeth. I sucked more air in and pushed myself off the ground and scrambled back up in the tree. Where was my gun? The javelina was just a few feet beneath me. Javelinas couldn't climb trees, could they? Why hadn't I asked Brian about that? I was so dumb sometimes! I climbed higher, holding on to the trunk. My skin stung where I'd scraped myself, and blood was smeared across my arm. I'd busted open the scabs that were left on my knuckles from the day I crashed my bike, but I barely noticed. I saw my gun! It was a few feet from where I'd fallen. The javelina was practically on top of it! How was I going to get it if the javelina didn't leave? It's not like Brian could come save me. He couldn't see! No one but me could see. What if the javelina never left…

And then the javelina fell over—just like that. I leaned against the trunk of the tree, shaking, still trying to take normal breaths. The javelina's legs twitched one last time before they were still.

It turns out that javelina meat tastes exactly like it

smells. Even Brian said I could stick with hunting rabbits, at least for now.

***

The day I found Molly was the first time I spent the night at Brian and Mary's house and after that I stayed almost every night. I set an air mattress up in the living room, and when we all went to bed that first night, Molly scrambled to her feet to follow me. She gingerly stepped up on it and sank, and then she took a few careful steps and plopped down next to me. Her face was just a few inches from mine. I could see the pebbly texture of her black nose in the shadows of the lantern beside me, and I could smell her breath. It smelled like peanut butter flavored treats.

"Molly," I whispered, trying it out on her again. It was the perfect name for my dog. She must have thought so too, because her tail gave one final, satisfied whump before she closed her eyes and fell asleep.

THE CHASE

I pulled the bike over to the side of the street when I got out of the neighborhood. It was almost the end of August, and Martha still hadn't died from all the cigarettes she smoked. She needed a few things: mostly water and cigarettes. She asked for food too, but she didn't seem to eat much, and she sure didn't eat anything healthy. She only ever asked for things like dry cereal, crackers, and spray-on cheese. She drank instant coffee that I don't think she even bothered to heat up on the camp stove I'd taken her when the power first went out, because she never asked for more fuel. Sometimes she had me bring her those juice pouches that Jeremy liked, or instant soup cups, but that's about it. How could she still be alive?

I was glad to be out of her house. Even after riding for two blocks, my clothes still stank. I promised myself I'd go to Jonathan and Rebecca's before I changed, just to irritate him by stinking up his house. I pulled a bottle of water from the holder on the frame of my bike and took a big swallow. Water dribbled down my chin. I heard a few birds and then suddenly, music! It wasn't the same song I'd heard last time, but it was definitely the same loud, thumpy style. For the first time, it was close enough that I heard a car engine, too. Whoever it was liked their music very loud. The car was close, then. Very close.

No, not close. It was here! I froze as the brand new black pickup truck sped past. The driver hadn't seen me! Relief made my body sag. I had just enough time to wonder why I was glad I hadn't been seen when the tail lights flashed and the truck skidded to a stop. The driver stuck his head out of the window and looked back at me. I almost threw up.

I knew him! How could that be? How could practically everyone I knew from before be blind and gone except him?

He yelled to me without turning the music off. "Hey, baby! I knew if I drove around enough I'd find out who's been breaking into all the stores around here!"

He looked me up and down. It was more than a hundred degrees outside but I wished I had a big thick coat to cover myself from head to toe. My skin crawled. He must have been so close all those other times I thought I'd heard music. He must have heard the gun when I was out shooting with Brian that day. What if he would have found us?

"Lose the bike and let's go for a ride," he said. Did he recognize me from the night he and his friends tried to pick me and Laney up? I sure recognized him. How could I not? He showed up in my nightmares, along with killer rabbits, people-eating coyotes, and mummified zombies. I would never forget him. He'd been the worst one, the one who had scared us the most. Maybe this was just another nightmare. It had to be, didn't it? Otherwise, how could he be alive? How come he could see?

The reverse lights came on as he started to back up. My body unfroze. I spun the bike around and sped back into my neighborhood. The bike trailer bounced over the cracks in the asphalt as I took the corners.

He yelled after me. "Hey, don't be like that! Come back! We're gonna be friends, girl, real good friends!"

I heard the tires squeal as he made a fast U-turn to follow me, but I was already around the corner, zig-zagging through the neighborhood. My house was closer than Brian and Mary's, but I heard him right around the corner. I wouldn't be able to unlock the door and pull the bike and trailer inside fast enough—not unless I wanted him to know which house was mine. I shuddered at the thought. I sped past him coming the other direction. In the background, I heard people shouting and screaming at him to stop.

I'd been seeing fewer and fewer people when I went out, but I thought maybe it was just my timing or the mosquitos, or because I stayed at Brian and Mary's house now and there were fewer people living in the houses on their street. But people came out of three of the houses on my street when the truck rumbled past. They jerked their doors open, covering their eyes, and waving their arms at him. They screamed at him.

"Help us! You've got to help us!" they shouted.

"We're starving and we need water!"

"We're here! Please help!"

I had to get away, but where should I go? It needed to be close or he'd catch me!

The man tried to swerve in front of me to keep me from going past, but I was too close to his truck and he couldn't swerve fast enough to block me off, not unless he wanted to run into me. "So you wanna play chase?" he yelled after me as I passed.

He tossed a nearly empty beer bottle out the window. The brown glass shattered when it hit the road and we were close enough that beer splashed up on my leg. He spun the big truck in a hard circle, going over the curb with a loud clunk. He swore. I went to the left and took a corner too fast. I skidded, and the bike almost fell but the trailer was stable and it kept the bike upright. The music thumped from a little farther away, and more people yelled and screamed for his help when they heard him pass. He'd taken a right turn instead of a left! I sped around the block and back to my house. I fumbled with my keys. Why didn't the key fit? I shoved it in harder but it just wouldn't go in. I stared at my hand. I had the wrong key! My hands shook. There were only two keys—the one for the door and the one for the mailbox. How could I grab the wrong one?

The music was closer. He was circling back again! Did I have time? Or should I run for it? I twisted the key in the lock and wrenched the door open. I gave the bike a shove. The door bounced against the trailer and slammed open again. I pushed it closed and dropped to the floor. My keys! They were still in the door! I yanked the door open, twisted them out, and slammed the door shut again. Had he seen me? I dropped to the floor and crawled to the window, peeking out of one of the broken slats of the blinds. He hadn't seen me! He was just turning the corner onto my street. I got a better look at him. I was right! It *was* him. He was the one that had reminded Laney and me of Rich. He had the same dangerous look in his face. Why could he see and not Brian or Mary or Susan? Why him? It wasn't fair!

Through the window, I could hear people still screaming at him over the sound of his music.

"Who are you—are you military?"

"Can you help me? Please?"

"I'll give you anything!—just help us!"

But he didn't stop to help anyone or even call out to them. I tried to tell myself that maybe the music was too loud for him to hear them, but I could hear them, so that didn't make sense. And he saw them. I know he saw them, and still he ignored them. I hadn't helped those people either, but somehow it seemed different to sneak past them so they didn't even know I was there. It *was* different. Wasn't it?

The truck dropped to a slow roll as he drove past my house. Did he know? Could he tell it was my house? I wanted to slink away from the window and go crawl under my bed, but I was afraid he'd see the movement or something else would give me away. The front of my house faced the sun, and I knew the light bouncing off the windows would keep him from seeing inside, but for one long, terrible moment, I thought he'd seen me. It wasn't until he was in front of the next house that I realized he'd been slowing down in front of all the houses without blocked off windows, not just mine.

He was hunting for me just like I hunted rabbits and that javelina.

PLAYING HOOKY

I left my house through the back door. I rolled my bike to the back gate and propped it against the house after I unhooked the trailer. I eased the back gate open and sucked in my breath when it squeaked. I hid behind the gate and listened. The truck sounded like it was a couple of streets away. I was just about ready to risk it and race to Brian and Mary's when the music suddenly got louder again. He was back! I slammed the gate shut and it shuddered. I pressed my body against it to make it stop vibrating and ran inside again.

Hidden behind the slats of the blinds, I watched as people screamed hysterically from their doorways again. Except I realized they weren't people anymore. They were skeletons. Nothing more than walking, talking skeletons. Had I looked like that back when I was starving?

The skeletons weren't yelling for help, they were begging for it, pleading for the man to stop, to bring them food or water, to bring them anything, or to take them with him. I sat, curled up in a ball, at the edge of the window for hours, watching and listening for him to return. It was dark before I got the nerve to race around the corner to Brian and Mary's house.

Mary knew something was wrong as soon as she saw me. She stopped stirring the pot of soup she was heating up

201

on the camp stove. She reached me the same time Molly did. "What's wrong, Jenna? What happened?"

I buried my face in Molly's fur and she licked at the sweat on my skin. She knew something was wrong, too. Normally, she wanted to play when I got home, but this time she hunkered close to me. Could she smell my fear? If she could, I must have stunk of it. Her tail, what was left of it, was curled between her legs. And what should I tell Mary? Did she even need to know? Had they heard the truck? They must have. Did they run outside and beg for help like the others who were still alive?

Brian came in then. He wiped dust and sweat from his hands with a rag. He'd been taping off the garage by feeling his way around it so no light would leak in. He wanted to move my driving lessons to an actual car even though we couldn't turn it on in the garage without risking carbon monoxide poisoning.

"What was the deal with the car that drove by earlier today?" he asked. He didn't notice anything was wrong.

"I don't know," I said, trying to think of a reason for not being excited to find someone else who could see. What could I say that wouldn't sound Suspicious? Finally I just said, "He didn't stop to help any of the people who came out of their houses begging for help."

Brian studied his dirty hands and picked at a fingernail. "You don't help them either. Maybe he's taking care of people like you are, and he knows he can't help everyone."

"Maybe."

I kept petting Molly so I didn't have to look at him.

Brian studied me. "One of the things we taught our students in the Air Force was that if you have the luxury, you always study the situation before you make a decision."

I looked at him then but didn't say anything.

"We didn't go out when he came by, if you're wondering. I heard that guy Jonathan down the street screaming at him to rescue them, though. It didn't sound like the driver even slowed down."

I shrugged. Brian squatted down with a groan and petted Molly. He changed the subject. "Her wounds are healing nicely. I pulled another couple of ticks off her this morning after you left. You might want to check for them every couple of days. The tiny ones can be hard to find until they're engorged with blood."

"Yeah, thanks."

Mary put a hand on my forehead. "I don't think she's feeling well, Brian. I've been feeling a little punky myself the last few days. I think Jenna might be coming down with something."

That was it! My excuse. "Yeah, I think you're right. I think I'm definitely coming down with something. Maybe I'll go lie down for a while. I should probably take it easy for a couple of days."

I stretched out on the air mattress in the living room, feeling a little bit like I was playing hooky, which is what my dad used to call it when students skipped his classes. I actually fell asleep too. In my dream, Laney and I were going to the dumpster again. Instead of a beat-up old car painted with primer, a black pickup truck with headlights that looked like evil eyes kept trying to cut us off. There were people trapped inside, and they pounded on the windows and screamed for us to help them escape. The truck turned and the headlights shined right in my eyes, blinding me in their glare. I couldn't see the driver. He revved the engine and came at me. He was going to run me down!

I woke with a jerk when I heard a car passing the house. If I'd been asleep in one of the back bedrooms, I might have slept through it. There was no music this time, but it had to be the same truck, didn't it? I heard it pass by once more a few hours later. I wanted to peel back some of the tape that kept the glare out of the house so I could look, but I was worried he'd notice.

After being up so late listening for his truck and with

the nightmare, I slept in later than usual the next morning. Mary tip-toed over to me when I started to get up. She knelt down and felt my forehead as she sniffled with the start of a cold.

"You don't seem to have a fever, but you should just lie here and rest for a while. I think we've started to take you for granted a little bit. Why don't you just take it easy for a day or two?" I didn't need any other excuse to stay in bed.

I was a few pages into a book Susan had given me when the truck drove by again. The music was loud and obnoxious, just like before. I put the book down and pretended to be asleep when Mary, Brian, and Susan snuck past me and put their ears to the door.

I heard Susan whisper, "Are you sure we shouldn't go out?"

I peeked through my eyelashes at them and saw Brian shake his head. "I don't know what's going on, but I have a bad feeling about that car, and I think Jenna does, too. She knows something she's not telling us. I'm not going to push her on it, but we're not going out there. None of us are."

After they tip-toed away, it was a long time before I could focus on my book again, and I got a headache from the flickering light of the lantern. It wasn't really bright enough to use for reading, at least not for very long.

Molly hadn't left my side except to eat. I sat there, staring at the ceiling while I petted her. It was the first time since the glare started that I hadn't spent most of the day outside, riding my bike and loading and unloading my trailer.

Usually, when I spent the night at Brian and Mary's house, it seemed normal for the light to be dim inside. But I was never really inside during the day, except to make deliveries. I could see flickering shadows coming from the other room where Brian, Mary, and Susan were talking quietly. The lantern beside me gave off the blueish light of long-lasting LED bulbs, but it wasn't bright enough. Except for the heat that pressed down on me, it seemed like the middle of winter when it was dark before school and dark soon after I got home. Was this what it was like for people blinded by the glare every day? Did they feel trapped in the dark? Did they crave light—real light? Did they want to tear the paper off the windows just to see the sun again? I dozed on and off for the rest of the day and the next night, wondering if I would be trapped inside, too—not because of the glare, but because of *him*. Could people live without ever seeing the sun again? Was that possible? Maybe I really was fighting off a bug. All I could think about was how awful it must be for all those people to be trapped inside and when I woke up the next day, I couldn't stay in bed any longer.

I wasn't brave enough to go to the stores like I normally did, but I had to get outside. I played out back with Molly and sat under the back patio, reading a little more. Brian came out and sat with me for a little while; he'd started making everyone spend a little time outside every day even though it meant wearing a blindfold. I hadn't understood that before, but now I did. I closed my eyes and tilted my face to the sun. The light was yellow through my eyelids, but even that made me feel better. Brian had said they'd all get sick or depressed if they didn't let their bodies absorb some sunlight and make a little vitamin D every day. After being trapped inside for the past few days, I believed him.

DRUG RUN

"I hate to ask, but Jeremy's cough is scaring us a little. How do you feel about going to the drugstore?" Mary asked. "Susan's getting really worried about him."

Susan had been cuddling him all day. The little cough he had when he woke up in the morning hadn't been so bad, but by the end of the day, his breathing was wheezy and his cough sounded thick and phlegmy.

It was late but I thought that might be a good thing. If the man was out there looking for me, I might be able to see him coming before he saw me since it was dark out. He didn't turn his music up at night. I don't know why. Maybe being outside at night creeped him out like it did me, and he wanted to be able to hear what was going on. But maybe that was good. Maybe it would be safer for me in the dark. He'd have to have his lights on to drive so I'd be able to see him coming. Plus, I could hide from him more easily in the dark. The dark was good.

"Of course I'll go." I said. Molly wagged her tail when she saw me heading for the door. She wanted to go with me. She wasn't limping anymore, but what if we came across a pack of dogs or some coyotes or javelinas? She was very protective of me; she might get hurt. And if the man was out, it would be harder to hide with her.

"Stay girl. You stay, okay? I'll be back soon and then I'll

play with you."

She whined but stayed inside when I slipped out the door. Brian had a roll of blue painter's tape ready to tape around the door when I closed it behind me.

The only other time I'd been out after dark since the glare had started was the night the man found me. I'd been so desperate to get to Brian and Mary's house when I was sure he was gone that all my attention had been focused on listening for his truck. This time I was hyper aware of everything, and I watched for any sign of movement that might be him hiding around a corner or driving by. I listened for the quiet sounds of the truck's tires and even smelled the air for exhaust.

The street lights that had once peppered the block with big circles of light were nothing but tall, useless poles. Had there always been so many stars? We talked about light pollution once at school, and we learned that lots of birds got tricked by the lights of big cities and dropped from exhaustion because the lights made them lose their bearings. Some animals, like sea turtles, got disoriented and headed toward bright city lights instead of out to sea after they were born, too. And some cities put out so much bright light that you couldn't see any stars at all.

It was never that way in Ahwatukee. Living in the desert, we could always see the stars at night. I stared up and saw two shooting stars streak across the sky. August was almost over, so maybe they were part of that meteor shower that came around every summer. One summer when I was seven, Dad drove us all out to the middle of the desert. We sat on the hood of his car, leaning against the windshield. We watched the comets shoot through the sky, leaving streaks. Now, without lights anywhere, it had probably been even cooler. Too bad I'd missed it. And too bad there was no one to watch it with.

I hadn't been back to my house for my bike trailer since playing hooky, so I thought I'd just hang some bags from my handlebars. I didn't like the idea of pulling the trailer behind me now anyway, not with the way it slowed me down. Plus, it had all that reflective tape on it that made it easy to see in the dark. I felt fast and invisible when I rode down the street without it. None of the packs of dogs I'd been seeing lately were out, but I did see the dark, thick shadow of a small group of javelinas cross the street in the moonlight not far ahead of me. I slowed down to give them space.

I was almost to the drug store when I heard it: the sound of an approaching engine. There was no music, just the sound of an engine—but it was him. I was sure of it! Who else could it be? I threw the bike down flat and crouched behind a bush. My gun went skittering across the sidewalk. I lunged for it, then glanced over at my bike. The tires were still spinning! I hesitated. Was he far enough away that it was safe to stop them? Or would he see me? I duck-walked three steps to the bike, staying as low as I could. I put my hands on the wheels to make them still and then hid again. The lights came closer. He turned onto the street I'd just come from, the one I'd been on when he first saw me. The sound of his engine faded away as he drove deeper into the neighborhood, hunting me.

I pulled my bike up and hopped on, tossing the gun into the basket. I thumped over the sidewalk and across the street, pedaling as fast as I could while I listened for the sound of the truck again. I got to the drugstore, pulled open the doors I'd broken weeks and weeks ago, and rolled my bike inside the entry way. I slammed the doors shut before stopping to catch my breath.

I started into the store. I'd been inside it often enough to know the layout really well, but then I panicked. My gun! I'd forgotten my gun! I ran the few steps back to the bike and pulled it out of the basket. I tucked it into the waistband of my pants. I felt a little better with it there. Safer. Braver.

I turned on the flashlight I'd brought with me. The light

was too bright! He'd see it! Something brushed against my ankles. I screamed and shined the light at the ground. Rats! They were everywhere! The light scattered them. Their scent drifted up to my nose. How had I missed that smell when I first walked in? I'd blocked off the broken glass in the doors with cardboard, but they'd gotten in anyway. I needed to turn the flashlight off, but what about the rats? I put my hand over the light to shade it and kept it aimed at the ground; the rats stayed at the edge of the beam of light, dancing in and out of it. I passed an end cap with an early selection of back-to-school items. Back then, stores were always months and months ahead of whatever season was next. Whole aisles in every store were full of folders and binders that featured the last popular singing group before the world changed, the last cartoon character everyone loved, and the last up-and-coming movie star.

I shined the flashlight up at the stuff on the shelves and the rats moved closer. I grabbed a big black backpack and shined the flashlight back down on the rats. They moved away again.

I found the Cold and Cough aisle and grabbed bottles I thought might work for Jeremy, but I didn't really take the time to read them. I shined the light on them only long enough to make sure they were safe for little kids, and then I aimed it back at the rats. I threw all sorts of different kinds of medicines into the backpack until it was so full I almost couldn't zip it closed. Once I got it shut, I settled it on my back. The boxes inside poked and jabbed me in the ribs.

I turned the flashlight off before I got back to the door. A rat squeaked at me and I kicked at it. It was fat but fast and it waddled away, not even a little afraid. I got closer to the door and peeked around the corner, staring out and trying to let my eyes pull in whatever light they could so I wouldn't be blind when I opened the doors. I eased the doors open and listened for the sound of the truck. Nothing. I stared into the darkness watching for movement.

Nothing. But it was so dark without the streetlights. Maybe he was on foot now...

My body thrummed with fear as I rolled my bike out. I was ready to hop on and race away. I couldn't let him catch me. But there was still nothing—no noise, no movement. Maybe he'd given up for the night. I closed the door behind me and studied the street again. I got on my bike and crossed the street. I stood on my pedals like I was running so I could get away faster if I needed to. The bike clunked and the backpack jammed into my back. The noise seemed too loud, and the jolt made my teeth slam together. I rode as close to the bushes as I dared and tried to avoid the rabbits and rats that darted out from under them when I brushed past. But I'd been careful for nothing. I got all the way to the entrance of my neighborhood before there was trouble.

THIS TIME I DIDN'T CRY

I was in trouble, but it wasn't because of the man. I stopped the bike and stared into the dark. There were small green-gold lights flashing on and off, but it was too dark for me to make out an outline. What were they? They seemed to be moving...wait! Was it people? It had to be! I felt a flood of relief wash over me. It *was* people! A whole bunch of people using flashlights as they walked down the street. I wouldn't have to worry about the man anymore. I was safe! They had to be close—just a couple of streets away, maybe. I raised my hand to call out to them and stopped. What if the man was nearby? I didn't want to attract his attention before I got to the people. And I remembered what Brian had said, too. It was better to watch and observe if you have that luxury. And I did.

I started to pedal toward them, then stopped and stared. Could there be that many people who could see? Why had I been the only one to break into the stores in Ahwatukee, then? Or maybe the glare was gone! That's it! The glare must have ended, and all the people who'd been trapped could see again—except it was night so they couldn't see very well, so they all had flashlights. But why hadn't they just waited until morning? Maybe they were afraid the glare would come back. Or maybe they were just *that* hungry and needed food now. I wondered where they'd been trapped that they'd gotten so many flashlights. A camping store, maybe? But why were they all that weird color? My flashlight put off a sort of blueish white light...

Then I heard it: a coyote howling. Then another, and another, and another, like they were singing and only they knew the words.

And the coyote song was close. It was much, much too close. I had that same horrible, shuddering sensation you get when you're taking a shower and suddenly run out of hot water. Those weren't people with funny flashlights. They were eyes, and they were blinking, not flashing. And they weren't a couple streets away, either. It was too dark and my depth perception was off. They were here. Now!

I fumbled one foot onto a pedal and pushed off the ground hard with the other. I glanced back, and caught sight of a dark shadow loping behind me. I looked again and saw more of them. I shuddered again. That's why I hadn't been seeing as many coyotes out during the day. That's why I hadn't seen any dogs when I rode to the store. They'd worked something out, somehow. Nighttime must have become the coyotes' time to rule. I rode faster.

The pack of coyotes trotted behind me, moving quicker now, keeping pace with me. I sped around the corner and almost slammed into a truck—a big black one with shiny chrome accents that reflected the shape of the sliver of the moon back at me. What had I done? The inside of the truck was dark and for a moment I thought it was empty, but then I saw him. How long had he been sitting there in the dark waiting for me? We stared at each other, neither of us moving. He took one long swallow and threw a bottle out the window.

He opened his door and got out. "I knew I'd find you one of these days." He turned his head and spat on the ground.

I glanced backwards. The truck was something new to the coyotes, but it didn't scare them away. They only waited, just out of sight except for their roving, blinking eyes that reflected the light. I let my bike drop to the ground, but I didn't move fast enough. The man grabbed my arm and pulled me toward him. I smelled alcohol on his breath and it seeped out of his skin. I tried to remember how smoothly Laney had handled him and his friends before, but my mind went blank.

"Let go!" I screamed. I punched and kicked at him. He laughed and pulled me closer, closing his fist on my other hand and twisting my arm.

"I know your type," he said. "Always playing hard to get, aren't you?"

"No, I'm not! Leave me alone!" I yelled. I tried to pull away, but he just held my arm tighter, digging his fingers into it and twisting my other arm more until I was sure he would break it.

He continued as if he hadn't heard me, "Well, I've got you now, so stop fighting it already and let's go have some fun." His words slurred together a little bit.

He dragged me to the passenger side of his truck and shoved me inside. The boxes in my backpack rammed into my back and made me gasp. I couldn't breathe! He slammed the door shut and jogged around the front of the truck. Did he really think I was going to sit there and let him drive off with me? I felt for the door handle. I pulled it open and jumped out. He sprang toward me again but he only managed to grab my backpack, not me. It came off my back. I ran across the street, ducking behind a bush, barely breathing. Rabbits and rats scattered from under all the bushes nearest to me. The rabbits' white tails almost glowed in the moonlight.

"You can't go far without your bike," he said loudly. Had he seen the rabbits? They must have given me away.

"Besides, I know where to find you, now." He kept talking. "You must live really close. I bet you have your house stocked with food and water, so you're not going to want to leave it. Maybe your family's even there and you're taking care of them. I remember you, you know. And your hot sister. I bet you won't want to leave her."

He stepped closer and my heart pounded harder. I could hear it thrumming in my ears. Could he hear it, too? I ducked lower to stay in the shadows. Something jabbed me in the stomach. My hand jumped to my waist and I felt the warm metal of the gun's barrel. I'd forgotten I'd put it there when I'd gone into the store! I shifted slightly and gravel crunched under my shoes. I winced and almost started crying. Why did everything have to go wrong in my life? I couldn't even hide without giving myself away!

"I heard that! I know you're close. Time to come out and play!"

He changed tactics and tried to coax me out. "I was just kidding before. Come out and we can have a beer and talk. We can get to know each other."

He was drunk enough that he thought he was being smooth. It just made him scarier. He lunged behind a shrub. There was only one more bush between us. I ducked further back into the shadows.

"I know you're here. I'll find you eventually. Why don't you just come out now before I get mad?"

He kicked the next bush, the one right beside me. I flinched. Another rabbit darted out and he jumped back, surprised. Then he laughed like someone had pulled a hilarious prank on him. I pulled the gun out of my pants, breathing in deep gasps but trying to keep from making a sound. And then I stood up, held the gun in both hands, and pulled the trigger.

I hadn't really aimed at him. That was a mistake. I knew it as soon as the sound echoed through the streets, but I got lucky. For once, I got lucky. I hit him even though it was dark, even though my hands were shaking, and even though I hadn't aimed well.

He screamed and dropped to the dusty road, moaning

with pain. I kept the gun trained on him as I stepped out from behind the bush. It weaved back and forth. I couldn't keep it steady so I just held it out in front of me. My stomach twisted when I saw him on the ground, squirming like that first rabbit had when I'd shot it. His hands were holding a slick, wet hole in the middle of his body.

"Don't kill me!" he begged. "I'll leave you alone, I swear. Just don't kill me! Please!"

He rolled over and threw up. Nothing but liquid came out, and it smelled like puke and beer and blood. I kept the gun aimed at him. It was easier to hold now, steadier. I looked around for the coyotes but they were gone, scared away by the gunshot.

My eyes stayed on him as I picked up my bike. "You can't just leave me here!" he moaned. "I'll die! You have to help me!"

I looked at him again. The slick circle of blood was bigger, and there was a growing puddle on the road. In what little light the moon and stars gave off, the blood looked black, like an oil slick. Should I at least help him into his car so the coyotes and the dogs wouldn't tear him apart? But what if he grabbed me, or worse, got the gun away from me? Then what?

His eyes were squeezed tightly closed, almost like he was blinded by the glare, and he shook with pain and fear, so I did the only thing that was left to do. I put him out of his misery, and this time I didn't cry. I moved quickly so he wouldn't know what I was doing and so I wouldn't lose my nerve. I leaned over and put the gun close to his temple. It went off again and fragments of his skull and brain exploded across the road.

DRIVING LESSONS

Jeremy's cough was scary for a long time, but some of the medicine I brought back helped him get better. Brian and Susan got sick, too, but they just got mild colds like Mary's. When Brian started to feel better, he took me out driving for real, and it wasn't too bad. Most of the drivers had pulled over to the side of the road when they couldn't see anymore, and even the ones who had crashed had mostly pulled away from the middle of the road. Plus, I knew where almost all of the pile ups were, at least the ones closest to my neighborhood.

With the scruffy man dead, I was free and I drove everywhere, even if I did drive almost as slowly as I could walk. Brian sent me to lots of different stores that had been too far for me when I only had a bike, and sometimes he went with me. The first time I drove for real it was in Brian's car. Once I knew how to drive a little bit, I took the black truck that the man had been driving because I was worried about wrecking Brian's car even though he didn't seem worried about it. The tank had been nearly full and the keys were still in the ignition, and I didn't care if I ruined the truck.

Brian had me get vegetable seeds and seedlings from a home improvement store, guns from a store that sold weapons and ammunition, camping supplies from every

216

store that carried them, and he even went with me into the archery store on the other side of the freeway. The store didn't have many windows so it didn't take too long to block the light out. Brian's eyes got bright when he swung his flashlight around the store the first time. He looked a little like Jeremy when I brought a new toy home for him. We brought back books on archery and different kinds of bows and lots of arrows, but we stayed so long that Mary was shaking with worry by the time we got back.

Driving on the surface streets wasn't too bad, but it was different on the freeway. The cars were packed against each other in long, horrible lines that went on and on for as far as I could see. Had there really ever been that many people in the world? Enough that each one of those cars represented one person?

There were bodies to go with all the cars, too. The farther we drove from the freeway exit, the more people there were. Their bodies were propped up against car tires where they'd died, seeking the little bit of shade the cars offered them. Some were still in their cars, their windows down, and their sunken heads leaning against their withered, leathery arms as if they'd been trying to catch a small breeze or talk to a neighbor. There were bodies of men all by themselves, and gristly-looking women who were frozen into position holding small children or little babies. There were dogs and foxes, and once in a while a lonely coyote that must not have had a pack. And they were all feeding.

I described everything to Brian—he sat in the passenger seat with his blindfold wrapped around his eyes. We made bad jokes about the things I described for him because that's all we could do. We didn't call them people because that's not what they were anymore. They were jerky. People jerky. We also talked about things we didn't discuss in front of Mary and Susan.

I told him how scared Laney and I had been the night we met the scruffy man. I'd rewritten the story in my imagination so I could talk about it. Laney and I hadn't been so desperate for food that we were going dumpster diving. Instead, I told him that we were just walking home from the library one night—that's all. I told Brian how I ran into the man's truck when I was trying to get away from the coyotes and I told him about everything that had happened afterwards. Brian slipped into Field Instructor mode.

He felt for my arm and patted my hand. "You did what you had to do, Jenna. You shot him to protect yourself, and you killed him to save him days or weeks of agony. He wouldn't have survived with that kind of injury—not now— not without a doctor. The wound would have gotten infected and he would have died a slow, painful death—and that's if the coyotes hadn't eaten him."

Then he added, "He probably deserved a long, slow death but that's another matter."

"But maybe I could have just run away instead of shooting him in the first place, and we could have all moved or something and he would have never found us," I said.

"And how, exactly, would you have moved all of us without him finding you? He drove around almost every day, looking for you. Do you really believe that would have been a viable solution?"

I shook my head, careful to keep my eyes on the road. "No," I finally said when I remembered he couldn't see or hear me nod with his blindfold on.

"But I killed him. I killed a man!"

It was silent for a moment. I looked over at him to see if he was going to say anything else.

When he did, he spoke slowly and carefully. "I hope you never have to kill another human being again, Jenna, I really do. Because it haunts you, even when it's in self-defense like this was. Even veteran soldiers who are trained to kill are haunted by memories of the lives they've taken. I know I am, even after all these years.

"If you need someone else to blame for what you did,

you can blame me. We're not in the middle of a war and you're not a soldier, but there's a reason I spent so much time drilling you with your stance and your aim, trying to make it automatic for you to shoot."

His smile was sad when he said, "I haven't been entirely honest with you, kiddo. I haven't been asking you to bring home rabbits every day because we need the food, or so you'll learn to skin and prepare them. It's true those things are important for our long-term survival, but it's the killing that's the hard part. It's called being inoculated, and it's not much different than when a doctor inoculates you against a disease by giving you a vaccination. I was inoculating you against the act of killing. You have to survive, Jenna, even if you have to kill to do it. Otherwise we all die."

We didn't talk the rest of the way home. I was getting better at driving—it's not like it was that hard when there were no other moving cars on the road. After I led him back inside, I went back to my own house. I hadn't been there in weeks, but I needed to be alone to think. It was mid-September and the nights were just a little bit cooler than they had been. I lay under my bed and traced designs in the dust that had collected there. Had it always been so hot and stifling under there? Had it always been so cramped? Why had the small space made me feel safe? Now I just felt trapped. I pulled myself out and stretched out on my bed, staring at the ceiling. That was better. I could think again.

Brian had trained me to kill that guy. He'd tricked me, kind of. But if he hadn't, I might be dead, or worse. I thought about Laney and how her friend said she'd last seen my sister getting in a white van with some guy. Had someone like the scruffy man hurt my sister? I wanted to turn my brain off so I didn't have to imagine something so horrible. The thought of it was so much more horrible than shooting the man had been. It was worse than killing that first rabbit or seeing the zombie man and the bloody body the coyotes had been pulling apart. It was worse than seeing those mummified women holding onto their mummified babies on the freeway, and worse than seeing the dogs gnawing on their bodies like they were giant chew toys.

Laney was so much smarter than me—why couldn't she have gotten away? And why had she gone with that guy in the first place? None of the reasons we'd used for the things we'd done made sense anymore. Would the police have really thought we'd killed Mom and Rich? And we were old enough that even if we'd been separated, we wouldn't have forgotten each other. She would have been eighteen in a couple of years. Even if they had put me in a foster home, she could have gotten a job close to me. We would have found a way to see one another. And what about food? What if we'd told someone, just one person—Amber maybe. Would that have been enough? Could we have made it then? Amber and I had known each other forever. Her mom had liked me. I know she did. She would have helped us. She might have even let us move in with their family.

I flopped over and buried my face in my pillow. It smelled like dust. None of our choices made sense anymore. There was no reason for any of it!

Except there was. That little voice that sounded like Laney said, "That's not true." All the survival stories Brian had told me scrolled through my mind like a movie on fast forward. He'd inoculated me to kill that man with baby steps. But what if I hadn't been starving when the glare happened? How long would it have taken me to get the nerve up to break into a store? And what if Laney and I had called the police the night Rich killed Mom? We would have been somewhere safe, even if we hadn't been together. But we wouldn't have been used to living alone and taking care of ourselves. And if Laney hadn't disappeared, I wouldn't have been used to being completely alone either. Could I have survived the glare if none of that had happened?

I flipped back over and wiped my face with my shirt. My shoulder was still stiff from the way the man had wrenched my arm. I forced it to move. My other arm was covered with green and purple bruises where he'd dug his fingers into my skin. The bruises still hurt, even when I just barely brushed them with my fingertips.

I thought about that night again. Even if I'd been able to run faster or could have gotten on my bike and pedaled away, the coyotes might have gotten me. Or the man would still be driving around, day and night, hunting for me, making me afraid to go outside. I'd be trapped just like the people blinded by the glare. Wasn't it better that he was dead? It had to be. It felt less scary knowing he was gone, but killing him changed something inside of me. If I could kill another person—even a bad one like him—what else was I capable of? What else could I do?

AUTHORITY FIGURE

Brian, Mary, and Susan were in the living room talking when I walked in with Rebecca, Jonathan, and Martha. I was practically dragging Martha because she coughed and wheezed so much that she couldn't do much more than shuffle along. I made her put her cigarette out before we walked in, and I think the only reason she did it was because I threatened to stop getting them for her otherwise. Rebecca and Jonathan came for the same reason: because I threatened them. I told them that I was probably leaving Ahwatukee and that unless they walked down to Brian and Mary's house to talk about it with the rest of us, I would leave them behind. I meant it, too.

Jonathan got in my face and cussed me out. "Do you know who you're talking to? I don't take orders from dumb little teenagers! How dare you threaten me!"

Spit flew from his mouth and hit me on the cheek. I wiped it off with the back of my hand and stared back at him. Laney's calm face flashed through my brain when I answered. I hoped my face looked something like hers would have. Brian had told me how to talk to him and what to say, but I didn't think Jonathan would buy it.

"I'm not threatening you. I'm just telling you how it is. You can come with me now—both of you—or you can stay here in Ahwatukee when I leave. That's it."

Jonathan's face got red and a blue vein on his forehead

bulged. He pulled his hand back like he was going to hit me
like I thought he'd started hitting Rebecca. Then he balled
his shaking fist and forced it to his side instead. "Watch
yourself, kid. You don't want to make me mad."

Beside him, Rebecca tugged on his arm. "Let's just go
with her, Jon. I can do it this time. I promise."

He shoved her away and she hit the wall. She yelped like
Molly did when Jeremy pulled her tail too hard, but I stayed
where I was and I kept my Laney-face on. Brian had said I
had to act like I wasn't scared—the same way Laney had
acted the night those men stopped us.

I took a deep breath. "Or what? If you hurt me or make
me mad enough, I'll leave and you'll starve. If you try to
stop me, you'll eventually run out of food and water so
you'll die. And if you actually killed me, you'll die, too.
That's just how it is. You're the one who needs to watch it.
You really don't know what I'm capable of."

That part, at least, was true. Even I didn't know what I
was capable of anymore. He stepped back, and for a second
I wondered if he could see the image I saw in my mind: the
body of a man lying in a pool of his own blood while I shot
him in the head.

Rebecca had whimpered and clung to my arm when I
led them out into the street. I thought it would be good for
them to think the walk was longer than it really was, so I
took them with me to get Martha before we turned around
and went back to Brian and Mary's house. Jonathan didn't
say anything. He looked like he was concentrating really
hard—so I marched us back and forth across the street a
few times. I even twirled us around in a circle once and
pretended like I'd heard a noise. There was no way he'd be
able to find his way back to Brian and Mary's house or even
back to his own house without my help.

Jeremy was wearing nothing but a diaper when we came
in. He toddled past, chasing Molly through the house. She
stayed just out of reach, trying to tempt him to chase after

her. He'd get close and she'd back up, put her butt in the air, and yip at him with her tail beating fast. He'd giggle and reach for her again. When he started to get tired of the game, she pranced up to him and licked the sweat from his body, making him squirm and giggle. Then he was ready to play some more. Meatball usually played too, but this time he was sleeping in one of the back bedrooms.

I shut the door and slapped the tape back in place around the frame so the light wouldn't bother the others. Once he could see again, Jonathan stalked into the living room ahead of me. Rebecca followed behind him, trying to neaten her hair. Martha shuffled in last, wheezing. The smell stale cigarette smoke came in with her. Susan started to cough immediately and had to excuse herself—she had really bad allergies and had a hard time with certain smells. Everyone else shook hands, just like people used to do back before the glare happened. Mary smiled at me and patted the spot beside her on the couch. She gave me a quick hug when I squeezed in next to her. Brian settled back into his recliner while Jonathan stood in front of him with his arms crossed.

I studied Jonathan as he stood there. When I'd first met him, his dark hair had been neatly clipped. It had grown out since then, and he'd put on a few pounds from being stuck inside his house with nothing to do but eat and drink and sleep. The whites of his eyes were bloodshot from drinking and whiskers shadowed his jaw. For a moment he became Rich in my mind, and my heart raced. He towered over Brian, staring down at him and trying to intimidate him, but that didn't work with Brian. All my fear dissolved. What I'd told Jonathan was true. He couldn't hurt me. And I wouldn't let him hurt anyone else.

He glared at Brian. "Let's cut to the chase, shall we? Why are we here?"

Brian looked up at him kind of blandly. He pushed the recliner back and yawned as if he were bored. I tried hard not to smile. Then he folded his hands behind his head. "You'll need to ask Jenna. She's the boss."

I cleared my throat and said what I'd been practicing for days. "You're here because I'm leaving."

Mary and Brian sat quietly with carefully blank expressions. I saw Susan peek around the corner. She had Jeremy in her arms. She grinned and winked at me before she sneezed, and then she was gone again. I think she was afraid she'd start laughing and give me away if she stayed. The others kind of freaked out. I don't blame them. I mean, without me, they were dead and they knew it.

Brian said it would be best if I made it sound like I was doing them a favor by inviting them to come along and that I should make it clear that I was going, even if they didn't want to. He said it would set me up to be the Authority Figure. And yeah, he said it like that, like it was capitalized. It's funny how I didn't have to worry about Arousing Suspicion anymore, but now I was an Authority Figure.

So that's what I pretended to be: an Authority Figure.

Rebecca started sobbing. "Oh my God! We're going to die! We're all going to die!"

Out of the corner of my eye I saw Mary hide a smile behind her hands as she pretended to scratch her nose. Brian had asked how I thought everyone would respond. I think he was worried that Jonathan might get violent or something; I'd told Brian how angry he got sometimes. I'd imitated Rebecca for them too, but I don't think they believed that a grown woman could be that much of a drama queen.

Jonathan got all worked up again. "When this is all over, I'll make sure the authorities know you abandoned us. You'll be sorry! If anything happens to me, you'll pay! This is murder! That's what it is! Premeditated murder!"

With her playmate out of range, Molly had wandered over and sat next to me. Her tongue hung out of her mouth, and her ears were pricked up, like she was listening to the conversation. But when Jonathan shook his fist at me, she sprang forward. The fur between her shoulders stood on end and her lips were pulled back, showing sharp teeth. A deep growl came from the back of her throat, and Jonathan stepped backwards, surprised. Molly stepped toward him. I slid off the couch and squatted down, calling her over to me. Her tail dropped between her legs, and she lowered her head as if she thought she'd been a bad dog. I rubbed her head and whispered, "Good girl, good dog," in her ear so she would know I wasn't mad. She sat down next to me and mostly relaxed except for an occasional quiet growl when she looked over at Jonathan. He stood there, shaking with fury.

Beside him, Martha tried to wheeze something, but she had a coughing fit. The only words I could make out through her sputtering and choking were, "…more cigarettes."

I had to admit, for an old guy who never had to pretend to be something he wasn't in order to survive the way Laney and I did, Brian was a pretty good actor. Mary, too. She sat there looking very worried about her future.

Brian cleared his throat. "So where are you going, Jenna? And are you going alone? Because even though we can't see outside, I wonder if we might be able to help you. If you'd take us all with you, of course."

Rebecca stopped weeping immediately. "Oh, yes! I'm sure he's right! I'm sure we could be helpful." She gave Jonathan a meaningful look. He clenched his jaw but nodded curtly. His fists were balled tightly at his sides like he wanted to take a swing at something. Probably me. "I can't imagine how we could possibly help you," he said. "But I suppose we could try."

Mary pretended to be nervous. "So where are we going, then? If you'll take us with you, that is."

I turned around to hide my smile. I pulled out a big map of the United States that I'd found at the convenience store, and I taped it to the wall. Mary, Brian, Susan, and I had already traced a thick red line on some of the freeways.

"At first I thought it would be good to go someplace like California, where the weather's good all year around," I said as I pointed to the left of Arizona.

I glanced at Brian and he winked at me. "But then it occurred to me that California has a really big population, and I remembered how people always used to talk about how bad the traffic was there. That means it might be really hard to get anywhere on the freeways if there are accidents or even just traffic jams from the day the glare happened. Plus, there might be more people who didn't make it inside before the glare got really bad. That means there could be diseases from the bodies, and more wild animals eating them, and stuff like that. Oh yeah, and there are bad earthquakes there too, and sometimes wildfires."

I pointed at Oregon, just above California. "So I thought maybe this would be a better place to go. It'll be cold, especially compared to what we're used to here, but not freezing cold most of the time. Anyway, it will be easier to warm up with a fire than it is to cool down with no electricity, like we've been trying to do all summer. There's water there all the time too, so we won't have to worry about that. We'd only have to boil it to make sure it's safe to drink. And there are probably fish and deer and other animals to hunt when the food from the stores runs out. And we should be able to start a garden. We might be safer from diseases and from fires if the cities start to burn, too. I've been seeing a lot of smoke in the distance lately, so I think downtown Phoenix has been burning, you know."

There really wasn't anything anyone could say. Brian, Mary, and Susan were in on the plan, and the others, well, they seemed kind of stunned by the dumb teenager who was their new Authority Figure. Before I walked them home again, I said, "I'm leaving in a few weeks, so you need to let me know soon if you want to come too."

***

I got us a van from the daycare center down the street. It wasn't hard to find the keys, but it was really horrible seeing all the mummified bodies of the kids who had never gotten picked up by their parents. Some of them weren't any bigger than Jeremy. It wasn't until Brian warned me that the van wouldn't get very good gas mileage that I even thought about getting gas.

"We can't go anywhere! How am I supposed to get gas when the electricity's out?" I'd been driving the black truck around for a couple of weeks thinking I'd have to find a different car once the tank was empty.

"You said that gas pumps have to have electricity to work!" I was shocked and a little angry that Brian hadn't thought of that.

"Relax, Jenna! You don't think I'd let you get stuck in the middle of nowhere with a bunch of blind people, do you? Look. Here's what you're going to do..."

He poured water into a cup from a water bottle and sat it on the kitchen counter. "Pretend this is a tank of gas in a car."

Then he put an empty cup down in the sink. "This is an empty gas can."

Next, he taped together a couple of straws. "Here you go. I want you to bend this straw a little so one end is inside the cup of water and the other one is inside the empty cup. Pretend the straws are plastic tubing."

I did what he asked and then looked at him. "Did I do something wrong? Nothing's happening."

He grinned at me. "That's right. Nothing's happening. You have to get the flow of gas—or in this case, water—started. In order to do that, you have to provide some suction. That means you have to suck on the end of the straw in order to get the gas moving."

I sucked on the straw and the water was pulled near the top.

"Now, quick, before any gets in your mouth—because, remember, this is gasoline—put the other end back in the empty cup.

I shoved the straw into the cup that sat in the sink and water came flowing out. We watched the level of water drop in the cup on the counter as the one down below, in the sink, filled.

"Hey! That's pretty cool! I said. "So we don't have to stop at gas stations or anything, do we? We just have to find cars, and there are tons of those all over the place!"

I thought for another second and said, "But isn't there some way to get the gas out without having to suck it out? That's going to be really, really gross! Especially if I have to do it all the time!"

Brian tousled my hair. "Now you're thinking kiddo!" He pulled a long tube with a skinny handle out from behind his back. It looked sort of like a vacuum cleaner hose.

"This is a battery-operated siphon pump. Next time you go out, go to Target, or to one of the home improvement stores, or maybe an auto parts store. See if you can grab a couple of these and lots of batteries. I had this one because I used to siphon gas out of my car so I could fill the weed trimmer without having to keep a tank of gas around for it. They're pretty cheaply made, though, so it'd probably be a good idea to have one or two for back up."

***

I turned fourteen later that week. Laney was fourteen when Dad died, and now I was fourteen and Laney was dead. They had a birthday party for me, and Mary and Susan made a cake. Or at least they tried to. There were no eggs, so they used some powdered egg substitute I'd found. With no electricity, they couldn't bake the cake either, so they cooked it in a skillet on the camp stove.

"I'm not sure you can call this a cake," Mary said. The edges were burnt and the middle was still a little gooey, but it smelled just like any other chocolate cake. She shook her head at their creation as she stuck fourteen candles in it.

Susan and I looked at each other and started giggling. "Let's call it mush. Birthday mush," she said. "Or how about mushday cake?"

When it was cool, Mary put a piece on each of our plates, carefully cutting away the burnt parts. Jeremy grabbed his piece with both hands and got more on his face than he managed to stuff into his mouth.

Susan shook her head at him, "What you need is a bath, little man!" She sighed. "It's those little things I miss the most, I think: being able to run the bath water or turn the faucet on to get a drink." She leaned over and kissed the top of Jeremy's head. He grabbed her face, leaving a smear of chocolate on her cheek.

We all started laughing.

We didn't talk about any of the usual things that night. We didn't talk about how big of a jerk Jonathan had been that day, or how I'd seen new bruises on Rebeca's arm. We didn't talk about the packs of dogs that were everywhere now, or how the coyotes had formed larger packs, but didn't come out until it started to get dark. We didn't talk about how bad the smell was getting, the new columns of smoke I'd seen in the distance, or the way the last monsoon had flooded some of the streets and ripped chunks of concrete away.

Except for the heat and the flickering light from the lanterns, it was easy to pretend like we were just having a party. We played that game where you put a card on your forehead and try to guess what it says by asking each other yes or no questions. And we ate the whole pan of burnt mushday cake.

"Aren't you having any?" I asked Brian. He hadn't had

even one bite of the small piece on his plate.

Mary put her nose up in the air and winked at me. "Apparently it's not up to his standards."

He chuckled. "It might be mush, but it smells heavenly. I'm just trying to cut back on the sweets, that's all." He pointed at his midsection. "Haven't you noticed how much more suave and debonair I've become lately?"

I hadn't noticed until he mentioned it, but he did look like he'd lost a few pounds. The solid round stomach that made him look like he was about to have a baby wasn't nearly as big as it had been.

Mary patted his hand and grinned at him. "All these years and it just took the end of the world to get him to take his diabetes seriously. Who knew?"

All I knew about diabetes was the little bit we'd learned in Health class—that there was a Type 1 and a Type 2, but I could never remember which one was which. I just knew—because Mary had told me—that Brian had Type 2 diabetes.

He smiled and shrugged his shoulders. "The doctors have been telling me for years that if I lost some weight I might be able to go off my meds, but I've never been able to lose more than fifteen pounds. Not and keep it off, that is. There was always dinner at a restaurant, Halloween candy, a birthday to celebrate, Christmas parties with cookies and cake, or Thanksgiving to make it hard to diet. Mary tried to get me to eat more salads and vegetables, of course, but always being on a diet just didn't seem like any way to live, not when it was so easy to take my medicine and get a check-up every year. It's a little different now, though. Maybe this time I'll be able to stick to the diet. All this fake food in boxes and cans just isn't as appealing as the real stuff, anyway. I've actually been craving salad lately. Isn't that crazy? Salad!"

Mary leaned over and kissed him on the cheek.

That night I wrote two things on the list I'd packed when I'd gone back home one last time: mushday cake and fake food. I wanted Brian to live a very long time, not like my dad.

It was strange being back in the house when I went to pack up. I'd only been staying at Brian and Mary's for a few weeks, but everything seemed so different now. I was different now. I didn't pack much—a few changes of clothes and my list from the fridge. Mom's old cell phone was still sitting on the kitchen table where I'd left it. I picked it up, but it was dead and useless.

I was excited to leave, but scared too. Leaving meant that Laney was really dead. But what if she wasn't? She would find a way to come back to the house and I wouldn't be there!

I knew it was stupid—she'd never see it—but I wrote Laney a letter anyway. I told her where I was going, and I promised that I'd find a way to leave her a message if I had to change my route. I told her how to get gas from the cars on the street and I even left one of the siphons I'd gotten and a GPS unit. I left them on the table with Mom's cell phone on top of the note like a paperweight because that's really all it was anymore.

***

I had a hard time backing the daycare van into the garage.

"Don't worry about hitting anything, Jenna." Brian said as he stood in the doorway of the garage with his eyes squeezed shut. "Just don't hit me, that's all!"

I turned off the engine and closed the garage door, then put the tape back around the frame of the garage. Brian felt his way over and helped me slap it back in place by feel. It took nearly a day to load the van, even with Brian helping. We had to keep taking stuff out and repacking to make everything fit so there would be enough room for everyone to sit.

Finally, it was time to leave! We got about an hour outside of Phoenix before I knew it wasn't going to work. Jeremy hadn't stopped screaming since we pulled out of the garage; he couldn't see, and he was too little to understand why. Susan and Mary took turns trying to console him.

"Here, honey! Listen. Do you hear it?" Susan said as she plinked her fingers on the light-up piano he couldn't see. He arched his body and threw himself around so violently I thought for sure he'd bang his head on the back of the seat whenever I glanced in the rearview mirror. Molly whined at him and tried to lick him. Jeremy grabbed a fistful of her fur and pulled. She yelped and dropped to the ground with her ears back. Meatball sat cowering in Brian's lap, whining too.

At the back of the van, Martha crabbed at everyone, not really talking to anyone in particular, just grumbling and complaining. "This infernal nicotine gum tastes like crap! I might as well be chewing on my shoe. And these blasted nicotine patches aren't doing a thing, either."

I wasn't sure how that was possible since she had three of them on her arms even though the directions clearly said to use only one every twenty-four hours. She picked at one of them and blindly flicked it away when it peeled off her skin.

It landed one seat ahead of her, on Rebecca. Rebecca screamed. "Oh, my God! Oh, my God! Something's on me! Something landed on me! What is it? Get it off me! Get it off!"

Behind her, Martha chuckled quietly; she knew exactly what had happened even though she couldn't see. I glanced back at her to make sure she hadn't turned into Hansel and Gretel's witch. No. She was still herself: a crabby old lady who loved her cigarettes more than anything else. The only thing that had changed about her since the day I'd come to her door was that she was just a little more hunched over and wrinkly.

Rebecca flapped her arm around wildly, smacking

Jonathan, who was sitting next to her. The wine he'd been drinking straight from the bottle splashed out, but he managed to catch the bottle before it slipped out of his hands completely.

"What is your problem?" he shouted at her, pulling a pair of earbuds out of his ears. Brian had me get a car charger at the store and all sorts of electronic devices so people could listen to music and do stuff while we drove even if they'd have to throw a blanket over their heads to block out the glare. Jonathan had stuffed his earbuds in his ears as soon as we got in the van. "And will someone please shut that stupid kid up?"

He shoved the earbuds back in his ears and shook the wine off his hands. He cranked the music up so loud that I could hear it when Jeremy took a breath between screams.

Rebecca continued to shriek. "Someone get it off me!" She finally managed to flick the flesh-colored patch off, and this time it landed on the back of Jonathan's hand, startling him so badly he choked on a sip of wine.

I hit a bump in the road and his bottle went flying. At the same time, a box of all the papers Brian and Mary had printed off on their computer slid down the aisle and slammed Mary in the shin. She shrieked. Molly slid down the aisle, scrabbling to stay in place, and she yipped when she hit the edge of a seat.

Up front, I started to shake. "I can't do this…I can't do this…!" Brian's voice was flat when he said, "That's it. Turn around. This isn't going to work."

***

We tried again a few days later. This time Brian really did think of everything. He told me his plan and insisted that, as the Authority Figure, I had to explain it to everyone else, just like before.

He went with me to the U-Haul store. I helped him

climb up into the back of a moving truck and then I closed him inside with a battery-operated lantern and a roll of tape.

After a while, he pounded on the wall. "Alright! Go ahead and open it up," he yelled.

I helped him down and then tied his blindfold back on for him. "I think this fourteen-footer will work just fine. Hopefully it won't be too hard to drive, either. It's not like there will be anyone else out on the roads."

After we got it packed up, I told everyone the plan and pretended that I had thought of it myself. "You're all going to start sleeping during the day—everyone except Brian— starting tomorrow. That means you're not going to bed tonight. You're not going to sleep until you get in the truck tomorrow morning.

"You'll sleep during the day while I drive so I can concentrate." I looked at Brian and told him, "You're going to have to sleep at night when I sleep so you can help me if I have questions while I'm driving. When I get tired of driving, I'll find a place to stop, maybe someplace like a hotel, where it will be easier to block off the windows so you'll all be able to see. I'll sleep and you guys do whatever you want."

Martha shrugged. She didn't care what we did as long as she had her cigarettes. Everyone else except Jonathan seemed to think it was a good idea. He scowled at me. "Why should I have to change my sleep schedule? They're the ones with the problem. Did you hear a peep out of me? No, you didn't! They're the ones with the problem," he said again, jabbing his finger toward Jeremy and Rebecca.

I looked at Brian out of the corner of my eye and saw him nod, just slightly, from behind Jonathan's back. I crossed my arms and scowled right back at him. "You're going to do it because I'm not stopping so you can pee, and I'm not stopping to find food for you or to get you a drink. Not even once. So you might as well sleep because you're going to be miserable otherwise."

***

So that's what we're doing. Brian rides up front with me wearing his usual blindfold, and when it starts to get dark, we stop at a house or hotel, and I tape off the windows and doors so the others can see while they're inside. And then, if there are any bodies, we drag the corpses out or pull them into another room and close the door. The smell is the worst part. The stench of their decay has a way of sinking deep into the furniture, the carpet, even the curtains, and it takes a while to get used to.

Sometimes, before I go to sleep, I write about everything that's happened. I'm not sure yet if I'll let Brian, Mary, and Susan read all of it, or just the parts that happened after the glare. Maybe my secret isn't so important anymore. I killed a man, and they know about it. If I told them how Rich killed Mom and how Laney and I buried them both, maybe they'd still like me. Maybe it doesn't even matter anymore with so many people dead and dying.

Everyone else has projects they're working on, too. Brian is putting together all the survival information he printed off the computer before we lost electricity; Mary and Susan are collecting books so they can teach Jeremy to read in a few years and Susan makes me read and do math problems. Jonathan is writing a business plan for when the glare ends—Brian rolls his eyes at that, but at least it keeps Jonathan busy.

Now that she's not stuck being alone with Jonathan all the time, Rebecca seems a little more normal. She's starting to help with Jeremy and talks to Mary and Susan a lot. Sometimes she reads magazines I find for her—the trashiest ones are her favorites. I don't know how she can read about all of those celebrities when they're probably dead now, though. Martha just smokes. We make her do it outside but as long as I tell her I've checked for wild animals, she's content to sit by the door, smoking cigarette after cigarette.

As we travel, I look for signs of others who can see, and sometimes I find them; I've seen stores with broken windows or doors that aren't blocked off with newspaper or cardboard, and sometimes we come upon a string of cars that look like they've been shoved off the road, as if a giant has pushed them aside. Brian thinks that someone might have driven a big semi-truck through them to clear the road.

The trip has been mostly uneventful so far. I tell Brian what I see as we drive, and he sometimes tucks his head under a blanket so he can check the GPS I picked up. So far it still works. Brian thinks that as long as we have a way to charge it, it should work for a very long time. He says that as long as the satellites it relies on are still up there, orbiting the earth and transmitting data to us as if nothing ever happened, it should keep working. I tell him about the things I see: there's always smoke coming from one direction or another—big tall columns of black smoke, or wider, slower clouds of gray smoke, depending on what's burning. There are animals everywhere, too. Molly and Meatball usually sit at opposite sides of the extended cab behind us and they stare out as we drive. Sometimes I wonder if they're jealous when they see other animals—do they wish they were free, too?

The predators and the scavengers are busy eating the people who got stuck on the side of the road—the people jerky. They flinch when the truck approaches, or they lope away, but they never go far. It was coyotes and dogs in Arizona, and once in a while, a fox. Now there are dogs and sometimes wolves. I still see coyotes but not as many of them. Once I thought I saw the lumbering body of a bear, but it slipped into the tall grass before I could be sure. Do bears eat people? I thought they only ate berries and fish. Maybe dead people taste a little fishy. Sometimes they smell that way, especially since we've left the desert and the bodies aren't mummifying anymore. Now they're puddles of bloated goo that barely look human. Brian and I call them marshmallows.

I've seen cats, too. Big ones with golden coats and green eyes that might have been cougar. When I get out of the truck to squat down in the bushes to go to the bathroom, I always keep one of my guns—I have three now—handy, and Molly always stays nearby. Her fur bristles, her lips pull back and she growls, deep and low. I don't think any animals will attack me with so much easy food available, but Brian says that they will eventually.

"The predators are going to have a lot of babies in the next few seasons because they're eating so well now. When the easy food is gone, they'll hunt whatever they can find, and since they've been eating humans, they'll see us as prey again. We aren't at the top of the food chain anymore."

When we detour through towns in order to get around traffic jams on the freeway, I describe that for him, too. Trees and bushes are no longer carefully manicured. Grass is overgrown. In some places, trees or big branches block the road. Whole blocks of houses have been burnt to the ground, sometimes leaving one random home scorched but otherwise untouched. Once, we came across a downed power line.

"I'm sure it's dead," Brian said when I described it to him. "But it's better to be safe than sorry, kiddo. Back up and find another way."

I had to drive in reverse for nearly a block to find a spot that was wide enough for me to turn the truck around. In the back, the others slept on, unaware of the way things have changed.

And things *have* changed. I mentioned that I have three guns now, right? I keep a pistol on my hip in a holster. I feel silly wearing it, like I'm pretending to be a cowboy, but I wear it just the same. I carry a hunting rifle with me sometimes, too. I don't like shooting it—it kicks back so much that it almost knocks me over every time—but I'm not *afraid* to use it. I guess I'm not afraid of much anymore.

As we get closer to Oregon, it's getting greener and it's been raining more. Even so, lots of houses have burnt to the ground. I'm not sure when we'll stop. Brian has been talking about going up to Washington if we can't find a good place to stay in Oregon. He doesn't seem too worried. He says we have lots of options. We could go into the national forests where there shouldn't be as many bodies and look for a big cabin. Or we might go to one of the ports along the shoreline and see if there are any empty warehouses. If they don't have windows that are up too high for me to get to in order to block out the light, it might be nice for Jeremy to have a big area where he can run and play.

I haven't seen any people yet—not ones like me who can see—but I know they're there. If they're smart, they'll watch to see what kind of people we are. If I see them first, that's what I'll do, too. I'll study the situation before I make a decision, just like Brian taught me. I'll make sure they're the right kind of people before they get too close. And if they're not the right kind of people—if they're like the scruffy man who hunted me—well, they might be surprised at what I'm capable of.

I still think about Laney all the time. I know she's dead, but maybe what they say about people living on in our memories is true because she doesn't *feel* dead. I guess that's why I left that note for her. Sometimes when I do things I never would have imagined I could do, I wonder what she would think of me. Would she think I'm as strong as I always thought she was? Would she be proud of me? When I have the dream, the one where I'm swimming into Dad's arms, she's always there. She's on the shore next to Mom and they're both jumping up and down, waving at me and cheering me on. I think Laney *would* be proud of me. I hope she would, anyway. I hope she'd be really, really proud of me.

THE END

Please review this book on Amazon or GoodReads before you pick up the next books in the series:

The Glare Continues
The Glare Ends

There are also two companion books available for this series:

Since the Glare: Susan's Journal
Before the Glare

You can learn about new and upcoming releases on www.StringerStories.com. Don't forget to sign up for **The Newsletter of the Apocalypse** and check out the freebies available on the site while you're there.

ABOUT THE AUTHOR

Anissa Stringer is a long-time resident of Ahwatukee, a suburb of Phoenix. She lives there with her husband, their daughter, and their dogs. Anissa has written for several local magazines, and she occasionally conducts author visits.

Made in the USA
Middletown, DE
24 July 2019